Acclaim for Denise Hunter

"A fun weekend read with equal parts spunk and spice, Denise Hunter's *The Accidental Bride* will keep readers lassoed up tight 'til the cows come home."

—*USA Today*

"The best kind of love story—completely believable, wonderfully real, with a *Sleepless-in-Seattle*-esque vibe that just makes you want to cheer for love's ability to be reborn."

—Susan Meissner, author of *Lady in Waiting*, regarding *A Cowboy's Touch*

". . . a romantic adventure about unconditional love and forgiveness."

—*Library Journal* review of *Surrender Bay*

"[In *Surrender Bay*] Denise has turned the spotlight on the depth of God's love for His children in a story that will remain with you long after the last page is read."

—RelzReviewz

"No one can write a story that grips the heart like Denise Hunter . . . If you like Karen Kingsbury or Nicholas Sparks, this is an author you'll love."

—Colleen Coble, best-selling author of *The Lightkeeper's Bride*

"In *Finding Faith* Denise Hunter once again brings me to tears with her thought-provoking story. For depth and emotion, this author always hits her mark."

—Kristin Billerbeck, author of *What a Girl Wants* and *She's All That*

What Readers Are Saying

"Thank you for being faithful with the talents God has given you. Your Nantucket Island series has really opened my eyes to a deeper understanding of God's love for me. I love being reminded that God's love is steadfast and undeserved. I can't begin to fathom it, but your books do help scratch the surface."

—Tanya

"I just read *Sweetwater Gap*, and I wanted to say that it was such a powerful and compelling novel. I LOVED IT. I finished and just cried myself to sleep because that's how much of an impact it had. It was amazing! I thank you for writing such a novel."

—Kelsey

"I just read *Surrender Bay*, and I loved it! I'm 16 and I hate to read, but I just couldn't set the book down. I'm so excited to read more of your books!"

—Destiny

"I finished *The Accidental Bride* at 3:00 in the morning. I loved the story. I wished it could go on and on."

—Lori

"I'm so thankful that I ran across one of your books one day at the bookstore a month ago. I do not like to read, but you've got me hooked now! I've got just about all your books in a short amount of time. My favorite ones are the Big Sky Romances."

—Martina

"Thanks for being fabulous! I am an avid reader and have worked at a bookstore for seven years. Finding authors and books that I love sometimes seems impossible even with the thousands that get released every year! I picked up *Seaside Letters* and could not put it down. Now I am in the middle of *The Convenient Groom* and cannot get through it fast enough. Keep 'em coming!"

—A Reader

"Just wanted to know how much I loved *The Accidental Bride*, I woke up last night at 2:00 a.m., and started reading it. I read it all the way through and am now trying to face the day with very little sleep, but a wonderful story rattling round in my brain. Thank you so much for your wonderful work."

—A READER

"I am about thirty pages away from the ending of *Sweetwater Gap* and I am in the middle of a dilemma . . . I am so scared to finish it . . . because then it will be over! I cannot tell you how much I have enjoyed your book. [I've] become closer to God by realizing that he is always there!"

—CARRA

"A friend gave me *Surrender Bay* to read. I could not put the book down! It kept me up until 2:00 a.m. one night, and past 1:00 the next! I've never read a book so quickly in my life!"

—EMILY

"There are no words to explain how amazing your book *Surrender Bay* was. I read it in two days because I couldn't stop reading. You have to be my favorite author of all time. I am going to read all your books because I am sure they are all amazing."

—DAISY

"I just cannot put your books down. Your novels are contemporary, humorous, and moving to tears. I am such a fan now."

—LANA

"Was in a local store and picked up a copy of *A Cowboy's Touch* . . . and I ABSOLUTELY loved it. I have been reading romance novels since I was a teenager, and this one is one of my favorites. Thanks for such a well-written and inspiring book."

—A READER

"I just read *A Cowboy's Touch*, and I enjoyed it so much. I am so amazed at the gift God has given for you to bring forth such a beautiful work."

—CATHY

"Oh my goodness, I just wanted to stop by and say that you are truly amazing! I just finished reading *Surrender Bay*; I've never read a Christian based novel before, but I am SO glad I decided to read your book. It was so touching!"

—A READER

"I'm a librarian . . . I read *A Cowboy's Touch* and was hooked. I started searching for every book I could find by you. I've read all the Nantucket series and loved every one. I highly recommend your books to all my patrons. Thank you so much for writing such good Christian books."

—JOY

"Why haven't I discovered you sooner! I read *Seaside Letters* and am finishing up *Driftwood Lane*! Headed to get *The Convenient Groom* and *Surrender Bay* tomorrow! Then *A Cowboy's Touch*! Keep the books coming! I'm trying to catch up!"

—BRENDA

"I have fallen in love with your books. I work in a high school media center . . . I try to point all the young girls and teachers your direction."

—BILLIE ANN

"I must admit that I never used to like romance novels, but your books have changed my mind! Keep writing, and I'll keep reading!"

—BETHANY

"A friend introduced me to your books a couple of months back, and I have not been able to put them down since! I read the entire Nantucket series first, then went on to *Sweetwater Gap*. I also especially loved your metaphor in the Nantucket series of God's love for us, by using the characters to show His love the way Jesus would. AWESOME stuff!"

—JEN

"I just finished *Seaside Letters* . . . WOW! This is definitely on my favorite books list. I loved every aspect of this story! I am looking forward to reading more of your books. You have a devoted reader in me!"

—ERICA

The Trouble with Cowboys

Also by Denise Hunter

THE NANTUCKET ROMANCE SERIES
Surrender Bay
The Convenient Groom
Seaside Letters
Driftwood Lane

THE BIG SKY ROMANCE SERIES
A Cowboy's Touch
The Accidental Bride

Sweetwater Gap
"All Along" in *Smitten*

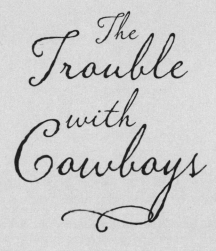

The Trouble with Cowboys

A
Big Sky
Romance

Denise Hunter

THOMAS NELSON
Since 1798

NASHVILLE   DALLAS   MEXICO CITY   RIO DE JANEIRO

Published in Nashville, Tennessee, by Thomas Nelson. Thomas Nelson is a registered trademark of Thomas Nelson, Inc.

Thomas Nelson, Inc., books may be purchased in bulk for educational, business, fund-raising, or sales promotional use. For information, please e-mail SpecialMarkets@ ThomasNelson.com.

Publisher's Note: This novel is a work of fiction. Names, characters, places, and incidents are either products of the author's imagination or used fictitiously. All characters are fictional, and any similarity to people living or dead is purely coincidental.

Library of Congress Cataloging-in-Publication Data

Hunter, Denise, 1968-
  The trouble with cowboys : a big sky romance / Denise Hunter.
    p. cm.
  ISBN 978-1-59554-803-0 (trade paper)
  1. Ranch life--Montana--Fiction. I. Title.
  PS3608.U5925T76 2012
  813'.6--dc23

                          2012022635

Printed in the United States of America

12 13 14 15 16 QG 5 4 3 2 1

Dear Pushover,

Horse temperaments differ by breed and personality. A stallion requires a firmer hand. Don't be afraid to let him know who's boss.

Annie Wilkerson was sitting in the Chuckwagon, minding her own business, when he mosied in. He was with a crowd, of course. He always traveled in a pack—him and his handful of ardent admirers.

Annie opened the menu, propped it on the table, and slouched behind it. The Silver Spurs belted out some country-and-western tune her sister probably knew by heart. The clamor in the crowded restaurant seemed to have increased twice over since Dylan and company walked in. But maybe that was her imagination.

The chair across from her screeched against the plank floor. Finally. John was already ten minutes late. She lowered her menu, smiling anyway.

An instant later the smile tumbled from her lips.

Dylan Taylor plopped his hat down and sprawled in the chair like he owned the table, the restaurant, and half of Park County besides. His impertinent grin slanted sideways, calling his dimple into action—a fact of which he was no doubt aware.

"Annie Wilkerson. Why's the prettiest filly in Moose Creek sitting all by her lonesome on a Saturday night?" Dylan's Texas drawl had followed him north, sticking with him like a stray dog.

Ignoring the heavy thumps of her heart, Annie tilted her head and deadpanned, "Well, Dylan, I was just sitting here waiting with bated breath for you to come rescue me."

He put his hand to his heart, his blue eyes twinkling. "Aw, Annie, don't tease me like that. It smarts."

She scowled at him and settled back in her chair, propping the menu between them. "What do you want, Dylan?"

"Maybe just the pleasure of your company."

"Maybe you should find another table."

He tsk-tsked. "So cruel. You wound me with your hurtful words."

If Dylan had a heart, she was sure it was unwoundable. Made of something springy and elastic that sent oncoming darts bouncing off. Typical cowboy.

She skimmed the menu, unseeing. "That seat's taken."

"Your sister joining you?"

Like she couldn't possibly have a date? "What's that supposed to mean?"

His hands went up in surrender. "I was hoping to join you."

"I have a date."

His head tipped back slowly, his eyes never leaving hers. "Ah . . . who's the lucky guy?"

"What do you want, Dylan?"

He tilted the chair onto its back legs, and she found herself wishing it would fall. But that kind of thing never happened to men like Dylan.

"I have a proposition," he said, his eyes roaming her face.

Her cheeks grew warm and she hated that. Cursed Irish blood and fair skin. She swore he said things like that on purpose. She focused on the menu. On the photo of barbecue ribs that were actually better than they looked.

"Not interested."

"Now, come on, give me a chance to explain. It's business—not that I'd have any problem picking up socially where we left off last time . . ."

She narrowed her eyes at him. "There was no last time."

"Whatever you say, sugar."

She gritted her teeth and slumped until she could no longer see him over the menu.

"In all seriousness," he said, his voice dropping the teasing tone, "I got a horse that needs help. Wondered if you'd drop by next week and take a look at him."

Oh no. She wasn't stepping foot on Dylan's property again. Not after last time. "I'm busy next week."

"It's my best horse—Braveheart. He's got moon blindness."

"I'm not a vet—have Merle look him over."

"He did."

There was something in his voice she couldn't define and didn't care to try.

"He thinks I ought to put him down."

Annie lowered her menu. Dylan's dimple was long gone. "Is he blind?"

"Not completely. But he will be. Started bumping into things in the spring, and by the time it was diagnosed, it was too late. He's not himself now. Spooks easy, won't let anyone near, not even me."

His eyes pulled her in. She'd never seen him without that cocksure grin, much less with that sober look in his eyes.

Careful, Annie.

She looked away, toward the dance floor where her best friend, Shay, was dancing with her husband. They moved like two pieces of the same puzzle. She wondered how long it would take that cowboy to erase the pretty smile from her friend's face. In her experience, it wouldn't be long.

"Annie . . . ?"

She pulled her eyes from the couple. "There's a trainer over in Sweet Grass County, Roy Flint. He's supposed to be really good. I'll get his number for you."

"I don't want him. I want the best. I read your column; you know what you're doing."

Brenda Peterson appeared tableside, flashing a bright smile. "You two ready to order?"

"We're not together."

"Large Coke, please."

They spoke simultaneously, and Annie glared at Dylan as Brenda walked away with her menu—never mind that she hadn't ordered yet.

Dylan propped his elbows on the table. "I can't put Braveheart down, but he needs a lot of work, and I don't have the time or expertise."

Annie leaned back, putting space between her and those puppy dog eyes. She was a sucker for a horse in distress, but if she was at

Dylan's place for days on end, she'd be the one in distress. Besides, getting him to pay up last time had been like collecting pollen from the wind.

"You're right," Annie said. "It is going to take a lot of time—time I don't have right now."

He leaned in, trained those laser-precision eyes right on her. Heaven have mercy, it was easy to see why he made women lose their wits. What was God thinking, combining all those rugged good looks with cowboy charm and tossing in dimples for good measure?

"I want *you*," he said.

The double meaning—intended or not—was a needed reminder. She pulled the napkin from the table and spread it across her lap. "Roy can help him, I'm sure of it. I'll get his number for you Monday."

Someone nearby cleared his throat. John Oakley had somehow arrived unnoticed, thanks to Dylan's annoying habit of usurping her every thought.

"Hello, Annie." John bent and placed a kiss on her cheek.

"Hi, John." Annie couldn't tear her eyes from Dylan, whose left brow had shot up.

"Oakley." Dylan nodded, coming slowly to his feet. He towered over John, who looked out of place at the Chuckwagon in his banker clothes.

"Dylan. Thanks for keeping my date company." His flat smile and flaring nostrils said otherwise.

"Anytime, Oakley, anytime." Dylan's gaze held hers for a beat too long, the corners of his lips twitching in a way she was sure annoyed John. "Annie, talk to you Monday." He pointed at her, winking. "And don't think I've given up."

Warmth flooded her face as John sank into the chair and jabbed his glasses into place with his index finger. She watched Dylan amble away and told herself the feeling spreading through her limbs was relief.

Dear Spooked,

Horses often spook when the rider is fearful. You will both feel more confident if you have a safe place to go when things go awry.

2

Annie knew something was amiss the minute she entered the Mocha Moose the next week. For starters, it was too quiet—there were only a few patrons. Even the music whispering from hidden speakers was all wrong. A soft classical tune, not a blaring rendition of "Ladies Love Country Boys."

She looked behind the bar where the owner, Tina Lewis, was stacking fresh cups beside the coffee carafes. Her short brown hair swung forward.

She gave Annie a chagrined look. "Hey, Annie."

Annie proceeded with caution toward her afternoon caffeine fix. "I thought Sierra was working tonight."

Tina glanced away and caught her lip between her teeth.

"What happened?"

Brown eyes met hers. "She didn't tell you. I'm sorry, Annie. I kept her as long as I could, but she didn't show up again last Friday, and Monday she brought Ryder with her—some trouble with the sitter. Now don't get me wrong, he's a little darlin', but . . . well, he's a four-year-old boy . . ." She finished with a wince.

Annie's stomach dropped to her dusty cowboy boots. "It's okay. I understand."

"I hated to do it in this economy, honey, and I tried to warn her, but it didn't help. I mean, your sister's a hard worker, and she was super for business—when she was here. "

Cowboys had lined up for their coffees on Sierra's shift.

"It's okay."

"And she took some great photos for me . . ." Tina gestured at her new board menu with the close-ups of their most popular drinks. "She's just got a lot on her plate with college and a little boy."

She filled a to-go cup with French roast and passed it across the granite counter with a lid. "On the house today."

Annie protested but gave up when Tina insisted. They made small talk for a few minutes while Annie sipped her coffee. Tina peppered her with questions about her new Arabian mare.

"We got our issues of *Montana Living* today." She gestured toward the stand of magazines. "I always read your column first. It's your fault I went out and bought a horse for Rachel, you know."

Annie's grandfather, a veterinarian, had started "Ask Avery" in the biweekly magazine. When he'd passed, they'd offered the column to Annie, changing the focus to horse training. It made her proud to carry on his legacy. Maybe the magazine was free, but it was offered in every store in Montana and read by residents and tourists alike.

"You won't regret buying the horse. If you have more questions, just give me a buzz."

Annie left the shop with a fresh cup of coffee and a massive headache. *What will we do without Sierra's income, God? And why didn't she tell me she lost her job two days ago? What am I gonna do with that girl, Lord?*

She thought of Dylan's request for help and wondered if she'd been too hasty in turning him down. No point crying over that spilt milk. She'd already given him the other trainer's number.

Annie turned toward her house rather than going to check on Mr. O'Neil's new gelding as she'd planned.

Outside her car window the sun shone brightly, casting shadows across the rocky peaks of the Gallatin Range, where snow still clung for dear life. Though spring hadn't reached the higher elevations, it had wakened the valley, greening the grass and birthing colorful wildflowers alongside the rippling creeks. The sight lifted her spirits.

When she pulled into the drive, she spotted Sierra's rusty Buick by the barn. Pepper grazed in his pen, his long nose following her truck up the drive. She wanted to saddle up and head for the hills, let the cool spring wind whip her hair from her face, chase the worry from her mind.

Instead she exited her truck and took the porch steps two at a time. Inside, the TV blared a cartoon. Ryder sprang from his spot on the floor. "Aunt Annie! You're home!" He smothered her legs in an exuberant hug.

"Hey, buddy." She ruffled his soft, dark hair and fought the urge to pinch his chubby cheeks—an action he hated—when he gazed up at her with adoration.

"Where's your mommy?"

The blender roared to life in the next room.

"Never mind."

After Annie removed her boots, Ryder tugged her hand. "Watch Batman with me." He pleaded with his wide green eyes.

"Not right now. Aunt Annie isn't finished for the day."

Ryder plopped onto a pillow, the sulk fading from his baby face as he became reabsorbed in the cartoon.

In the kitchen her sister shut off the blender, lifted the lid, and dipped her finger into the jar.

"I just stopped by the Mocha Moose."

Sierra turned, wide-eyed. The dab of chocolate something on her finger fell to the linoleum floor.

"You're home early." Sierra grabbed a paper towel and wiped up the drip.

"Why didn't you tell me you got fired?"

Her little sister swiped her long auburn curls from her face with the back of her hand. "I tried."

"When?"

"You've been gone a lot . . ."

"Working!"

"I know, I know. I just . . . I knew you'd be upset."

Annie wondered where Sierra had been the last two nights while Ryder had been with Martha Barnes. No doubt at the Chuckwagon, chatting up every cowboy within a five-mile radius, while the sitter tab ran up.

She sank into a chair at the kitchen table and ran her hands over her face. *Deep breaths. Help me out here, Lord. I don't want to lose it, but she just doesn't get it.*

Sierra perched on the chair across from her. Her small frame and delicate features had always made Annie feel protective. She was young, only twenty after all, and she'd hardly had a chance to be a kid.

"I'm really sorry." Sierra looked at the table.

"I know you are. It's just—" Annie sighed. She'd already said it a million times. After Sierra lost her jobs at Pappy's Market and Food 'n Fuel. She didn't have the energy for another recital of the Responsibility Speech.

"You're passing your classes, aren't you?"

Sierra lifted her chin. "Of course."

If Annie could just keep her sister going the right direction for one more semester, they'd be home free. Or so she told herself.

"Maybe I can apply at the bank? Or the clinic?"

"You need weekend hours. And I know for a fact the bank isn't hiring."

"That's right. How goes it with you and John anyway? What is it, two dates now?" Sierra shrugged, a crooked grin tugging her lips. "Not that I'm changing the subject or anything."

"John's fine." Annie didn't want to talk about John or the fact that his first kiss had been about as sizzling as a damp firecracker.

"You could do better, sis."

"He's very responsible, and he has a stable job."

"Boooorrr-ring."

Annie didn't know why she bothered. Sierra was just like their mother had been, falling for every cowboy who passed by, every sweet line thrown her way. It was the reason for Annie's promise— one that seemed more impossible to keep by the day.

Her cell phone pealed, and Annie glanced at it. The magazine. She left the table and walked toward the patio door, glad for the interruption.

"Hi, Midge. How's life in Bozeman?"

"Looking good, like summer almost. I'm so ready."

Beyond the patio door the sky spread like a blue blanket over Paradise Valley.

"Me too. The sun feels great today. Hey, my compliments on the new edition. I loved the article on upcoming rodeos."

"Yes, that seems to be a popular one."

"I turned in my next column last night. Did you get it?"

"Yes . . . yes, I did."

"Is there a problem?" The readers' questions had centered on a horse that wouldn't take a bit and another that disliked shots.

"It was fine. It's just—I'm afraid there have been some changes at the mag. We're doing a little restructuring."

"Restructuring?" *Oh, please, Lord, not my column. Not now.*

"I'm sorry, but I was instructed to tell you that 'Ask Avery' is being cut."

"Cut?"

"I'm sure you've noticed we're only getting a trickle of questions these days. My boss doesn't think the column is relevant anymore."

A chair squawked across the floor, and then Sierra was beside her, frowning.

"Half the state owns horses, Midge. How can you say it isn't relevant?"

"Back in the day we got dozens of queries a month. Even when you first took over, we received a lot. But now . . . seems everyone's finding their own answers online with Google and Wikipedia and such. It's a self-serve culture. I'm sorry, I realize it must feel like the end of an era, what with your grandfather starting the column."

"It is hard to hear." She'd felt as if she were keeping a little piece of him alive. It wasn't supposed to happen this way. Sierra was supposed to graduate with her journalism degree and take the reins, shifting the column to a topic that better suited her. Or that had been Annie's plan.

On top of that, there was the matter of money. First Sierra's job, now her part-time income. What was next? Her own business?

"I do have an offer for you, Annie. You're a wonderful writer and you have great judgment and a big heart. The higher-ups recognize that—I made sure of it—and we want to offer you first chance at a new column."

"What kind of column?"

"Well, my boss was talking to a friend who writes for a regional magazine in Wyoming. They started a column last year, and it's taken off like wildfire. He wants to do something similar at *Montana Living*, and he was on the cusp of asking the Wyoming columnist to write it, but I convinced him to give you a try. I think you'd do a wonderful job, if you're interested."

"I am. Tell me about it." Maybe it was a full-length column on horse training.

"We want to start a lovelorn column."

"A—lovelorn column?"

Sierra's brows shot up.

"I know it's completely different from what you're used to, but writing advice columns is more about voice and common sense, and you have both in abundance. The submission process is the same, and so is the pay. We'd call it 'Ask Annie.' There would be a three-month probation, since this is a new venture, but I have no doubt you'll pass with flying colors. And if all goes well, there'll be a raise down the line."

"Advice to the lovelorn." Annie was the last person on earth qualified to write such a column.

Sierra was smiling, nodding until her auburn curls bounced.

"As I said, it's been extremely popular in Wyoming. Specific relationship help is hard to find online, and women love reading about relationship issues. You have a way of being direct without being rude, and most importantly, you're decisive. The best advice columnists are black-and-white. I think your style would be a nice fit."

Annie had an idea that grew roots in two seconds flat. It was brilliant. "Maybe you'd consider a different direction, Midge. My sister, Sierra, is nearly finished with journalism school—I've mentioned her before. Would you consider letting her give the column a try?"

Sierra shook her head.

Annie continued anyway. "I could send you some samples of her work. She's a terrific writer."

"I'm sorry, Annie. I'm sure she is, but I barely convinced my boss to give *you* a try."

"I see." Annie still hoped Midge might hire Sierra once she had her degree. She hadn't worked so hard for nothing.

"Are you not interested?"

It wasn't as if she could afford to turn it down. Besides, with the redheaded bobblehead next to her, all momentum was pointing toward yes.

"Annie?"

"Yes, of course. I'll do it. Thanks for the opportunity, Midge." A niggle of worry flared in her stomach.

"Super! I'll let my boss know, and I'll send the first batch of questions as soon as I get them."

"Terrific. I appreciate the opportunity."

Sierra was clapping silently, her eyes twinkling like Ryder's on Christmas morning as Annie closed her phone.

"This is going to be so fun!"

"A real riot."

"Oh, stop it. I'll help you."

Annie didn't point out that Sierra had been in love a grand total of one time, or that her Prince Charming had left her high and dry with a baby.

Ryder appeared in the doorway. "Is my shake ready, Mommy?"

"Oh! I forgot about it, puddin'." Sierra dashed to the blender and began scraping the shake into a plastic cup.

"I have to get back to work. I'll try to be home for supper."

"I'll cook tonight," Sierra called, and Annie knew she was trying to make up for getting fired.

"Sounds good."

Outside Annie turned the key in her truck. The niggle of worry had spread through her body, leaving her limbs weak and shaky. Midge might have all the confidence in the world in her ability to write this column, but that was only because Midge didn't know the truth: Annie Wilkerson had never even once been in love.

Dear Concerned,

A horse can become stressed when losing his sight, but that doesn't mean he won't adapt.

3

ou look tired," Dylan said over the loud hum of the propane heater. With the help of his neighbors, he'd vaccinated and branded all his calves in one afternoon.

Wade shut down the heater, ushering in blessed silence. "That's what happens when you're working on four hours' sleep."

"Don't tell me the Code-meister was up all night again."

"This teething business is for the birds. Maybe Cody needs to spend a night with his Uncle Dylan tonight."

Dylan smiled. "Think this is a good time to remind you I'm only your kids' honorary uncle. Maddy, however, is welcome anytime she'd like."

Wade pulled off his hat and wiped the sweat from his brow. "Wouldn't want to interfere with your swinging-singles lifestyle."

"Is that a little jealousy I hear, pal? Married life getting you down?"

"Not a chance. I feel sorry for *you*, coming home to bologna sandwiches and a lonely bed."

Wade was joking, but his words hit the mark.

Dylan grinned anyway, shaking an image of Annie Wilkerson from his head. "Well, we can't all have an Abigail. She still taking classes?"

After years as an investigative reporter, Wade's wife had gone back to school for a teaching degree. Dylan couldn't imagine anyone more suited for the job.

"She just got out for the summer. Good thing, since she's not getting any more sleep than me."

They put away the tools and horses, working mostly in silence. Braveheart snorted and tossed his head.

Wade stopped by the stall. "He's no better?"

Dylan hung the saddle in the tack room and approached the stall where Braveheart stamped restlessly. "Don't know what to do with him. Had a horse trainer from Sweet Grass out several times this week, but he's getting nowhere."

"Never thought I'd see Braveheart go bronc-y like this."

"He's afraid—can't say I blame him. Just wish I knew how to help. Any ideas?"

Wade shoved his hands into his pockets. "Maybe if he weren't cooped up. Tried letting him out?"

"I'm half afraid to, the way he spooks." Dylan put out his hand, and Braveheart settled a bit, nickering softly. "Maybe you're right. Nothing else is working."

He fetched a halter and lead and put them on the horse. "Better stand back," he said, opening the gate.

Braveheart snorted and tossed his head but followed Dylan's lead through the barn. "That's right, buddy. Let's get you some fresh air."

At the threshold Braveheart stumbled and reared. Dylan tried to soothe him, but the horse darted sideways, squealing. His body barreled into Dylan and a hoof clipped Dylan's knee.

He hit the dirt hard, the breath leaving his body. Braveheart tore off for the field.

Wade jogged toward Dylan. "You all right?"

Dylan sucked in a breath, then accepted the hand up, dusting off the dirt. "Fine." He frowned at his horse, now bouncing around the field, the lead swinging. "Getting him back in will be a challenge."

"Guess it wasn't such a bright idea."

"Maybe he'll settle soon. Just hope he doesn't hurt himself." He was glad the horse was well away from the fence. Poor thing might just slam into it.

"Need to get Annie Wilkerson over here," Wade said. "Bet she could help him."

"I already asked her at the Chuckwagon last week."

"And here I thought you were only putting the moves on her."

"Yeah, that too." For all the good it had done him. He'd had plenty of company that night, but he couldn't deny his attention had been on the table for two in the corner instead of on his dancing partners.

"She can't do it," Dylan said. "Too busy."

Wade tossed him a wry grin. "Time for some of that famous Taylor charm, then."

Dylan pressed his lips together. "Already tried. That's about the time she gave me the other trainer's number."

Wade laughed. "Immune to the Taylor charm. Love it. Maybe she discovered a vaccine. Maybe she'll inoculate all the other gals in town."

"You're a real hoot." Maybe he should ask her again. That Roy was getting nowhere with Braveheart, and neither was he.

"You know, one more woman isn't going to scratch that itch of yours. One of these days, you're gonna have to deal with what's really stuck in your craw."

"And what would that be?"

Wade stuffed his hands in his pockets again. "You're running just as scared as Braveheart, and you know it."

Dylan clamped his jaw. Mighty brave of his friend to broach that subject. Brave or stupid. "My itches are getting scratched just fine, thanks very much." He reached for a change of topic. "Anyway, I thought you liked Annie."

"She's a sweet gal. But she's seeing John Oakley, isn't she?"

"That's just because she hasn't had a taste of me yet," Dylan said. He could hardly forget that the one time he had touched her she'd responded as if he'd jabbed her with a branding iron.

"If Oakley's the type she goes for, you're dead in the water. 'Sides, best I could tell, she wasn't looking so receptive at the Chuckwagon."

"Yeah, well, I know how to handle a woman who plays hard to get."

"Trouble is, pal"—Wade tossed him a sideways grin—"don't think she's playing."

Dylan watched Wade walk away, for once at a loss for words. Because deep down he knew his friend was right.

Dear Ready to Surrender,

The old saying is true. You can lead a horse to water, but you can't make him drink.

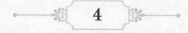

4

$\mathcal{A}$nnie left her bedroom and made her way down the narrow hall. The tired wood floors creaked under her feet. The house might be old and small, but it was hers. When she reached the living room, the morning light flooded through their picture window, coloring the walls with sunshine.

She wished she hadn't checked her e-mail before church. She didn't need another distraction today. Midge had sent her only one reader question to use for the first column, and Annie had no answers.

She turned into the small kitchen where Ryder was slurping Cheerios at the table. He was still in his Batman pajamas, a striped towel-cape tied at his throat. His dark hair stood at attention on the left side.

She ruffled it. "Morning, Bed Head. Where's Mommy?"

"I dunno."

Annie headed into the living room and saw her sister's reclining form on the couch.

"You're going to be late," she said, though it was obvious Sierra was skipping church.

"Not going. I'm extra tired."

This made three weeks in a row. "Late night?"

"Way too late. I met up with some of Wade Ryan's old friends from his rodeo days—they're passing through for that rodeo in Bozeman. You should've come—it was a single woman's palooza last night. We had a blast."

She wondered how much all that fun had cost. "It was too late for Ryder to be out. Besides, you know how I feel about cowboys."

"Wouldn't kill you to have fun once in a while, you know."

"And it wouldn't kill you to come to church now and again."

"I know, I know." Sierra pulled the quilt over her shoulders. "I'll go next week."

Annie checked her watch. It was too late to get Ryder ready. She had to be out the door in three minutes. "Have you applied anywhere?"

"Not yet, but I will."

Annie smothered a complaint. "Tomorrow?"

Sierra sighed. "Yes, Annie."

"I need some help on my first 'Dear Annie' letter. Will you be home this afternoon?"

"Sounds like fun."

Annie slid on her boots, said good-bye, and left, her heart heavy despite the beautiful sunrise cresting over the Absaroka Range. She didn't understand Sierra's sudden lack of interest in church. She knew it was symptomatic of a faltering spiritual walk, but what had caused it? She missed the days when Sierra had been full of godly passion, when she'd taken a stand with her high school friends, when she'd begged to go on mission trips.

If anything, Sierra should be seeking God's help now. She should be feeling anxious with no job in sight. But no, worry was Annie's territory. Sierra would smother the negative emotions with fun, fun, and more fun.

Annie got in her truck and turned the key, looking heavenward. "I'm trying, Gramps, but it's harder than I ever figured. Way harder."

"I don't see the problem." Sierra handed Annie the paper and forked her last bite of salad. "Tell her to give the guy the boot."

Outside the patio door Ryder let out a squeal as he descended the slide.

Annie stared at her sister. "It's not that simple."

"Sure it is. He cheated on her."

"They have a child."

"Well, they're not married yet. If she leaves him now, it'll save her the trouble of divorcing him later."

"You know God hates divorce."

"He also gives permission in the case of adultery. And if she marries him, that's what'll happen."

Sierra had a point. Still . . .

"Just because we have permission doesn't mean we *should*." They were getting off subject. Annie shook her head. "You have to consider that there's a child involved. He's sorry, and he still wants to marry her."

"So he says. Look, once a cheater, always a cheater. Isn't that what Mom always said?"

"Mom was married four times."

Sierra rolled her eyes. "Life isn't like your Jane Austen novels, Annie. Times have changed. Women don't have to put up with that stuff, nor should we. If she lets him off the hook this time, he'll just do it again."

Sierra seemed so sure, but Annie still didn't know. How could she advise a woman to break up with the father of her child when she wasn't certain? What if she steered the reader wrong?

"Why did Midge have to give me this one on my first try?"

"I'm telling you, it's clear-cut. Betrayed in Billings already knows what to do—she just needs you to tell her she's right so she can find the courage to do it."

Annie frowned at the letter. "I didn't get that at all."

"It's in the subtext."

She read it again. "Or maybe she's trying to find the courage to forgive him and only needs to hear me say it."

Sierra shook her head. "If you don't believe me, ask Shay."

Maybe she should. "Or maybe I'll just pray about it."

"When's it due?"

"This Wednesday. Midge wants to avoid a lapse." She'd already written a note to the readers for her last horse column.

"Well, you still have time to mull it over—not that I think you need to."

Annie took her dishes to the sink and rinsed her bowl. "Olivia asked about you at church." Shay and Travis's daughter adored Sierra.

"She's a sweetheart. She always asks me how I fix my hair and where I get my clothes."

"She looks up to you." Unspoken message: pull it together or you'll lead a little girl astray.

"I'll finish those," Sierra said, ignoring her hint altogether. "You should go for a ride. The weather's gorgeous."

"I think I might. Pepper's probably forgotten who I am."

"You don't forget the one who feeds you."

A few minutes later Annie headed out the front door and toward the barn. Pepper nickered softly as she approached the pen. The Arabian was mostly white, with tiny flecks of gray. When her grandfather had presented him for her fifteenth birthday, he'd said it looked as if God had shaken some pepper over him. The name had stuck.

Annie finished saddling the horse and struck out toward her friend's pasture. Shay and Travis McCoy had a huge spread, doubly so since they'd married and joined properties the year before. Shay had told her she was welcome anytime, and since her own property was so small, Annie took her up on it regularly.

She nudged Pepper to a canter and felt the wind take her shoulder-length hair. It tugged at her shirt and smacked her cool cheeks. She gave the horse his head, and he galloped across rolling green hills toward a ridge that dipped down to a bubbling creek.

They rode as one, their bodies moving together effortlessly. It reminded Annie of the way Shay and Travis had danced in tandem the weekend before. Much as she loved her horse, she couldn't help thinking it would be nice to share that kind of easy harmony with a man someday . . .

John Oakley sprang to mind then, and the sinking feeling that accompanied the thought of him did nothing to buoy her spirits. Maybe she *had* been reading too many romance novels. Or maybe

God wanted her to remain forever single, like Paul in the Bible. She hoped not. She was hardly old at twenty-four, but she felt much older.

Lord, I hope there's someone out there for me, she prayed as the sun dipped behind the clouds. *Between keeping Sierra on the right track and my financial struggles, I feel like I'm carrying the world on my shoulders. And this new column isn't helping. Show me what to tell this woman. I don't want to steer her wrong.*

She rode and prayed until Pepper grew winded, then she headed back to the barn, dismounted, and unsaddled the horse. Pepper's sides heaved, but she could tell he was happy by his high head and tail, by the way his ears turned forward.

Annie patted his withers, then scratched along his neck and back. He accommodated by stretching, then grunted his pleasure.

Normally, riding cleared her head, and she returned soothed and refreshed. This time she felt no better than before, despite her prayers.

She remembered what Midge had said about needing to be decisive. But Annie had never been decisive when it came to relationships. She could see both sides of an issue. It was the reason she'd constantly been in the middle, first between Sierra and their mom, and then between Sierra and their grandpa after their mom had passed. Annie was the perfect buffer, but it wasn't a role she enjoyed.

Midge was right, however. She couldn't be wishy-washy or readers wouldn't want her advice. It had been easy with "Ask Avery." There was a right way to train a horse and a wrong way, and Annie had the knowledge and experience to make that call.

Maybe she should take Sierra's advice and ask Shay for help. Her friend had managed to find love, after all. But Shay was busy with two kids and a prospering ranch, and Annie hated asking favors of friends.

She was just going to have to figure it out herself. But how was she supposed to have the answers for everyone else's love life when she had nothing but questions about her own?

Dear Betrayed in Billings,

It sounds as if your boyfriend is sorry and willing to make amends. If you love him, you should try to work it out.

5

ylan shut off his truck and got out of the vehicle. Annie's truck wasn't in her drive, a bad sign. Her house, painted a cheery yellow, was small but well kept. Just behind the gravel drive an old barn, big enough for a horse or two, leaned slightly toward the Gallatin Range.

He took the porch steps, wondering if he should've called first. He'd been hoping to catch her off guard. That hadn't worked out so well last time, but he had to use surprise to his advantage if he was going to get help for Braveheart. And Annie could help the horse, he was certain of it. As certain as he was that Annie Wilkerson was, bar none, the most intriguing woman in all Park County.

None of that, Taylor. You'll scare the filly away. And he couldn't afford that, no matter how attracted he was.

He knocked on the hollow green door and shoved his hands in his pockets, looking down at his dusty clothes. Why hadn't he taken time to shower? He'd been in an all-fired hurry to see Annie, that's why.

A heartbeat later the door opened and Sierra appeared, holding a bulky camera lens. Dylan felt the sting of disappointment.

Her eyebrows rose. "Hey, Dylan."

He smiled, removing his hat. "Howdy, Sierra. How are you?"

"Super," she said, then called over her shoulder, "Ryder, don't you touch my camera!" She faced Dylan again. "Sorry."

"Don't suppose Annie's home."

"She's not, but she just called. She's on her way, ten minutes or so. Ryder, you better not be near that camera!" She opened the door. "Come on in, I have to . . ." She gestured toward the other room.

"That's all right. I'm a mess. I'll wait here."

Sierra disappeared, her auburn hair swinging over her shoulder as she trotted away. "Ryder . . . what did I say?"

Dylan smiled as he walked to the edge of the porch. He set his hat on his head and looked around Annie's property. A fenced-in corral lay to the left of the house, and a neighbor's property butted up against hers on the other side.

In the distance the Gallatin Range had turned dusky purple in the waning light. Having been born and raised in Texas's prairie region, Dylan appreciated the mountains. They were like sentinels standing guard over the valley, always there, always constant.

Behind him the screen door squeaked. Ryder appeared, his dark curls poking out every which way.

"Hey, little man," Dylan said.

The screen door clacked behind Ryder, who tilted his head. "You're a cowboy."

"That's right, I am. Are you a cowboy?"

Ryder snickered. "I'm only four, silly."

"That's all right. I was roping cattle and wrestling calves to the ground when I was your age."

Ryder frowned thoughtfully, and Dylan caught a glimpse of Annie in that look. "I can't do none of that."

Dylan shrugged. "All it takes is a piece of rope and a little practice. I could teach you."

The boy's eyes lit up. "You could?"

"Why, sure, it's not that hard. Got a lariat in my truck if you want to learn."

"Okay!"

Ryder followed him to his truck, asking questions the whole way. Dylan showed him how to tie a Honda knot.

Ryder's brows pushed together. "I can't even tie my shoes."

Dylan ruffled his hair, chuckling. "Well, we'll just skip that part then."

He led the kid to the nearby fence and showed him how to hold the rope and swing it. He gave it a toss, and it settled around the fence post.

"Wow, I wanna try!"

Dylan collected the rope. "It's gonna take some practice, now. You gotta be real patient." He placed the lariat in Ryder's hand and helped him swing and throw the loop.

The lariat dropped to the ground at the base of the post, sending up a puff of dirt.

"That's awful close," Dylan said. "Keep it up and you'll be a real cowboy in no time." He set his hat on Ryder's head. "Looks good on you."

The boy looked up at him and smiled with adoring eyes, and Dylan remembered the kid didn't have a father.

"Try again, now."

A few minutes later he heard a rumble and looked up the drive to see Annie's truck approaching.

Ryder's loop fell at the base of the post as Annie shut the truck off. She got out and walked toward them. Her jaw was set, her back stiff.

Ryder dropped the rope and threw himself into her legs. "Aunt Annie!"

Her face softened as she embraced him. "Hey, Bed Head. How was your day?"

She was striking, with that black silky hair swinging around her shoulders and that skin, pretty as porcelain. He bit his tongue before he went and said so.

"Mr. Taylor is teaching me to be a real cowboy!"

Her lips stretched in a smile that didn't meet her eyes. "Is that so?"

"If you keep practicing," Dylan said, "you'll be roping cattle in no time."

Ryder let go of Annie. "I don't have a rope."

"Take this one. I have plenty." Dylan picked up the lariat and wound it up.

"You really shouldn't," Annie said.

"No problem." He handed the rope to Ryder, who jumped up and down.

"Thanks, Mr. Taylor."

"Anytime."

"Ryder," Sierra called from the doorway. "Time for your bath."

"Aww, I don't wanna."

"Being a cowboy is dirty work, right?" Dylan said. "Every day ends with a nice, hot shower . . . er, bath."

"Come on, Ryder!" Sierra called.

The boy made a face, but he handed back Dylan's hat and scuttled off with his rope.

Dylan turned a smile on Annie. "Cute kid."

She crossed her arms, none too inviting. "Thanks."

Maybe she didn't like unannounced visitors. "Sorry to drop by. Wanted to thank you for passing on Roy's number. He worked with Braveheart last week."

"Glad to hear it."

" 'Fraid it didn't go too well."

"That's too bad."

He felt like he was talking to a tree stump. If he could just get her to sit down and loosen up. "Listen, you have a minute? Maybe we could take a load off."

Annie's eyes darted to the house and she swallowed. "I—suppose we could sit on the porch."

When they reached the house, Annie disappeared inside, then returned with a plastic chair she set against the brick façade. She sat down and tucked her hands under her thighs. "What's up?" Her eyes darted away from him toward the darkening mountain range.

Dylan looked around her property. It was small by Montana standards, but the grass was neatly clipped, and the flower bed had already been given a spring spruce-up.

"Nice place you got. How many horses you have?"

"Just one. You need some advice about Braveheart?"

He called on his dimple; it rarely failed him. "Eager to see the backside of me, Annie?"

She banked a look off him as a pretty blush bloomed on her cheeks. "I'm busy, Dylan. If you have a question, spit it out. If not . . ." She looked ready to bolt.

"I'll cut right to the chase then. Braveheart's worse than he was last we spoke. Roy wasn't working out. I let him go."

"You shouldn't have done that."

"The horse needs your help."

"I already told you—"

"You're busy, I know. I'm getting desperate here, Annie. He won't even let me near him anymore. His eyesight's worse, and he's wreaking havoc in my barn. He's going to hurt himself or someone else."

Dylan planted his elbows on his knees and twisted the brim of his hat in his hands. He hated seeing Braveheart like that. It was as if the horse was going mad, only he wasn't. When he looked up, he met Annie's eyes.

"Maybe Merle was right," she said softly.

"I'm not putting him down." They'd been through so much together. Braveheart had gotten him through the worst days of his life. How could he turn his back on his horse in his hour of need?

"I'm not," he repeated.

Annie looked away from Dylan. He had that dogged look Ryder sometimes got when Sierra said it was bedtime. Only the expression was ten times as formidable on Dylan's face and probably wouldn't precede a temper tantrum that left him thrashing on the porch.

It had disturbed her to see Ryder in the cowboy hat, swinging a lariat. Last thing she needed was Dylan coming around influencing the child.

"You're the only one who can help him," he said.

"You don't know that. These things take time. Roy's not a miracle worker."

Dylan shook his head. "Braveheart knows you. You'll be able to get through to him, I know it. You're the best trainer in all Park County, maybe even the whole state."

She steeled herself against his flattery and forced herself to remember last summer. She'd been working with his stubborn mustang, and the animal had kicked at her. She jumped back just in time. Right into Dylan's arms.

"Whoa there," he'd said, his low Texas drawl tickling her ear.

His strong arms curled around her stomach. The heat of his chest burned into her back. The feel of him against her sent a shiver down her arms despite the summer heat and turned her legs to noodles. Her mouth went as dry as Spring Creek in July. Her breath seemed stuffed in her lungs.

"Why, Annie Wilkerson . . . ," he'd whispered, fluttering the sensitive hairs near her ear. "I had no idea you felt this way."

His words brought her around quick enough. She pulled herself from his arms and gave him a shove for good measure, noting that it didn't make him budge one iota.

"Keep your hands to yourself, Taylor." She was amazed her voice hadn't betrayed the chaos inside her.

He'd tugged the brim of his hat down, his eyes twinkling. "Whatever you say, Miss Annie."

She looked at him now. The twinkle was long gone, replaced by hues of desperation.

Too bad. Her heart pounded from the memory. She'd rather wrestle a rattlesnake than spend another day at his place—she'd probably stand a better chance of coming out unscathed.

"You're his last hope, Annie. Please, you gotta help him."

The man had a way of working people over that reminded Annie too much of her own father and all the other smooth-talking cowboys she'd had the misfortune of meeting. Even now he was buttering her up, tugging at her heartstrings, making her want to do something she had no business doing.

"I'll pay whatever you want."

He didn't have the money to make an offer like that, but his desperation twisted her heart. And she hated seeing an animal suffer. Too bad she couldn't bring the horse here, but Braveheart already had enough change going on. He needed a familiar environment, familiar smells, familiar people.

"Come on, Annie. I'll do anything."

He was getting to her with his sad eyes. She could feel her resignation crumbling away like the old stone schoolhouse on Mill Road.

"Anything," he repeated.

The letter surfaced in her mind, the one she still had no answers for. The one that was due tomorrow even though she still didn't know what to say.

Maybe Dylan could help. No doubt the man knew his way around the maze of love.

She blinked, shaking her head. What was she thinking? She was not talking about something as personal as love and relationships with Dylan Taylor. Not with the way he made her feel all . . . distracted and unsettled. She'd be a ninny.

"And I swear," he said as if reading her mind. "No funny business. " He held up his hands. "Strictly professional."

She wavered. Maybe it could work. Helping the horse would take awhile. If they traded, he'd owe her a lot of help. Maybe even enough to get her through her probation period, long enough to get her legs under her, long enough to get that raise.

"Annie? Will you do it?"

"I'm thinking." Annie stood and paced the length of the porch. Could she handle Dylan? He said he was busy. Maybe she'd hardly see him. She did want to help the horse.

But they'd have to work on the column together. She imagined sitting in his cozy living room going over the nuances of love and shivered. All her red flags were waving high.

But what else could she do? Sierra had no job in sight, and their savings had dwindled down to nothing. She couldn't afford to lose the column.

Before she could change her mind, she turned. "All right, on one condition."

Dylan straightened. "Name it."

She crossed her arms, a barrier between them, and lifted her chin. "I need help with a project. I'll make a trade."

"What is it?"

"An advice column," she said, suddenly reluctant to mention the topic. "You help me, I'll help you. Equal hours."

He shrugged his broad shoulders. "Not sure how I can help with your horse column, but I'll do whatever you want."

Might as well just get it out on the table. "It's not the horse column. It's a . . . lovelorn column."

She watched the emotions flicker in his eyes. Understanding dawned like the sun, tinged with the colors of amusement and ego. "So you think I'm an expert in the love department."

She leveled a look at him. "Never mind. It was a bad idea."

His smile fell as he stood, his eyes sobering. "All right, all right," he said in a tone he probably used with a nervous horse. "I'll do it, whatever you want. Done deal." He extended his hand.

She paused a minute, her heart skittering across her chest like a marble over a hardwood floor. She told herself she had no choice. She told herself she could handle Dylan Taylor and his flirtatious ways just fine.

Then his hand closed over hers, and she felt the same shiver run through her as last time, and no matter what she told herself, she knew she'd just signed up for all kinds of trouble.

Dear Betrayed in Billings,

It sounds as if your boyfriend is unworthy of the love and respect you've given him. A marriage won't fix the problem and may, in fact, end up being the biggest mistake of your life.

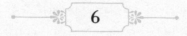

6

From the barn Dylan watched Braveheart running wild in the field. His mahogany coat gleamed in the waning daylight, and his black mane flopped as he bucked.

The horse had bolted like a wild mustang from the paddock when Annie opened the gate, and only now, a full thirty minutes later, was he beginning to settle. Dylan had winced as he watched the horse bump into the fence twice and trip several times on the uneven ground.

Now his sides heaved. He tossed his head and snorted. At the fence, Annie's head tilted.

Dylan approached her. "What do you think?" He propped his foot on the fence beside her. The sweet smell of her shampoo wafted over on a breeze.

"You were right, he's a mess."

He tugged his hat lower. "But you can help him . . ."

Braveheart caught the sound of his voice and turned toward them.

"I think so. It'll take time though."

"You got further tonight than Roy got all week."

"It was a risk to let him out again. Wasn't sure I was doing the right thing."

Braveheart tossed his head, cocked his ears.

She opened the gate. "Why don't we go say hello."

"Sure that's a good idea? He 'bout trampled me last time."

She started toward the horse, walking slowly. "He still has some sight in his right eye. Stay where he can see you and keep talking. He'll be reassured by your voice and know where you are."

Annie stopped, letting Dylan approach alone.

"Hey, buddy. How's my big guy? Yeah . . . it's okay."

Braveheart lifted his head and whinnied as Dylan neared.

"Keep talking."

"How you doing, Braveheart?" Dylan held out his hand, and Braveheart nuzzled it. A moment later the horse nickered quietly, greeting him.

"That's my boy." Dylan tossed Annie a smile over his shoulder, then patted Braveheart's side and scratched his neck, murmuring softly. Hope surged through his veins. Maybe the horse would make it after all.

Dylan smiled at Annie as she approached. "You're a miracle worker. Last time I tried this, he wouldn't stand for it."

"He still has a long way to go." She let Braveheart sniff her hand.

"What's next?"

"I'm afraid we're losing daylight. Go ahead and lead him back to his stall. Stay on his right side and keep talking."

He started toward the barn, instructing Braveheart to walk, and the horse followed. The woman knew what she was doing.

"He'll have to rely on your verbal cues now," Annie said, trailing behind them. "Treat him normally, or you'll have a real mess on your hands."

Braveheart lost his footing on the threshold and grew agitated as he entered the barn with the other animals.

"Use your cues."

Dylan did, and Braveheart snorted but followed a moment later, stopping when Dylan cued him.

When he had the horse settled in a stall with fresh hay and water, he gave Braveheart a final pat and followed Annie into the darkening yard.

"He hasn't let me near him since I let him out last week. I was starting to think—" He turned his eyes on her. Gratitude welled up inside him. "You're flat amazing, Annie."

She lowered her eyes, then looked out over the pasture. "It's not rocket science."

"Don't discount your skill." He set his hat back on his head.

"Let him out again tomorrow, but remember, stay on his right, and make sure there are no other horses in the field. Lead him around the fence line again so he knows his boundaries. And keep using verbal cues."

"All right."

"I'll stop by next week and check on him."

"We'd better get cracking on your column. Stay for supper?"

Her lips went lax, drooping at the corners. Had she forgotten about his end of the deal?

"Just sandwiches, but you must be hungry."

"No thanks. This shouldn't take long. Let's just sit on the porch—it's a nice evening."

He shrugged. "Suit yourself." He had to admit, he'd felt a little guilty since he'd agreed to this deal. He wasn't sure how much help he was going to be. After all, he'd only been in love once, and that hadn't ended so well.

His phone vibrated in his pocket as Annie stopped by her truck to collect her things.

It was Wade's cell. He grinned. Probably Maddy calling with boy troubles again. She'd called for advice three times in the last two days.

"'Scuse me." He continued walking as he answered. "Uncle Dylan, at your service."

"It's Wade. I need a favor." His voice was tense, and Cody bawled in the background.

Dylan stopped at the foot of the porch steps. "What's wrong?"

"It's Maddy. Calf stepped on her hand—think it might be broken."

"What can I do?"

"Abby's in Bozeman, and Cody's screaming bloody murder—"

"Say no more. Be right over." In between Cody's cries, he could hear Maddy sniveling in the background.

"I'm headed toward the clinic now. You home?"

"Yeah, bring him over."

Dylan closed his phone. He hoped Maddy hadn't broken her hand.

"What's wrong?" Annie asked, approaching.

He repeated the information as he took the porch steps. "Come inside. I should get some things up off the floor."

Annie stepped toward her truck. "I should go."

"No, have a seat. I'll be right out." Dylan went inside, hoping she'd hang around, but too concerned about Maddy to give it much thought. He snatched a pocketknife off the end table and a glass bowl from the coffee table. Last time they'd brought Cody over, he'd put everything he could grasp into his mouth.

What else? He set the fireplace tools in the closet and was shoving the ottoman in front of the staircase when he heard Wade's truck barreling down the drive.

He rushed out and met Wade as he shoved the truck into park. Cody was still wailing from the backseat. Dylan opened the back door and looked at Maddy in the passenger seat. She held her hand suspended in midair.

"Sorry," Wade said over his shoulder. "He's tired and not one bit happy about being put in that thing."

Dylan unlatched the seat belt and worked the car seat loose. "How ya doing, tough girl?" he asked Maddy.

Her lip wobbled. "Fine."

He grabbed the car seat and lifted the wailing eleven-month-old baby. "Hang in there, Maddy."

"Don't forget the bag," Wade said.

Dylan shouldered the diaper bag and shut the door.

"Thanks, buddy," Wade said through the open window. "Don't know how long it'll be . . ."

"I can keep him overnight if that'll help."

"I'll let you know." Wade nodded once, turned the truck around, and headed down the drive.

The outdoor light on his barn had kicked on, making a puddle of light in the dirt. Annie sat on the porch in the shadows. He took the steps and set the car seat down, then flipped on the porch light and freed the wailing Code-meister. Tears clung to his dark lashes, and his bottom lip quivered with righteous indignation.

"Come here, little guy."

Annie made to stand. "We can do this another time."

"Sit tight. Please. He'll settle down real quick." He pulled Cody to his shoulder. The baby's back was hot, and his forehead felt damp against Dylan's neck. He bounced Cody, pacing the length of the porch. The little guy smelled baby fresh and was already in his pj's.

"Shh, Uncle Dylan's here."

Within a minute Cody's cries petered out to wobbly sniffles. "Thatta boy." He rubbed the baby's back as he passed Annie and took a seat on the swing, setting it into motion.

A moment later Cody dropped his head to Dylan's chest and gave a long, shuddery sigh.

Annie watched the baby nuzzle into Dylan's neck. His thick arm supported Cody's weight, and he rubbed the baby's back. The motion of the swing made Cody's eyelids flutter until they remained closed.

The picture in front of her seemed contrary to everything she knew about Dylan Taylor. But she couldn't deny there was something inordinately appealing about a man with a baby. She decided she preferred her preconceived notions to the ones forming now.

"He asleep?" Dylan whispered.

She nodded, smiling despite herself at the way Cody's chubby cheeks were smooshed against Dylan's shirt. "He's a doll."

"He's a keeper. I sure hope Maddy's okay."

"I'm sure she'll be fine. You've probably broken a bone or two yourself."

He tilted a smile. "Or seven." He settled back into the swing, shifting Cody. "Why don't we get started on your letters?"

"Just one this time." She filled him in on the column and her instructions from Midge, then she handed him the letter.

She watched him discreetly as he read. He took up most of the swing with those broad shoulders. His brim hid his eyes but exposed his well-trimmed sideburns and five o'clock shadow. His lips, unsmiling for once, were nicely shaped and bowed on top.

Okay, so she saw the appeal. She could appreciate God's handiwork without wanting him for herself. So long as he kept that cowboy hat on to remind her what he was, she'd be just fine and dandy.

He looked up and passed her the letter, setting his hand on Cody's back. "Seems pretty clear to me," he said quietly.

"She should give him another chance?"

"You kidding me?" His lips tilted up as he shook his head. "Sugar, you're way off. She's gotta dump the dude, the sooner the better."

Not him too. "Seriously? Look, I know he blew it, but he shows clear indication of remorse, and there is a child involved, after all. Isn't it worth a second chance?"

"They're not even married yet. What's she gonna do when he cheats on her then?"

"Who says he will? She said he's willing to make it up to her. Maybe a little counseling would get them back on track."

He gave a wry laugh. "Counseling."

"It can work."

"Sure it can."

His grin was getting on her nerves. "Maybe he's learned his lesson, did you ever think about that?"

"He's a cheater."

"Oh, come on, like you've never cheated."

The smile fell and the fun fizzled from his face, his eyes going as flat as day-old soda.

She wished she hadn't said it, but it was too late to call it back. Still, you couldn't tell her a skirt-chaser like Dylan was true blue.

"You wanted my opinion and you got it," he said quietly. "Sorry if it doesn't jibe with yours."

Her stomach twisted at his calmness. Maybe she shouldn't have said it, but if the truth hurt, was it her fault?

Her phone rang and vibrated in her pocket. Cody didn't so much as stir.

She checked the screen. John. She didn't want to take the call, but she was desperate to extricate herself from the awkward moment.

"Do you mind?" she asked.

He dipped his head and gestured toward the phone.

Annie stood and answered as she crossed the porch. "Hi, John."

"Annie. I tried you at home, but Sierra said you were still working."

"Yeah, a late one tonight."

"One of Dylan Taylor's horses?"

She was going to thump Sierra upside the head. "Yes."

"You're losing daylight."

It didn't take a mind reader to pick up on his jealousy. "I'm about done. Can I call you when I get home?"

"Well, I was just wondering if you wanted to go to the Chuckwagon again this Saturday. The Silver Spurs are playing—I know you like them."

Behind her, the swing squawked rhythmically on its hinges. She'd been thinking about calling it quits with John after their first kiss, but she hadn't made up her mind yet. Maybe the dud first kiss was a fluke. Maybe she needed to give it more time. Or maybe she was feeling desperate.

"Sure, that sounds fine."

He set a time to pick her up, and she closed her phone and tucked it into her pocket.

"Date with your boyfriend?"

"He's not my boyfriend." She began gathering her things.

"Leaving so soon?"

"We're pretty much done here."

"Didn't take long."

"There'll be two or three letters next time."

He rose, supporting Cody's weight. "How are you going to answer?"

She hitched her handbag on her shoulder. "I'm not sure." She had to write the column tomorrow, and so far it was two against one.

She made to leave, but he took her arm. "We still have a deal, right?"

The porch light hit his face, highlighting the worry lines on his forehead. His eyes looked like melting caramel. His hand loosened on her arm, and his thumb moved back and forth, sending a shiver up her arm.

"I'm not going back on my word just because we don't agree." Or because he looked like heaven with a baby in his arms. Or because his touch made her feel things that made her want to run for the hills.

"I could just tell you what you want to hear."

Yeah, he was good at that. She shifted away from him. "You keep telling me what you think, and I'll keep helping your horse."

The lines faded as his lips lifted. "Thanks."

She said good night and scurried down the porch steps before the sight of his dimple beckoned her back.

Dear Jealous,

Nothing brings out the green monster like seeing your woman with someone else . . .

7

"Here you go, darlin'."

Dylan accepted the Coke from Brenda Peterson and tossed her a wink. "Thanks, Brenda."

The Chuckwagon was bustling tonight. The Silver Spurs cranked out their first tune, a country-and-western song that had drawn half the place to the dance floor. His date, Marla, was chatting up an old friend across the room.

Dylan's eyes swung past the dancing duo of Annie and John Oakley. He wondered if she'd ever considered what her full name would be if she married the banker.

He shook his head even as he took a second look. Oakley's beady little eyes gawked at Annie. His eyebrows jumped at something she said, bumping his receding hairline farther north. What did she see in the guy? He was stiff as a two-by-four and twice as square.

Dylan scowled. John Oakley. If she wanted a good time, Spreadsheet wasn't the answer.

"Hey, Dylan. Where's Marla?" Abigail Ryan settled into the seat across from him. Her green eyes sparkled under the lights. Motherhood agreed with her, teething baby or no.

"Over there," he said over the music, gesturing. "Leave the Code-meister at home tonight?"

"Shay's got him. We traded him for Olivia." Abigail nodded toward the floor where Shay's daughter was dancing with Wade's fourteen-year-old Maddy. Her hand, though badly bruised, hadn't been broken after all.

"I'd say you got the easier end of that bargain."

She smiled. "I'd say you're right."

"Right about what?" Wade settled next to his wife, drawing her into his side and setting a kiss on her head. She turned into his chest.

Show-off. Dylan looked away.

"Our trade with Shay. She's probably up to her eyeballs in smashed squash and zucchini, poor girl."

Dylan made a face as his eyes swung toward Annie in time to see the couple part as the song ended. Annie returned to their table while Oakley headed toward the restroom. Just before he hit the door, he withdrew his phone from his starched pants and detoured out the back door with a hand over his ear.

"Now's your chance," Wade said.

Dylan shot him a look, then watched Annie accept a basket of food from Brenda.

"Am I missing something?" Abigail said, looking between them.

"Our friend's got a crush."

"What are we, in kindergarten?" Dylan said.

Abigail turned around, then faced him again, her smile widening. "Annie Wilkerson? Oh, Shay is going to love this."

Dylan stood. "Excuse me. There's a lady in need of my attention."

"You be nice to her," Abigail called. "She's a good girl."

He made his way toward Annie's table and sank into the opposite chair, treating her to his best smile.

Her blue eyes widened and her lips parted before she clamped them closed and blinked away the surprise. "Seat's taken."

"How's the prettiest filly in all Park County?"

She rolled her eyes, and her long eyelashes got tangled in her bangs. Mesmerized, he watched her blink.

"What do you want, Dylan?" She cast a look toward the restroom hall.

"If you're waiting for Spreadsheet to save you—"

"Spreadsheet?"

"You'll be waiting awhile. He took a call."

Annie glared, but he wasn't fooled. Deep down she liked the attention—she just didn't know it yet.

"If you don't mind, I'd like to eat."

He gestured toward her food, then leaned his elbows on the table, watching her pick up the loaded burger. She took a bite and dabbed her mouth with the napkin, chewing.

"How'd the article finish up?"

She gave him a look, pointing to her full mouth.

That was okay. He was a patient man. He propped his chin in his hand, waiting.

She swallowed and took a drink. "It turned out fine. I have a

new batch of letters to go through for next week. How's Braveheart?"
She took another bite.

"He misses you. When you coming back?"

Annie pointed to her full mouth again, finished chewing, and
pushed the basket away with a sigh. "What day works for you?"

"Any evening."

She pursed her lips. "Thursday, I guess. Let's just make it every
Thursday."

"Perfect." The song ended and the Spurs started a slow tune.
"Dance with me."

"I'm here with someone else." She looked at him pointedly.
"And so are you."

She'd noticed. He tried not to let that go to his head. "It's just a
dance. My feet are itching."

"I'm sure you can find another partner." She glanced toward
the exit again, clearly hoping for the timely arrival of her date.

He remembered what Wade had said about Annie being hard to
get. He was starting to think his friend was right. Well, there were
plenty of other willing fillies.

He rose to his feet, winking. "All right then, be that way."

As he made his way back to his table, Marla appeared at his side
and pulled him onto the dance floor, laughing. But as he held her in
his arms, all he could think of was whether or not Annie saw them
and if it bothered her the way it bothered him to see her and Oakley
together.

And half an hour later, when Annie and her date slipped out
the back door, he wondered if she'd wind up in Oakley's arms yet
again before the night was over.

Dear Frustrated,

Sometimes loving someone else means letting go.

8

$\mathcal{A}$nnie turned off her alarm and crawled from bed, her thoughts turning immediately to the night before. An image of Dylan appeared unbidden. How vexing that the man whose face surfaced first wasn't even her date.

She washed her face and trudged to the kitchen to start a much-needed pot of coffee. Dylan and his winsome ways. So annoying. The way he just plopped down like he belonged there, never mind that she had a date or that he had one too. Love the one you're with, that was his philosophy. And then show up at church on Sunday with a Bible and a happy-go-lucky grin. It was so Dylan. But what did she expect?

So stop thinking about him, Annie Wilkerson.

She'd think about John instead. About his sort-of cute face and the kind-of endearing way he poked his glasses into place. About his soft hands and his gentle good-night kiss. He'd be a good husband to someone, a faithful provider. He'd be a good father too. She'd never once heard him raise his voice or lose his temper. Though, come to think of it, she hadn't yet seen him with a child. Ryder was always in bed by the time he brought her home.

Dylan, on the other hand . . . If he ever managed to narrow the field down to one woman, she was sure it wouldn't last long. He'd get bored in a month or two and be on to the next. And there would, no doubt, be a line of silly ninnies just waiting.

And here she was, thinking about him again. What was wrong with her?

"Aunt Annie, where's Mommy?"

She turned from Mr. Coffee to find Ryder rubbing his sleepy eyes. The night before, Sierra had headed out the door minutes after Annie had returned.

"Morning, Bed Head. She's probably still asleep. We get to go to church this morning. Wanna help me feed Pepper?"

Ryder shook his head. "Mommy's not in her room."

Annie frowned, ruffling his hair as she passed, even as her stomach clenched. Thinking back, she hadn't heard Sierra come in. She'd started her favorite book, *Pride and Prejudice*, read until eleven, and then fallen into a sound sleep.

At the end of the hall she stopped. Sierra's bed was empty and unmade. But then, it was always unmade. She checked the bathroom. Empty.

Ryder appeared at her side. "I'm hungry."

Annie smiled and fixed him a bowl of Cheerios with a calmness she didn't feel. Sierra liked to stay out late, but she always came home. Always. She'd said she was going to the Chuckwagon, but it closed at midnight. Where had she gone after that? What if she'd had an accident on the way home? What if she'd met some dangerous drifter passing through town or hooked up with some weirdo? She was so young, only twenty, and she didn't have the best judgment.

Annie put away the milk and checked her cell phone, hoping for a message. Her heart beat up into her throat. No voice mail, no text.

Just then a rumble sounded. She peeked through the curtains and saw her sister's car coming up the drive. The adrenaline drained suddenly, leaving her weak, shaky, and angry. She paced across the room, waiting, catching her breath, and trying to calm herself.

Her jaw ached from clenching by the time Sierra crept through the door in last night's jeans and spangled top, her mascara smudged under her eyes. They widened when she saw Annie, and she gave up on sneaking in.

"Where have you been?" She kept her voice down for Ryder's sake.

Sierra dropped her bag on the recliner. "Sorry, I meant to make it in before you woke."

"You didn't even call. You have a child, Sierra—you can't just stay out all night like an irresponsible teenager."

Sierra's elfin features hardened. "I *know* I have a child. He was perfectly safe here with you. And I didn't call because I didn't want to wake you both."

"Where were you?"

She pulled off a pair of heeled boots that looked ridiculous on a quiet Sunday morning. "With a new friend."

"A man?"

Her eyes narrowed. "Stop treating me like a child."

"Since when do you have one-night stands?"

"That isn't what—"

"Is that who you are, Sierra? Where is all this leading?"

"All *what*?"

"All this—cavorting with men, staying out till all hours on Saturday nights, skipping church—"

"I'm going to college, I'm raising a child—"

"You should be out looking for a job instead of trying to turn the head of every man you see!"

"On a Saturday night? I am looking for a job. What more do you want from me, Annie? I'm the oldest twenty-year-old ever!"

"Where was you, Mommy?" Ryder appeared, drawn no doubt by Sierra's raised voice.

Sierra lifted him, kissed his milky mouth, and set him back down.

"I was—outside, puddin'." She ruffled his dark hair and smacked his rump. "Go finish breakfast, then I'll put your new movie in."

"Yippee!" Ryder scampered toward the kitchen.

That should keep him busy while Sierra slept. So much for her promise to go to church this week.

Annie crossed her arms. "So you're lying to your child now too."

Sierra set her small chin. "Stop judging me, Annie. And stop trying to tell me what to do. You're not my mom!"

"You're my responsibility. How do you think I felt when I couldn't find you? I was imagining all sorts of awful things!"

This was exactly what their grandfather had feared. Annie was doing a terrible job. She wasn't keeping her promise at all. Tears stung her eyes.

Sierra's face softened. She looked so young with her makeup all smudged under her sleepy eyes. She tried for a smile. "Sorry I worried you. I promise I'll call next time."

She couldn't believe her sister. "Next time? What if something had happened? All moral implications aside, you can't go running off with strangers!"

"He isn't a stranger, exactly. He's a friend of Dylan's from the rodeo circuit, in town for a few days. Dylan introduced us at the Chuckwagon and we hit it off. We didn't—"

"Dylan?"

Sierra grabbed her bag, sighing hard. "You don't even listen to me, Annie. I'm an adult and it's time you started treating me like one." She turned and strode into the kitchen.

Annie could hear the clang of the silverware drawer, hear Sierra chatting with Ryder, hear his laughter. It all sounded like a perfect little family.

Annie put on her boots and left the house, seething. Even her chores didn't soothe her temper, and by the time she got to church, all she could think about was getting hold of Dylan Taylor, wrapping her hands around his thick neck, and squeezing the daylights out of him.

Dylan slipped into the pew late. Chores had set him behind, and he'd been trying to take extra time with Braveheart every morning. That hadn't happened today. As it was, the music had already begun.

He let out a breath and gave himself over to the worshipful words of "Great Is Thy Faithfulness," letting the cares of the week drain away. The music was his favorite part. He was convinced God could speak through lyrics, even through the melody, if He chose to. And the reminder of God's bountiful provisions spoke to him this morning.

When the music ended, the congregation was seated and Pastor Blevins began preaching on letting go of earthly cares. It was a fine sermon, but Dylan found his thoughts, and his eyes, drifting. As luck would have it, Annie was in his line of vision, her silky black hair glistening under the chandeliers. She sat straight as a ponderosa pine. He wondered for the dozenth time if Oakley had kissed her good night the night before, then he chided himself for caring.

When the service ended, he intended to wend his way over to Annie and confirm their plans for Thursday. Not because he was unsure, but because he needed an excuse to talk to her.

But when the service ended, Wade and Abigail appeared at his side, and then Travis and Shay, and he got caught up in Founders Day plans.

He scanned the crowd, hoping to catch sight of Annie, but she was nowhere to be seen.

By the time they wrapped up, the church was nearly empty, save for Miss Lucy, who was tidying the hymnals. Even the pastor had left his post at the door.

Dylan scowled as he left the building and set his hat on his head with a firm push. So much for that.

"Dylan." Annie pushed away from the brick building. She looked fresh as a daisy in a baby blue shirt that matched her eyes to a T.

"Annie . . . you're looking quite fetching this mor—"

"Save it, Taylor. I want to talk to you about that, that *cowboy* you set my sister up with."

He remembered the introduction at the Chuckwagon. "What's wrong?"

"I'll tell you what's wrong. He kept Sierra out all night. All night, Dylan, when she has a child at home to care for."

That didn't sound like Sutter. "Is the little guy okay?"

She tossed her hair over her shoulder. "I was home with him, but that's not the point."

"Sutter's a good kid, Annie. Wouldn't have introduced him to your sister otherwise. Listen, I don't think—"

"No, you listen." Annie's eyes glittered, and two dashes had formed between her brows. "My sister's young, and she's trying to get her life together, which isn't easy considering she had a child at sixteen. She doesn't need the distraction of some Rodeo Romeo sweeping her off her feet."

"Calm down, Annie. Sutter's not like that. 'Sides, I only introduced them and—not that I approve of what they did—they are both adults."

Her eyes narrowed and her lips tightened into a flat line. "Just keep your friends away from my sister."

He held up his hands. "Whatever you say."

Annie shot him one final look and stalked away, her hair blowing in the breeze. He admired her spirit and her desire to protect Sierra, but if you asked him, she was holding the reins a smidge too tight.

Dear Confused,

There's no reason to be confused. He already left you once. Taking him back is an open-ended invitation for heartbreak.

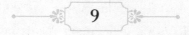

9

Sierra went out with her new cowboy three nights in a row, leaving after Ryder was asleep and returning late. Each time her sister left the house, Annie bit her tongue. Then she called Shay and whined until she got it out of her system.

On Tuesday night she lay in bed flipping through the copy of *Montana Living* she'd snagged from Pappy's Market. "Dear Annie" was on page eight. She read it for the fourth time, then looked at the title again. It felt good to have her own name in print. Folks in town had waved her down today, telling her they'd read her new column. Maybe this was going to work out after all. It had better since Sierra seemed in no hurry to get a job.

She closed the magazine and turned out the lamp but lay awake awhile. It was hard to sleep when Sierra wasn't safe and sound in her bed.

For what seemed like forever she watched the glow-in-the-dark hands on her clock slowly pivot around the face. What if Sierra fell for the guy? What if she got pregnant again? It was all they could do to keep their heads above water now. And she knew better than to count on a cowboy for child support or anything else, despite Dylan's glowing reference. Hadn't all her mom's cowboys proven that? Hadn't their own father?

She'd been watching the clock on that long-ago night when he'd left them. Watching the clock and listening to her mom's sniffles from the next room. She was glad when the rain started. The pattering on the metal roof covered the sounds.

She'd been five years old. Sierra was still a baby—Annie checked on her on the way to her mom's bedroom.

The light in Mom's room was off, her door pulled almost shut. It squeaked on the hinges when Annie pushed it open and the sniffling stopped. The smell of her mom's paints filled her nostrils, a comforting smell.

"Mom?"

"What is it, honey?" She sounded like she had an awful cold.

Thunder cracked, rattling the windows. Annie didn't like storms. They were loud and scary. She crept closer to the bed. The wood floor was cold on the bare balls of her feet, and her toes felt like ice cubes.

When she reached the bed, she climbed in, and her mom pulled her close, tucking her into her soft belly. Annie's head sank into her dad's pillow, and his musky smell filled her nose. The words she'd heard earlier echoed in her head.

"He didn't mean it, Mom." She'd closed her bedroom door, but she could still hear her father's cruel, calm words. Then the front door had slammed, and the crying had started. Annie's tummy had been aching ever since.

"Oh, honey, I'm afraid he did." Her mom smoothed her hair, sniffled again.

Annie was sure her mom was wrong. Daddies weren't supposed to leave. They were supposed to come home from work and call you princess and feed the horses. They were supposed to tickle your belly and help you with the hard puzzles and put you on their shoulders so you could see the parade.

But what if Mom was right? What if he didn't come back? What if . . . "Doesn't he love us anymore?"

The ache in Annie's tummy spread all through her body.

"He does love you, sweetie, very much."

"See? He'll come back. He was just mad." But he hadn't sounded mad. Just flat and empty.

Her mother's breath was a shuddery sigh. "Don't go getting your hopes up, honey. It only hurts when you're wrong."

Sometimes grown-ups didn't make sense. "If Daddy loves us, then he has to come back." She was sure of it.

"Oh, Annie, it doesn't always work that way."

"Why, Mom? Why would he leave us if he loves us?"

Her mom pulled Annie tighter, wrapped her arms around her middle. "Because, baby. That's the trouble with cowboys. They're always leaving."

Annie let the words sink in, frowning. Her daddy was the best cowboy ever. Was that why he'd left? She said no more but sank into her mom's arms and eventually drifted off to sleep.

Her mom must've been right, because her dad had never returned, not even to say good-bye. There were a few phone calls and postcards, just enough to keep hope alive. Just enough to hurt.

After the divorce, Annie's mom had brought one cowboy after another into their lives, had married three of them, only to have them leave in a matter of months. By the time her mom had passed, and Annie and Sierra had gone to live with their grandpa, she knew for a fact her mom had been right: cowboys left.

Now Annie turned to her other side away from the annoying hands of the clock. Only when she heard Sierra come in for the night did she allow herself to drift off.

And the next day when Sierra told her Sutter had gone back to whatever rock he'd crawled from, Annie breathed a sigh of relief. At least he'd left before he did any real damage.

Dear Undecided,

*A relationship rooted in friendship can grow to be the hardiest
of them all.*

10

Annie's day had been long and stressful. She'd started at the O'Neils' with a jiggy palomino that refused to walk. After that she'd checked on Mayor Wadell's four-month-old filly. Wadell didn't seem to understand that the filly's kicking problem would require more than one visit.

She'd finished up her afternoon at Travis and Shay's. He'd acquired a three-year-old abused quarter horse. They'd gotten nowhere with the gelding after four months of work. This was the kind of case that strained Annie the most. Not the fact that such horses were unpredictable or aggressive, but that their gentle souls had been wounded so heinously, so needlessly. Nothing raised her dander like a horse owner who took out his anger on innocent animals or neglected to learn proper handling.

She was just finishing up with the horse when Midge called. The editor got right down to business.

"Annie, we've received some feedback on your column already. I'm afraid it's not as good as we'd hoped."

Annie leaned against the stall door. "What do you mean?"

"Some of our readers thought you were off base with Betrayed in Billings. They thought the reader shouldn't write him off so easily."

"You know people are more likely to be vocal when they disagree. There were probably a hundred who agreed for each one who wrote."

"You may be right."

"I'm sure I am, but I'll keep it in mind. You can depend on me, Midge. I won't let you down."

After they hung up, Annie finished up with the quarter horse and headed toward her truck. Shay approached, sporting a low ponytail. Baby Austin was perched on her hip, gnawing on his slobbery fingers.

"What's wrong?" Shay asked.

Annie thought about brushing off the question but filled her in on Midge's call instead.

"Did you read the column?" Annie asked.

"I did. I thought your answer was fine. It was one of those situations—could've gone either way."

"Well, I'd better figure it out. With Sierra out of work, I need this job."

"Hang in there. I'm sure it was just a few complainers. The vast majority probably agree with you; they just don't take the time to write."

"Hope so." Annie gave Austin a kiss on his chubby cheek. "Gotta run. Tell Travis I said hello."

She waved bye as she pulled down the drive. Just when she was ready for her day to be over, she had to go to Dylan's house. She had to press him harder this time, make sure they were arriving at the right answer.

She found Braveheart much the same as he'd been the week before. He bolted from his stall and stumbled, but he let her approach so long as she kept to his sighted side. She walked the boundaries with him, talking constantly.

After working with him awhile, she led one of Dylan's gentle mares into the pasture with the gelding and retreated to the fence to watch.

The sun was going down over the Gallatin Range, casting the mountains in muted shades of purple. A wind cut across the valley, sending a shiver across her flesh, and she crossed her arms against the chill. She took a deep whiff of pine, hay, and the earthy scent of rain, then let out her breath as she watched the horses.

A few minutes later, when a drizzle began to fall, she put the animals away for the night. Dylan had watched her working most of the evening but had slipped into the house awhile ago. She was already dreading the column, and though Sierra's cowboy had left, Annie's frustration with Dylan had not.

She shut the gate to Braveheart's stall and headed toward her truck for her folder, then made a dash for the house as a bucket load of rain fell from the sky. She was drenched by the time she reached the porch. She knocked on the door, pushing her wet hair from her face. Thunder cracked, and she jumped just as Dylan opened the door.

"You're soaked." He pulled her in, his hand warm and firm on her arm, his scent filling her nostrils. "I'll get a towel."

Annie closed the door, pulled off her boots, then waited on the rug. The room was surprisingly cozy with its hardwood floor, braided rugs, and stone fireplace. Framed pictures, mostly old black-and-white shots, filled the mantel.

"Here you go," Dylan said, his voice lower than she remembered. He handed her a thick beige towel.

"Thanks." Annie dried her arms and face and soaked the moisture from her hair.

"Wrap up in this." He handed her a quilt and tossed the wet towel over a rocking chair as he left again. She watched him go, admiring the way his T-shirt clung to his shoulders, the way his damp hair curled at his nape. She couldn't deny he was nice to look at.

A moment later he returned with a hot mug of coffee. His fingers brushed hers as she took it, and she pretended not to feel the shock of electricity that zinged up her arm.

"You're tough to stay mad at, Dylan."

He smiled, his dimples showing up. "That's what I like to hear. Have a seat. Warm enough? I can get a fire going."

He already had—he just didn't know it. And if she were smart, she'd stick to the porch. But the thunder cracked again, making the light fixture overhead rattle, and she reminded herself she could handle Dylan Taylor just fine.

"That's okay." She sat in the recliner, leaving him the sofa, and opened her folder. "Braveheart is getting along okay. I put your mare in the field with him awhile to see how he did."

"What for?"

"Sometimes another horse will step in to guide and protect the blind one. You can introduce other horses into the pasture with him one at a time, but watch him when you do. If he gets bronc-y, it's a bad mix."

"Gotcha. Thanks for your help."

Annie pulled out the letters. "You're about to earn your keep."

He smiled. "Bring it on."

She handed him one of the two letters and snuggled into the quilt while he read. She wasn't going to tell him about the negative reader response. Shay was probably right. It was just the vocal few. She was sure her next column would fare better.

Dylan's lips moved as he read. His top lip had a dip in the center, the lower one was pleasantly full. Nice, she had to admit. Of course, they'd probably touched the mouth of every available woman in the tri-state area.

Annie being the exception. And Sierra. She frowned suddenly, wondering if that was true. How was she to know what happened on those nights Sierra went out?

He handed her the letter. She jumped as thunder struck again, piercing the air, rattling the windowpane behind her.

His eyes danced in the lamplight. "Want me to come over there and keep you safe?"

Dylan keep her safe? "I'll pass, but thanks for the offer."

He settled back into the sofa and gave her a cocky grin. "Suit yourself."

She held up the letter. "What'd you think?"

"Seems pretty simple. You should tell him to go for it."

Of course that's what he'd say. She sighed. She had to get these answers right. "What about their friendship?"

"A true friendship would weather the course."

"If he brings his feelings out in the open, it would make things awkward. What if she doesn't feel the same way?"

He shrugged. "What if she does, and she's just waiting for him to make a move?"

"He says there's no indication of feelings on her part."

"Maybe he's wrong. Anyway, what about honesty? You think this guy should hide his feelings?"

"Not hide them, just not wear them on his sleeve."

"Same thing."

"It is not the same thing. This is an eleven-year friendship; he can't just throw it away all willy-nilly because he's developed feelings. At the very least he should test the waters a bit."

"And how's he supposed to do that?"

"I don't know. You're the expert!"

His lips curled upward and his brow hitched higher, meeting the lock of hair that had flopped over his forehead.

Great. She'd done it now.

"Why, Annie Wilkerson, I had no idea you held me in such high regard."

Was this all just a joke to him? "Get over yourself, Taylor. I just think he should play it a little safe, that's all."

He stared at her, and there was something in his eyes that made her shift and look away.

"Safe, huh?"

She had the distinct feeling he was thinking of John Oakley.

"Yes, safe. It's not a dirty word, you know. Nor is *relationship* or *commitment*, though you wouldn't understand either of those."

He shrugged. "I advised the guy to start the relationship, did I not?"

Maybe he did, but his own life contradicted his advice. He was confusing her and she didn't like it. She took a sip of her coffee, realized she'd warmed up—more than she intended—and shrugged the quilt from her shoulders.

"Why don't we move on to the next letter?"

He took the paper and read. This time she kept her eyes averted. Instead, she sipped the coffee and took a good look around the room. The furniture was old and worn. A plaid sofa with an afghan tossed over the back, hurricane lamps with golden globes and antique brass trim. It seemed more like an elderly person's home than a confirmed bachelor's.

"Okay." He handed the letter back. "She needs to move on."

Annie's hopes sank to her toes. Could they agree on nothing? "Why do you say that?"

"They've dated almost three years, and he's clearly not interested in marriage. She's almost thirty—"

"Oh, and her biological clock is ticking, is that it?"

"I didn't say that. Look, she's not going to change his mind—why do women always think they can change their man?" He gave an exaggerated shrug as if they were talking about him.

Annie rubbed her temple. He was giving her a headache. "First letter you said drop the relationship, second one you said pursue the relationship, and now you're saying this woman should drop it. You're inconsistent."

"If it were that cut-and-dried, they wouldn't need help."

She sighed. He was right about that. Was he right about all of it? Was she really this bad at matters of the heart?

Of course she was. She was going to have to ignore her poor instincts, swallow her pride, and follow his advice. He was the expert, like it or not.

"Okay, suppose you're right. Let's talk about what I should tell her."

They spent twenty minutes chatting about the woman's situation, then went back to the first letter and discussed it awhile. She watched him closely as he talked, sensing another layer beneath his flippant façade. His answers went deeper than she'd expected, delving into the subtext of the letters. He was surprising her again, and people rarely did that. The more he talked, the better she felt about his answer.

She watched him now, rubbing the back of his neck as he talked, the curls at his nape now dry. He had nice hands with squared fingers and thick palms, no doubt rough with calluses.

She thought back to Saturday when he'd had those hands on Marla Jenkins's waist. There had been a brief moment, watching them move together, when Annie had regretted turning him down. He was a smooth dancer, after all, and John had been in the middle of a monologue on bilateral debt.

Okay, maybe John wasn't all that intriguing. Maybe his kisses didn't leave her weak-kneed. He was responsible and faithful and . . . lots of other good things.

If, when he'd kissed her good night, she'd imagined Dylan's lips on hers for the tiniest little second, it was only a silly flight of fancy. Everyone had errant thoughts. Even so, when John had drawn away, her face had burned with shame.

She looked up at Dylan now, realizing he'd gone quiet. Realizing her face burned again from the memory of her errant thought. Curses on her Irish skin.

His lips turned up. "Something you wanna share with the class, Miss Wilkerson?"

"No, there is not."

It was time to go, more than. The patter of rain grew louder as the storm picked up. But still, she began packing her things, because there was a more dangerous storm brewing inside.

"Stay awhile, sugar, I don't bite."

She seriously doubted that. "I have to get home."

"It's pouring out there. I'll freshen your coffee."

"That's okay," she called after him, but he had already left with her mug.

She heard the coffee carafe sliding from its cubby, the splash of liquid, and then he returned, handing her the mug.

"That was my grandpa's favorite chair," he said, nodding toward her seat before plopping on the sofa. "This used to be his place, you know."

Annie sipped the coffee, torn between her need to leave and her reluctance to be rude.

"I remember. I was a senior when he passed, I think."

"I forget you're several years younger than me. You're so . . ."

She crossed her arms, waiting. Stodgy? Old-spirited? Well, if he'd had the responsibilities she'd had, he wouldn't be so—

"Capable."

She was sure it wasn't the first word that came to mind, especially when his eyes danced in the lamplight.

She decided not to let him bait her. "Your grandpa was a good man. He got on well with my grandpa, I recall."

"They were childhood friends."

"They were?" How had she not known that? Then again, her grandfather hadn't talked much about himself.

"You didn't know?"

She shrugged. "Until Sierra and I came to live with him, we didn't see him much. He and Mom didn't get along."

"That's too bad. My grandparents were a big part of my childhood. Me and my brother came up here every summer, and we thought we were in heaven."

"You have a brother?"

"Luke. He's a few years younger."

"You're from Texas, like Wade . . ."

He nodded. "Why didn't your mom and grandpa get along?"

She settled back into the chair, cupping her hands around the warm mug. "Too different, I guess. Mom didn't make the best decisions—that was hard on my grandpa."

"Tell me about your sister."

"Sierra?" She gave a wry laugh. "What's to tell? She pretty much lets it all hang out. She's very much like our mother."

He templed his hands on his chest and rested his chin on his fingertips. "You're more like your dad?"

"I hope not. I guess I'm more like my grandpa."

"You were close."

"How can you tell?"

"Your voice changes when you say his name, softens. I'll bet you were the apple of his eye."

He was more perceptive than she'd given him credit for. "He took us in when Mom passed, without a second thought. He's the reason I pursued horse training. He was a great vet, the best."

"My grandpa used to say he could talk a breech calf from her mama."

She found herself smiling. "That might be a slight exaggeration. But he was pretty amazing. A godly man too. Not that he was very vocal about it—but he lived it, you know?"

Dylan nodded thoughtfully.

A pause stretched out as the grin fell from her face. Still, she felt reluctant to go. He didn't seem so dangerous when he wasn't trying to flatter her.

"Braveheart was a gift from my grandpa," Dylan said in the quiet. "The last thing he ever gave me."

Now Annie understood his desperation to save the horse.

Braveheart must feel like the last living piece of his grandfather. That was how Pepper felt to her.

"He's going to be fine. Going blind can be tough on a horse, but it's not usually insurmountable."

The rain had slowed to a quiet patter, and Annie realized they'd been having an ordinary conversation. She didn't know why that surprised her. Maybe she hadn't thought Dylan was capable. Or maybe she didn't think she'd ever drop her guard enough to permit it.

"Well." She grabbed her bag and stood, setting down the mug. "Thanks for the coffee . . . and the help."

He rose, towering over her. "Thanks for helping Braveheart." His smiling brown eyes sucked her in, holding her hostage for a long beat.

She cleared her throat and turned toward the door, suddenly eager to escape. At the door she gathered her boots and stepped into them. In her hurry she lost her balance.

Dylan took her elbow, steadying her.

"Thanks," she said, straightening, happy for the extra two inches the boots gave her. Still, now she was eye level with the V of bare chest above his unbuttoned shirt.

And he still had her elbow. She pulled away under the guise of hitching her purse onto her shoulder.

"Thanks again," she said, opening the door. "See you next Thursday."

"If not before."

She hustled outside, took the porch steps, and dodged raindrops all the way to her truck. As she turned the key in the ignition, she could still feel the imprint of his hand on her elbow.

Dear Boring in Bozeman,

Sizzle is overrated.

11

ounders Day dawned bright and sunny. The blue sky stretched from horizon to horizon, and the sun crested the mountains, bathing Paradise Valley with golden warmth.

Annie tried to work up some enthusiasm for the festivities, but part of her had hoped for a rainy day that would give her an excuse to stay home and curl up with her worn copy of *Pride and Prejudice*. That the novel held more appeal than an afternoon with John wasn't a good sign, but it was, after all, her favorite book.

She and John attended the wedding reenactment of town founders Prudence and Joseph Adams, played by Shay and Travis. After the debacle year before last when the pretend ceremony had culminated in a real marriage—thanks to the absentminded Pastor

Blevins—the couple had agreed to play the parts one more time. The joke being, since they were already married, the preacher couldn't possibly do any harm this time.

Afterward they made their way to the town square. John had gone to fetch them lemonade, and onstage, the Silver Spurs did a sound check. The wedding reenactment behind them, the towns-people now poured onto the lawn like ants onto a crumb.

"Annie, dear," Miss Lucy called from a nearby lawn chair on the outskirts of the crowd. "Would you like to sit with us?"

"Us" included Miss Lucy, her bingo brigade, and two of her handmade dolls. The women greeted Annie.

"Hello, ladies. Thanks, Miss Lucy, but John likes to sit in the middle."

"Wasn't it a fun day?"

"It was. Your doll booth seemed busy."

"I sold twenty-two!" She perched the prairie-dressed dolls higher in her lap. "You haven't said a word to the girls."

"Hi, girls." Annie waved at the blank-faced dolls. "You're, uh, looking festive tonight."

"They're very partial to Founders Day." She patted their yarn hair. "Not to rush you, dear, but you'd better claim a spot before they're all taken."

Annie said good-bye and carried her blanket toward the middle of the crowd. She spread her quilt, claiming the last open spot, and sat down.

Up front Sierra wrangled a spot close to the speakers, and Ryder helped her spread a quilt on the grass. Annie squinted at the blanket and pursed her lips. Her favorite quilt. Oh well, it would wash.

Riley Raines came by and ruffled the boy's hair, then pulled Sierra into his chest, laughing, and kissed her cheek. Another cowboy. Heaven help her. It would be a miracle if Annie got her safely through college. She was a bright girl, had gotten her GED in record time, and got good grades in college—when she applied herself.

Sierra backed away enough to snap a picture of Riley with the camera dangling from her neck.

A body plopped down next to her. Annie had a polite smile ready, but it wasn't John who nudged her shoulder.

"How's my girl?" Dylan's brown eyes twinkled and little lines flared toward his temples.

Annie leaned away, ignoring the impressive somersault her heart performed. She rolled her eyes. "Hi, Dylan."

"Not happy to see me?"

"My heart is all aflutter." She pulled her knees into her chest.

"That's more like it."

"Better find a seat, it's filling up fast."

He smiled flirtatiously. "That your way of getting rid of me?"

She sighed and looked away, cracking her knuckles. She could not win with him. And she didn't like the way his shoulder was rubbing hers or the way his breath fanned her cheek. He was entirely too close.

"I make you nervous," he taunted, a smile in the low drawl of his voice.

She stiffened. "You'd like that, wouldn't you."

There was a beat of silence. A breeze whispered by, carrying the scent of him, musk and leather.

"I think I would, Miss Annie."

His words, or maybe it was his breath stirring her hair, sent a shiver up her spine. She drew her knees in tighter.

"You're in my spot, Taylor."

She hadn't noticed John's approach and felt her face warming, though she'd done nothing wrong.

"Howdy, John." Dylan took his time standing. "Just keeping your girl company."

John's girl, Dylan's girl. How swiftly he changed. It really was just a great big game to him. She'd do well to remember that and stop getting caught up in the way he made her feel. In the way he made her insides heat, and the way his nearness pebbled the skin on her arms.

"See ya around, Annie." Dylan tossed her a wink.

Player. She frowned at his retreating back as John settled next to her, his slim shoulder bumping hers. She waited for the goose-flesh, tried to manufacture just a pebble or two.

Nothing. She wondered briefly if Dylan was her Mr. Darcy. Good grief, she hoped not.

"What'd he want?" John handed her the lemonade as she watched Dylan skirting people and blankets on his way toward the stage. He couldn't get three inches without someone stopping him.

"Not much. I'm still helping him with that horse." She hadn't mentioned the help he was giving her on the column.

"Well, if you ask me, he's overly friendly with you. Want me to say something?"

She had an instant image of John up in Dylan's face. 'Course, he'd have to get on tiptoe.

"That's just Dylan's way. He'll chase anything in a skirt." Case in point, Marla Jenkins, who just pulled him down on her blanket. And she actually was wearing a skirt, unlike Annie, who hadn't worn anything but jeans for as long as she could remember.

"Yeah, well, he'd better keep his distance if he knows what's good for him." John sniffed loudly, a punctuation mark on his threat.

Dylan settled on a blanket with Travis, Shay, Wade, Abigail, and their kids. Thank goodness she'd refused Shay's offer to share a blanket. What a miserable night that would've been.

Marla plopped down next to Dylan, sitting close. So he had another date with Marla. What was that? Three? Must be a record.

John began talking about the town square property and how the town had acquired it—some admirable feat of his uncle, so he had every detail and shared each one with glee.

When the Silver Spurs struck up their first tune, Annie was relieved that the volume made talking difficult, and when John slipped his arm around her shoulders, she forced herself to relax into his embrace.

"Good night, John." Annie turned at the door, preparing herself for a brief kiss. She was eager for her quiet house and soft mattress. *Pride and Prejudice* awaited.

Instead John took her hand. It was soft and not unpleasant feeling. She shook away the image of Dylan's thick squared fingers and calloused palm.

"Annie, we've been going out, what, five weeks now?"

She wondered if he could round it down to the nearest hour, then chided herself, bracing for what she was sure was coming.

"That's about right."

He nodded and poked his glasses into place. She tried to focus on his eyes—they were a pretty shade of green—but the porch light glared off his glasses, blocking them.

"I've come to care for you. I admire you more than you know. Life has handed you lemons, and you've made lemonade. I respect that."

"Thank you, John."

He patted her hand. "What I'm saying is, I'd like it if we could take our relationship to the next level."

She frowned, suddenly unsure, wondering if he was asking to come in. She didn't think John was like that. He was a Christian, after all. Surely he didn't think . . .

"What I'm saying, Annie, is that I'd like us to date exclusively."

Oh. *Oh.* Her knees went weak, not from his touch but from relief. "Well, we sort of already are . . . at least I am."

"Right, right. Well, me too, of course. You'd know if it were different—you can't blink in this town without starting the rumor mill." He laughed in that slightly nasal way he had. "I just, you know, thought we might make it official."

She wondered if Dylan's persistent flirting had anything to do with John's sudden desire for exclusivity . . . if John felt threatened by the cowboy's attention, regardless of the fact that Dylan treated her no differently from every other single woman.

Regardless, she hadn't expected this so soon. On the other hand, she'd planned to continue seeing John, and it wasn't like she had many other options. There were only so many single men in Moose Creek.

She squeezed his hand and smiled. "I'd like that."

He tilted his head back enough that the glare shifted, and she saw the relief in his eyes. "That's wonderful. I'm so glad, Annie." He lowered his head and his lips met hers.

They were cool and soft, not unpleasant. He touched her face and she sensed he wanted to deepen the kiss.

She ended the kiss and offered a smile instead. "Thanks for a lovely day. I had a good time."

If he was disappointed in the abrupt ending, he hid it well. "I did too." He squeezed her hands. "I'll call you tomorrow."

"All right."

Annie slipped into the darkened house, wishing she felt something. Anything but this vague ambivalence. Oh well. The feelings
would come in time. Love could grow from friendship, couldn't it?
Maybe it did fly in the face of all her favorite Jane Austen heroines—
but they hadn't been surrounded by a bunch of cowboys.

Dear Tom,

*Love is a choice. Decide to keep loving your sweet-tempered
boyfriend, and the feelings will eventually follow.*

12

*A*nnie pulled a mug from the cabinet and shut the door,
letting it bang against the frame. While the coffee brewed,
she pushed in a chair until it scraped across the floor. She came
back to the brewing coffee and thumped her fingers loudly on the
countertop, waiting.

The past two weeks of exclusivity with John had been . . . nice.
When Annie found out he had never been to Yellowstone, one of
her favorite places, she wanted to remedy that. So yesterday they'd
driven down and explored the park.

He'd seemed a bit out of his element in his button-up shirt and
Dockers, and in the way he'd insisted on driving from one attraction to another, even when they were only a mile apart. He'd put up

the windows to block the smell of sulfur from the springs and notched up the air-conditioning.

So he wasn't the outdoor type. That was no crime. At least he'd been a good sport, even if he hadn't been willing to wait at the creek in hopes of spotting a moose.

Mr. Coffee gurgled and the machine let out a nice, loud beep. She retrieved the creamer from the fridge, letting the machine go off a couple more times before turning it off and pouring a mug of the rich brew.

She slid the carafe into its cubby extra hard, satisfied with the loud clang. The spoon clinked against the inside of the mug as she stirred.

Sierra appeared in her nightshirt, her auburn hair rumpled. "You don't have to clatter all through the house. I had my alarm set."

A denial perched on her tongue but she pressed her lips together. Maybe she had been a little loud, but Sierra hadn't been to church in weeks despite her promise.

"Want some coffee?" Annie asked.

"Yes. I hope it's extra strong," Sierra said around a yawn, then collapsed on a chair.

"What time did you get in?" Annie asked, knowing full well where the clock hands had been when Sierra had tiptoed in.

"After midnight. A bunch of us went into Bozeman and saw this band. It was loads of fun. And before you ask, Bridgett paid for my ticket."

Annie sat down across from her and slid the coffee over, smiling. *You wouldn't be so tired if you got in at a decent hour.*

Sierra cupped the mug in both hands and took a sip. "Thanks for staying with Ryder. I know I don't say it often enough." Even with her sleepy green eyes, Sierra looked so young. She *was* young.

"You know I love spending time with him." Even if he did carry that stupid rope with him everywhere now. He'd even wanted to sleep with the thing, but Sierra agreed that the loop was a hazard. He asked for it upon waking, though, and spent hours practicing in front of that fence post. Annie hoped it was just a phase. A short one.

"Oh," Sierra said, her eyes lighting up. "Guess who's coming for our Fourth of July festival? Sawyer Smitten!"

"The country-and-western singer?"

"The totally hot country-and-western singer. He wrote 'Smitten' for his bride awhile back, remember?"

"I love that song. Too bad we won't be able to afford tickets."

"The town's footing the bill in hopes of bringing in tourists. Isn't that fab?"

"Awesome. I'll bet the town square will be packed. Maybe the stores will need extra help that weekend. You should check around town."

Annie's cell phone rang. It was early for a call, especially on a Sunday morning. She checked the screen and frowned.

"Hello?"

"Annie, it's Dylan." His voice was rushed and serious.

"What's wrong?"

"I came out this morning and found Braveheart banging into the stall door. He's spooked and going a little crazy. I've tried to calm him down, but nothing's working."

She could hear the horse neighing, then squealing. A loud clatter followed, and she imagined Braveheart slamming into the wooden stall door.

Her heart squeezed. "I'll be right over. Call Merle as soon as we hang up and ask him to come."

"Why?" His voice sounded tight and guarded. Maybe he thought she was suggesting Braveheart needed to be put down.

"He might be in pain or need a sedative, that's all, just to keep him from hurting himself. Don't worry, we'll get him through this."

She closed the phone and dumped the rest of her coffee.

"You're leaving?" Sierra asked.

"It's Dylan's horse." She was glad she'd already taken care of Pepper. She brushed her teeth and said good morning to Ryder as he came out of his room.

Good. Now Sierra wouldn't be able to go back to bed so she might as well go to church.

Annie tugged on her boots.

"So let me get this straight." Sierra leaned against the doorway. "You've been harping on me about missing church, and now you're the one who's not going."

Apparently the caffeine had kicked in.

"This is an emergency. I can't let the poor horse hurt himself." Her boots on, she grabbed her purse. "Tell John I won't be there, all right?" And then she was out the door.

As she drove up East River Road, she forced herself to ease up on the accelerator. She told herself it was the sound of the suffering horse that weighted her foot. But there had been something in Dylan's voice. A vulnerability she hadn't heard before.

Minutes later she pulled into the Circle D and eased up on the gas, passing under the log-style entry arch. When she pulled up to the barn, Dylan met her at her door, his brow creased below the brim of his hat.

"How's he doing?" she asked.

"No better."

She started for the barn. "You called Merle?"

"He'll be here soon as he can."

She heard Braveheart before she saw him. He neighed and blew, then rammed into the stall.

Dylan tried to soothe him as they approached. "It's all right, buddy. Settle down now."

The horse showed no sign of calming. His eyes, cloudy from the uveitis, looked frantic as he tossed his head. Annie approached on his right, talking as she went.

"What's wrong, fella? It's all right, Braveheart. Everything's okay."

When the horse lowered his head, she put her closed fist on his left side. He didn't turn to smell. He neighed and squealed.

"It's okay, buddy," Dylan said. "I'm right here."

Annie pulled her hand back. "I think he's lost the last of his vision," she said over the sound of his stomping hooves.

A nearby horse snorted.

"I was afraid of that. Why isn't my voice calming him?"

"He's just scared. He'll need time to adjust, that's all."

"But he will adjust . . ."

She knew how worried he was, but she wanted to be honest. "What was his temperament like before he started going blind?"

"Steady as a rock. Never gave me a lick of trouble."

"I don't think you have anything to worry about then. Some horses never adjust, but it's rare, and it's the jittery ones. I'm not going to lie though. It might take awhile. Days or even weeks. We'll just have to be patient with him."

A rumble sounded in the drive, and Dylan went out to meet Merle. After the vet looked Braveheart over and found no cause for pain, he gave him a mild sedative. The horse calmed within minutes, his eyelids drooping.

They discussed a plan of action as Dylan walked them both

outside. As soon as they left the coolness of the barn, Annie's phone pealed from her pocket.

"Excuse me," she said, walking toward her truck. She didn't want to leave yet, wanted to assure Dylan she'd put in extra hours with Braveheart over the next week. The horse was fine for the moment, but they couldn't keep him sedated forever.

John's name appeared on the phone's screen. She checked her watch and was surprised at the time. She hadn't realized she'd been there so long.

"Hi, John."

"Hi, Annie. What are you doing? I was worried when you didn't show up at church."

After all her efforts this morning, Sierra hadn't even gone?

"I'm sorry. I told Sierra to tell you I wouldn't be there. I guess she decided not to go."

"Oh no, she was there. She told me you were at Dylan Taylor's place," he said pointedly.

It was obvious from his tone that her sister had offered no explanation. *Thanks, Sierra . . .*

"There was an emergency with his horse."

"I thought you were helping him on Thursdays."

She gritted her teeth. "Horses don't keep a calendar, John. I'm sorry you were worried, but it couldn't be helped."

He sniffed. "Right, right. Well . . . how is he—the horse?"

Merle drove by, lifting a hand. She waved and watched the dust plume behind his truck.

"He's sedated now, but it'll take time to adjust to the blindness. He was pretty spooked this morning."

"Well, I'm glad he's under control. I have to say, it worries me that you work with reckless horses. A lot can go wrong when two thousand pounds are out of control."

She smiled tightly, staring out over Dylan's vast green pasture. "I'm well trained for this, John." She didn't know why everything he said today was lighting her fuse.

"Of course, of course. I just worry about you, is all."

"Well, no need. I'm always careful."

"I'm sure you are." He sniffed again. Allergies must be flaring up.

Annie watched the horses in the pasture, an appaloosa and a beautiful bay quarter horse. His tail flicked, and he lifted his head in the air.

"So are we still on for lunch in Bozeman? There's a premium steak house I'd like to take you to."

"Sure." Truth be told, Annie wanted nothing more than to spend a nice quiet afternoon at home. It had been too long since she'd ridden Pepper. Besides, she'd hardly had time to read lately, and she was coming to the part where Mr. Darcy proposes.

"I'll pick you up in twenty minutes then?"

"Fine. See you then." Annie closed her phone and turned.

Right into Dylan. He caught her arms before she slammed into his chest.

She pulled away, huffing. "Do you have to stand right on my heels?"

He fell back against her truck door, hitched one of his boots on the running board, and tilted his head. "Trouble in paradise?"

That stupid cocky grin.

She crossed her arms, pressed her lips to prevent the denial from escaping. It was none of his business.

His smile relaxed and his eyes became thoughtful, the lids dropping in a way that could be defined as either lazy or sexy—she refused to make the call.

"Know what I think?" he said finally. "I think Oakley's like a greenhorn with a wild mustang; he has no idea how to handle you."

She glared. "I do not need to be *handled*."

He tilted his head, studying her. She hated the way his brown eyes seemed to stare right into her, like he could read her every thought. So annoying. Even his posture, so relaxed and carefree, annoyed her.

"Treat her gently, meet her needs . . ." His words were slow as molasses, his deep voice barely above a whisper. "Let her know you're there, that you won't hurt her. Talk to her sweetly . . . touch her often . . . earn her trust."

She couldn't seem to inhale. "You're despicable."

"Am I?"

Her face grew warm. Just the image of him doing all those things to her . . .

She swallowed hard. "I was about to tell you I'd put in extra hours with Braveheart this week, but you're making me seriously reconsider that benevolent gesture."

"Except you'd never turn your back on a wounded creature just to spite his incorrigible owner."

"I'm sorely tempted."

He smiled again, one side of his mouth kicking up just before the other as if wanting to put that infernal dimple into effect as soon as possible.

"So am I, Annie Wilkerson, so am I."

If her breath caught, it was only the sudden warm wind that stole it away. "I'll be back to check on Braveheart tomorrow . . . *despite* his irritating owner."

"I think I might be growing on you . . ."

"Like a noxious mold."

He chuckled. "You amuse me, Annie—you keep me on my toes."

"You mean I don't fall at your feet like all the other women."

His eyes twinkled. "Jealous?"

Of all the— "Will you move out of my way, please? I have plans."

"Ah, of course." He pushed away from the truck and opened her door. "What exciting things do you and Spreadsheet have planned?"

"None of your business."

"Well . . . I hope you have a frolicking good time."

Annie skirted him, got inside the cab, and pulled the door from his grasp. "Don't worry. We will."

Now that she was in the truck, she couldn't get away fast enough. As she pulled away, she caught sight of Dylan in her rear-view mirror. He turned her way as he headed toward the barn.

Infernal man.

She was somewhat calmer by the time she reached the house. She hadn't much time before John arrived. Sierra and Ryder were eating when she entered.

"Hi, Aunt Annie!"

"Hey, Bed Head. How was Sunday school?" She dropped a kiss on Ryder's head.

"Nicky Peterson kicked Mrs. Franklin right in the knee!"

"Oh no. Did he get in trouble?"

"His mom came to get him."

"Want some chicken noodle soup?" Sierra asked. "It's from a can, but I added yesterday's chicken."

"Can't. Having lunch with John. Speaking of which . . ." Annie tilted her head, shooting her a look. "I think you might've left out some pertinent information when you spoke to him at church."

Sierra shrugged, her lips twitching. "Maybe a detail or two."

"That wasn't nice. He was worried."

"Worried he might lose his prize possession, you mean?"

Annie frowned. "What do you have against John?" She kept her voice neutral on Ryder's account. "He's a very nice man."

"He nearly ripped Shay's ranch right from under her last year."

"He feels terrible about that. Besides, Shay doesn't hold a grudge. She told me so herself."

Sierra rolled her eyes. "He's not good enough for you, Annie. I don't know why you can't see that."

"That's not your decision to make. Besides, it's not like there are scores of available men beating a path to my door. This is Moose Creek. And I would like to settle down someday, preferably before I'm old and decrepit."

Sierra scooped up a spoonful of soup and blew on it. "What's wrong with Dylan Taylor?"

"Hah! I hardly know where to start."

"Mr. Taylor is a real cowboy!" Ryder said.

Annie nailed her sister with a look. "Exactly."

"Where's my rope, Mommy?"

Annie sighed. "I'm going to change." Somehow she couldn't seem to get away from Dylan Taylor—even when he wasn't there.

Dear Overreacting,

It sounds as if you're carrying baggage from a past relation-ship. My advice is to check it at the gate. In this case, the fee is a lot higher for a carry-on.

13

ylan watched Annie rifle through her bag for the latest let-ters. She wore a green button-up that contrasted with her hair. When she set her bag on the porch, her hair swung forward, a black curtain of silk.

They were meeting on Wednesday since tomorrow was the Fourth of July Festival. The town was packed with tourists in antici-pation of Sawyer Smitten's concert on the town square, and the community buzzed with excitement. It wasn't often a big singer like him came through their little town.

Annie had been out every day since Sunday, working with Braveheart, but he was the same. Only time the horse was calm was when he was sedated. Still, she'd said it would take time.

"Here's the one I'd like to use." She handed him the letter, and he settled back in the swing and read.

Dear Annie,

My boyfriend and I have been together three years. I love him, we get along great, and we've been talking about marriage. But lately I've felt like something's missing. I work with a man whom I'm attracted to and have been for a while. Two months ago, during a moment of weakness, I slept with him. I haven't told my boyfriend what happened. It was a horrible thing to do, but there's a spark between my coworker and me that's difficult to resist even now. My coworker has kept his distance since then, out of respect for my relationship with my boyfriend, but my feelings for him have grown.

Five weeks ago I discovered I was pregnant. I'm not sure whose baby it is. I did tell my boyfriend I'm pregnant, and of course, he assumes it's his, and now he wants to marry me.

Should I tell my boyfriend about my indiscretion? Should I break up with him because I still have feelings for my co-worker? Should I marry him? Or should I wait until the baby is born and see what happens?

Signed,

Learned Her Lesson in Billings

Dylan kept staring at the page even after he finished reading. The details of the letter felt personal and familiar. Brought back memories he'd worked hard to bury.

He cleared his throat and handed Annie the letter. The swing squawked as he settled back into it. He'd felt guilty about helping her with these letters because of his lack of experience when it came to love. With this one, however, that was not the case.

"She has to tell him the truth."

He wrapped his hand around the swing's cool metal chain, fighting the memories that made his gut ache.

Annie's lips parted. Frown lines formed between her brows. Surely she agreed. True, they'd agreed on nothing so far, but she couldn't advise this woman to hide the truth.

"What?" he asked, his voice on edge.

Annie blinked. "I guess I'm shocked. We actually agree that the reader should be honest."

"The least she can do. She and her boyfriend can hardly go forward with that secret hovering between them."

"Oh. I thought you meant—"

"What?"

"I just—I think she needs to tell him the truth about everything— including her feelings for her coworker."

Dylan gave a wry smile. "You mean her one-night stand."

"She said she has feelings for him."

He waved that off. "Cold feet."

Annie frowned. "She said something was missing between her and her boyfriend."

"Yeah, ever since that idiot put the moves on her."

"Why are you getting so—"

Dylan stood abruptly, the swing darting out behind him. Annie jumped.

"I need some coffee." He went inside, the screen door clacking shut behind him. He rubbed his neck where heat had gathered at the base of his skull. What was wrong with him? It was just a stupid letter, words on a page, people he didn't know.

He grabbed two mugs and filled them, the stream of coffee wavering under his shaking hand. This wasn't like him. Not at all.

He palmed the edge of the counter and took a couple breaths, shaking off the heaviness that had settled over his shoulders like a lead blanket. *Get a grip, Taylor. This isn't you, just some poor chump miles away.*

He straightened and carried the coffees back to the porch. When he handed Annie the mug, her gaze bounced off him.

"Sorry." He sank onto the swing and sipped his coffee. "Subject matter too close to home, I guess."

Annie's eyes narrowed, and her lips softened into a tiny smile. It was a new expression, the kind that would make a lesser man spill his guts and thank her for it.

"Moving on . . . ," he said. "You should probably just go with your gut on this one. Is there another letter?"

Annie pulled out a second from a woman asking if she should move in with her boyfriend of eleven weeks to solve her financial crisis. Fortunately he and Annie agreed on this one. After a brief discussion they wrapped it up for the night and said good night.

Dylan stood watching her taillights fade into the darkness. He'd tried to lighten things after he'd overreacted, but even the air had felt different after that letter. Heavy, weighted with something. Even now it swirled around his shoulders, threatening to press him into the ground.

He had to stop this. It was a long time ago and he was over Merilee. He needed something else to think about. Some*one* else to think about. He thought of Annie immediately, of the way she'd looked at him earlier. He could see how a man might fall right into those baby blues and not want to come out. Ever.

He shook his head, turning back toward the house. Never mind that she was with Oakley. They'd no doubt be spending the Fourth together, dancing to Sawyer Smitten's love songs. Not that it mattered. Annie was the last thing he needed. He needed someone uncomplicated. Someone simple and fun.

He pulled his phone from his pocket and dialed.

"Hey, Dylan!" Marla answered.

Her cheerful voice made him smile a little. "Feel like spending the day with me tomorrow?"

"At the festival or concert?"

"Both, if you're free."

"You betcha! But I'll have to leave the concert early. I promised Pappy I'd help with the fireworks."

"No problem. Pick you up in time for the parade, say nine thirty?"

"Sounds like a plan."

They said good-bye and hung up. Good old Marla. He could always count on her for a good time with no pressure to take the relationship to the next level.

As far as he was concerned, the next level only brought pain.

Dear Tempted,

Your instincts are telling you he's not your Mr. Right. Don't ignore these feelings. Sometimes they're the only thing standing between you and a monstrous mistake.

14

The town square was packed. Annie had saved their place early in the day, but even so, they were midway back on the edge of the lawn.

Onstage, Sawyer Smitten struck up a quiet tune as the applause faded away. He looked the part of country singer in his jeans and cowboy hat. He had yet to play his most recent hit, "Smitten."

Beside her, Sierra lifted her camera and snapped shots of Sawyer and his band. Ryder was looking sleepy after a full day of carnival games, junk food, and friends. Miss Lucy had doled out a pocketful of dollar bills before the parade, and Ryder's eyes had gone wide as walnuts.

"Can I have another burger, Mommy?" he said over the crooning singer.

"You just had one an hour ago."

"But they smell good."

Sierra snapped another picture of Sawyer. "I agree, but I think you've had enough, puddin'. Here's your rope. Go over there so you don't block anyone's view."

"Yippee!" Suddenly wide awake, he gathered the coil, sprang to his feet, and threw it toward a planter.

Sierra snapped an action shot. "Careful you don't hit anyone."

The infernal rope went everywhere with the kid, especially since he'd managed to loop the fence post a few days ago. They'd heard little about anything else.

Turning away, Annie perused the area. Twinkling white lights were strung above the makeshift dance floor. Couples had gathered beneath them, dancing to the love song. She spotted Dylan and Marla Jenkins whirling around the floor. Date four?

Dylan could move, she'd give him that. And he seemed to be having a good time with his partner. She wondered if he and Marla were getting serious.

The thought had barely surfaced when Dylan spun Marla into someone else's arms, and then he was dancing with Tina from the Mocha Moose. Dylan, committed to one woman? Ridiculous. She suddenly wished she weren't sitting in front of the dance floor.

When the song ended, the band struck up another slow tune. Dylan gave Tina a high five as they parted ways, then he scanned the crowd. She got the feeling he was looking for her. Despite the absurd notion she slouched and turned toward Sierra, who was snapping more shots of Sawyer.

A moment later she spotted Dylan a few blankets away,

laughing with an unfamiliar woman. She tossed her blond hair over bare shoulders and tilted her head, gazing at Dylan like he'd hung the moon. Oh brother.

"For someone who doesn't like Dylan," Sierra said over the music, "you sure manage to find him in a crowd."

"For your information, I was just thinking how much he annoys me."

Sierra's eyes sparkled as she raised the camera and snapped a shot of Annie. "That's how it starts, you know."

Annie rolled her eyes. What did her sister know? "How could you wish that on me? The last thing I need is a philandering cowboy like Dylan Taylor."

"Oh, come on. How can you know he's like that?"

"Look at him. He's hardly with the same girl twice. If it looks like a duck and walks like a duck . . . it's probably a duck."

"Where's a duck?" Ryder asked, his lariat at the ready.

Sierra laughed. "There's no duck, sweetie."

"Oh, yes there is," Annie said under her breath.

"You're too cautious. If it were me . . ."

"It's not." The thought of Sierra and Dylan made her insides twist.

"Well, if it *were* me, I'd sign up for a little uncertainty before I ever settled for boring."

"John's not boring."

Sierra raised her delicate brows. "And yet you knew exactly who I was referring to."

"You're overlooking his better qualities. He's smart and reliable and steady. There's nothing wrong with steady, Sierra."

"Steady . . . boring, same thing. Where'd he run off to anyway?"

"He has to be in Billings early tomorrow morning. Now hush, I want to hear the music."

It was Sierra's turn to roll her eyes.

The world went black as a pair of large hands covered Annie's eyes. They were warm and rough and smelled of leather.

"Guess who?" His voice rumbled in her ear, his breath stirring her hair.

Gooseflesh pebbled her skin. She pulled Dylan's hands away in time to see Sierra's smirk. His knees were planted on the blanket behind her.

"Mr. Taylor!" Ryder dropped his rope and swooped in for a hug.

"Hey, little man."

"I did it! I can loop the fence now!" He shrugged. "Well, sometimes I can."

He ruffled Ryder's hair. "I heard about that. You know what that means, right? You're a real cowboy."

Ryder bounced on the balls of his feet, too excited to stay earthbound. "Really?"

"You betcha." Dylan picked up a bag she hadn't noticed. "Got you something just today." He handed Ryder the bag.

The boy opened it and pulled out a hat. His green eyes widened. "A real cowboy hat!"

"Should be just your size too," Dylan said, setting it on his head.

Annie tamped down her frustration. Why couldn't he just stay out of their business?

"Look, Mommy!"

"You look adorable. Say cheese!" When Ryder complied, she snapped the photo.

"Look, Aunt Annie, I'm a philandewine cowboy just like Mr. Taylor!"

Annie sucked in a breath. She looked away, toward the stage, toward Sawyer Smitten and his band, swaying under the lights.

Sierra laughed uneasily. "Now where'd he hear a word like that?"

"From Aunt—"

Sierra set a hand over his mouth. "Say thank you to Mr. Taylor, sweetie." She pulled her hand away.

"Thanks, Mr. Taylor!"

"You're welcome, big guy."

Sierra grabbed Ryder's hand. "Come on, Ryder, let's go show off your hat on the dance floor."

Annie nailed Sierra with a look. *Don't you dare leave me! Don't you dare—*

And then she was gone, trotting toward the dance floor with Ryder in tow. Traitor.

Annie hoped the darkness hid her flush. She could feel Dylan behind her, and she wished he'd just go away. Find some other woman to pester, someone who actually enjoyed it.

He plopped down in Sierra's spot.

Perfect. She picked a piece of grass and twirled it between her fingers.

"Where's Spreadsheet tonight?"

"Stop calling him that. He—he had to turn in early. He has a very important meeting in the morning."

"Ah, a meeting."

He baited her with his tone, but she wouldn't rise to the occasion. Instead, she watched Ryder trying to two-step his way around the dance floor with his mom. She hated to admit it, but he did look adorable in that hat. Still, she hoped he'd be back to Batman before his fifth birthday. Maybe she'd buy him a costume, complete with an official cape.

Dylan bent his legs and propped his elbows on his knees. "Seems like a great kid."

For all Sierra's flighty ways, she was a good mom. "He is."

Onstage, Sawyer leaned down, extending his hands to the ladies in the front row.

"Mind if I ask about his dad?"

Annie shrugged. "I'm sure you've heard the rumors." Everyone knew Sierra had gone away for the summer and come home pregnant. Just like they knew the father had never bothered coming around.

"Rumors aren't always true."

"Well, that one was."

Sierra had cried for months over a guy she refused to name, and it hadn't been the pregnancy hormones. Annie could only imagine the hurt and betrayal she must've felt at his desertion. It had brought up all the feelings of unworthiness they'd both felt after their dad had left.

"She's lucky to have you."

Annie gave a wry laugh. "I'm not sure she'd always agree with that. It's been an uphill battle. But she's so close to finishing college. If she can just get through without throwing away her life, I'll rest a lot easier."

"Without falling in love with some philandering cowboy, you mean?"

Her palms grew sticky and the piece of grass stuck to one. She flicked it off and pulled her knees to her chest. "I just want her to be able to support herself. I know Sierra. Some man comes along and promises forever, she'll drop out and be at his mercy."

"Interesting choice of words."

"Yeah, well, when your own dad takes off for parts unknown, it leaves you a little jaded."

"All men aren't like that. Your grandfather wasn't. Mine either."

"Nevertheless, she has a child to support. She needs to depend on herself, not some—man." She checked her watch, but it was too dark to see. Surely the concert was almost over. The fireworks would start soon, then he'd go away. But maybe he wouldn't . . .

"Some cowboy, you mean?"

"I said man."

"But you meant cowboy."

She turned a glare on him and ignored his flirty smile. "Anyone ever tell you you're exasperating?"

"Lots." His eyes softened and the world whittled down to the two of them. His smile was a table set for two, complete with flickering candles. "Usually just before I take them in my arms and change their minds."

Her breath seemed locked in her lungs. "Exasperating *and* cocky. How can they resist?"

He bumped her shoulder. "I don't know, Annie, but you could sure give lessons."

"I really should. It would save countless heartaches."

"You think I'm a heartbreaker, huh?"

"Do you mind? I came for the music." His shoulder was still against hers, warm and hard, entirely too close. She shifted away.

"There's nothing wrong with having a little fun. You should try it sometime."

"Isn't there someone waiting for you? It's almost time for the fireworks, you know."

"Come to Yellowstone with me Saturday. Just you and me and God's beautiful creation. I know a spot where the moose come to feed in the water."

How did he know it was her favorite place? That seeing moose wade into the water was the highlight of her trips—when she managed to spot them.

"Last time I was there a mama and her calf showed up," he said. "It was amazing. I watched them for an hour."

She'd just been with John, but she imagined a different kind of day with Dylan, camped out by some rippling brook, behind the brush, waiting for moose. They'd huddle together on a blanket, waiting, talking. Then he'd point and say, "Shh, look over there," his mouth next to her ear, and—

"Whaddaya say, Annie?"

She shook the image from her head. What was she thinking? He'd probably toss her in the creek and think it was all great fun.

"I just went Saturday. Anyway, I can't."

"Can't or won't?"

She straightened her legs and leaned back on her hands. "John and I are seeing each other exclusively now. I'm sure you can find someone else to keep you company."

Dylan's expression went unchanged, but something in his eyes flickered. "Exclusive, huh? That was quick."

"Not really. We've been going out—" *How long?* "Awhile. Two months," she guessed.

"Barely time to know his boot size. Not that he owns a pair."

She ignored his dig. "We're thinking long term and looking to settle down. Besides"—she gave him a pointed look—"there's no one else I want to go out with."

He grinned. "Ouch. You wound me, Annie."

"I'm sure you'll get over it soon enough. Isn't Marla waiting somewhere? I'm sure she'd like to watch the fireworks with you."

"She's helping load them."

Oh, great. Now she'd never get rid of him. And she really did need to get rid of him. Her breath felt trapped in her chest and her palms were damp against the quilt.

As he straightened his legs, his thigh brushed hers. Her heart shot out a warning flare. *Danger. Danger. Danger.*

The man couldn't take a hint. But if she couldn't make him leave, at least Sierra and Ryder would be back soon. She would set Ryder right between them, a squirming four-year-old buffer. Dylan would find another blanket to sprawl on soon enough.

The tune ended, ushering in thunderous applause. Sierra and Ryder left the dance floor, skirting chairs and blankets on their return. Finally.

They stopped near Shay and Travis, talked a minute, then plopped down and made themselves comfortable.

Thanks a lot, sis.

Sawyer began the intro for "Smitten," and Annie applauded with the crowd.

Dylan nudged her. "Dance with me."

"No, thank you."

"I won't step on your toes."

She sighed, tired of being pestered, tired of being polite, tired of getting nowhere. "Please go away, Dylan. This is my favorite song."

"I'll go away if you dance with me."

She shot him a look.

"Otherwise . . ." He shrugged. "Well, I have it on good authority it's a veeerrry long fireworks display this year. I have nowhere else to be and I find your cute little quilt extremely cozy."

Of all the—

"One little dance or forty minutes of fireworks . . . your choice." He leaned back on the quilt and crossed his feet at the ankles like he was settling in for the night.

"Oh, all right. Fine. I'll dance with you if it'll shut you up." Besides, she'd take four minutes over forty any day of the week.

Dylan smiled broadly. "Thought you'd never ask." He sprang to his feet, surprisingly spry.

She walked slowly, pretending it took all her attention to navigate the obstacles. She didn't settle for the fringe of the dance floor but wound her way into the heart of it. Not only did it eat away the clock, but she didn't want news of their dance to reach John's ears.

She turned and Dylan walked right into her arms, not stopping until she planted her palms against his chest. *Close enough, buster.*

His lips twitched and his eyes danced under the brim of his black hat. He took her hand and she set her other on his shoulder.

She focused on the music, on the rich melody wrapping around her, on the words Sawyer crooned.

> *And I'm just gonna say it.*
> *Gonna lay my heart*
> *there on the line.*
> *When I wrap my arms around you,*
> *whisper in your ear, I realize*
> *that I'm smitten*
> *by your love.*
> *Baby, I'm smitten by your love.*

Dylan moved effortlessly to the tune, making the dancing part easy. It was the breathing she struggled with. Thank God he was so much taller. It was easy to avoid his eyes, which, she was sure, were mocking her even now. She needed something to talk about. Something to distract her from her thrashing heart, from the romantic words and stirring melody.

"So . . . you haven't told me how Braveheart's doing today."

When he didn't answer, she looked at him and found a little smile on his lips.

"What?"

"Searching for a safe topic?"

"It's called small talk." She huffed and looked away, but his broad shoulders blocked out everything. She settled for the white pearly button on his black shirt.

"You can't fool me, Annie. I know you feel it too."

She swallowed. "I don't know what you're talking about."

His thigh brushed hers as if to provide a case in point. Like she needed one. She put some space between them. *It's just the music. Sawyer Smitten and his magic melody.*

"Call it chemistry or electricity or whatever you want . . ." His voice rumbled low. "There's enough of it between us to make my neck hair stand on end. And believe what you want, I don't say that to just anyone."

"First one this month, huh? I'm flattered."

She wondered if he could see her thumping heart through her shirt. She drew in a slow breath and exhaled as casually as she could.

"Actually . . ." He lifted her chin until their eyes met. "I've never said that to any woman."

Have mercy, his eyes were serious as a county bake-off, and there was something in them that hinted at vulnerability. His smile was long gone.

His lips looked soft and oh, so kissable, and she suddenly realized why every other woman in Park County had fallen prey to his charms. It wasn't the boisterous, flirtatious Dylan. It was *this*. This quiet, unguarded, you're-the-only-woman-in-the-world Dylan that was so dangerous.

And tempting. Heavens to Betsy, yes, he was tempting. She wasn't going to lie to herself. No sense in that. Her thudding heart and empty lungs had already figured it out.

He looked as if he meant every word. As if he were somehow more attracted to her than anyone else. More than pretty, outgoing Marla Jenkins, more than sultry Bridgett Garvin, more than the gorgeous blonde who'd thrown herself at him ten short minutes ago.

He was still staring at her with those wounded puppy dog eyes . . . Oh yes, he was good. No wonder he left a string of broken hearts in his wake. It was cruel of him to tease women this way. To tease *her* this way.

She pushed him away. "I think I've had enough."

"What's wrong?"

"I danced with you, now leave me alone." As Sawyer belted out the bridge, Annie walked off the dance floor and swooped her quilt off the ground. She'd had enough fireworks for one night.

Dear Bowled Over in Billings,

There's a lot more to love than chemistry.

15

Annie stifled a grin as she watched Dylan read the letter from someone signed *Brokenhearted.* The temperature had cooled as the sun sank behind the mountains, and now a slight breeze made her shiver. Nevertheless, after last week's dance she wasn't about to step foot inside his house, not even if a snowstorm rolled through.

She'd had a full week to review those moments, and review them she had. At first she'd felt guilty. It didn't help that Dylan had managed to stir more with mere words than John had been able to rouse with lengthy kisses.

But after thinking it through, she put her guilty feelings aside. It was just Sawyer's song. It got to her every time. And maybe a little pheromones mixed in. All she had to do was keep her distance from Dylan, stay upwind, and all would be fine.

Dylan looked up from the letter with a smirk. "Cute, Annie."

She widened her eyes and shrugged. "What?"

He squinted at the paper. "Let's see . . . in love with a Casanova cowboy . . . promises me forever even while he dates others . . . string of broken hearts . . . can't resist his smooth-talking ways . . . Should I go on?"

So she'd handpicked the letter. "Does that sound familiar or something?"

"It's the way *you* see me—not the way I actually am."

She laughed. "Okay . . . let's go with that."

He handed her the letter and settled into the swing, still smiling congenially. "That's not me, Annie."

"You haven't left a string of broken hearts?"

"I don't lead anyone on. They know right from the get-go I'm not looking to settle down."

She thought of the way he'd looked at her during their dance. The way his eyes had said so much. "Promises aren't always verbal, Dylan. They can be a look or a touch. People's feelings are fragile. You should take more care."

She pressed her lips together. She'd said too much. She could tell by the way his eyes narrowed, by the way his easy smile fell away.

"Is that what's bothering you? What I said the other night when—"

"Of course not—"

"—we were dancing?"

"No."

"That's just the bare truth, Annie. Since you're all hung up on total honesty, you should appreciate that."

Her face burned against the cool night air. It had been stupid to choose that letter, but she'd wanted to put him in his place. Had she really thought she could best him in a game of verbal sparring?

Dylan watched a flush bloom on Annie's cheeks. Tough if she didn't want to hear the truth. It had taken courage to admit his feelings, and her response had been humbling.

He'd been uneasy about having her over tonight. She'd dashed in and out of church on Sunday, and he hadn't seen hide nor hair of her all week, even though one of his hands said she'd been working with Braveheart in the afternoons.

Truth was, he liked her. She challenged him with her smart comebacks and sassy attitude.

Good thing she already had a boyfriend.

Annie cleared her throat. "The point is, Casanova Cowboy hasn't been honest with Brokenhearted. Can we agree she needs to keep her distance?"

He set the swing in motion, thinking. The rhythmic creaking was the only sound breaking the silence.

"He leads her on," she said. "She's looking to settle down and he's not. It seems obvious she should look elsewhere, right?"

"That'll be hard since they work together."

"Well, maybe she should quit. There's a lot at stake here." Annie squirmed in the chair.

There was a lot at stake. Not for Brokenhearted but for him; he wasn't oblivious to the undertones of this conversation. Last thing he wanted was Annie running for the hills when Braveheart still needed her.

Besides, Dylan enjoyed her company. Got a kick out of getting her riled, seeing those blue eyes freeze over. And he hadn't minded the way she'd felt in his arms either. All those sparks had triggered some pleasant daydreams in the saddle this week.

Back to the letter, Taylor. He hooked his thumb around the cool metal of the chain. "Okay . . . *since* he's been lying to her, I agree she should look for greener pastures. And if she can't move on while working together, she should probably find another job."

Annie's brows shot up. "So we agree."

"Stranger things have happened."

"If you say so." Annie made some notes. Her hands were small, as was the rest of her. Sometimes it amazed him that she worked with horses that weighed hundreds of pounds. He admired her skill and competence. Even with all the responsibilities riding on her slight shoulders, she'd managed to find her passion.

"I heard your sister got a job at the Tin Roof." Travis McCoy had seen her waiting tables the day before.

"Just for tourist season, but I'm grateful. It's good of Mabel and Roy to give her a chance. Sierra doesn't have the best track record."

"She'll go back to school in the fall?"

Annie nodded. "Last semester. We're almost there."

"What's her major?"

"Journalism. She's got this great creative streak. You should see what she writes. I'm hoping she can take over this column when she graduates. Or write something else for *Montana Living*. At least we have a foot in the door, and in this economy, that's critical."

Ahh, that was why the column meant so much to her. "She'll get there."

"I won't rest easy till she does." The corner of her lip tucked in. "She has a way of turning all your expectations upside down. Like, she used to be so passionate about God, and now she never talks about Him, and she's practically dropped out of church. I feel like I'm failing her most of the time."

"You're like a second mother."

Annie shrugged. "That's a big sister for you."

"I wouldn't know. It was just me and Luke. Well, and Wade. We were close as brothers."

"That's right. You rodeoed with him in Texas."

"Wade rodeoed. I was just along for the ride."

"I've seen you in a trophy buckle or two."

"Wade was in a league all his own."

"Now he's up to his eyeballs in dirty diapers." Annie smiled. "He must be missing his rodeo days about now."

He'd never seen her prettier than right now, with the porch light casting a golden glow on her porcelain skin.

"Actually, I've never seen him happier."

"True love will do that, I suppose."

It had made him happy once upon a time. Just before it smashed his heart to smithereens.

"I guess his first marriage wasn't so happy."

He shook his head. Wade's wife, Abigail, had written an article about it in *Viewpoint Magazine* just before they'd married. "After his first wife had Maddy, she wasn't the same. Depression, I guess. You probably know she took her own life."

Annie nodded. "So sad."

"But God brought Abigail into their lives, gave them the Code-meister, and now they're a family. If anyone deserves a slice of happiness, it's Wade."

Annie began gathering her things.

He frowned. "Where you going? Don't you have another letter?"

"Not this week. My answer to Brokenhearted will be on the long side."

He'd just bet she had plenty to say about Casanova Cowboy. He was suddenly loath to see her go. "Stay for supper."

"No, thank you."

He thought about what kind of food he could tempt her with and came up empty. Bologna sandwiches wouldn't do it. "Come check on Braveheart again before you go?"

"I have to pick up Ryder from the sitter's."

He'd never had so much trouble getting a woman to stick around. Next time he'd have a plan in place. Maybe he'd offer to show her the cabin her grandfather was raised in. It was on his property, set way back in the hills. Not tonight though, with darkness closing in fast.

She stood, placing her bag on her shoulder. "Thanks for your help. I'll be by as much as I can next week to work with Braveheart."

"Appreciate that."

"Good night."

"Night." He watched her slide into her cab and turn the truck around. He recalled seeing her and Oakley on Sunday, in the third pew, her hair brushing his shoulder when she turned. He bet Oakley didn't have to work so hard to get a few minutes of her time, and he doubted the man had any idea how lucky he was.

As the red taillights of her truck disappeared into the darkness, an unwelcome feeling swept over him. He turned around and headed into his big, empty house.

Dear Fretful,

    Expect the unexpected.

16

The next Thursday Annie decided to stop by home to shower before she went to Dylan's. She smelled like horseflesh. She'd spent the bulk of her afternoon with the twelve-year-old gelding Tina from Mocha Moose had bought her daughter. The horse, otherwise a sweet thing, kept kicking from behind and had put a nasty bruise on Rachel's thigh.

Annie suspected the previous owner had mistreated the horse. They'd found a couple spots he liked rubbed, and Annie encouraged Rachel to love on him often. Once Rachel established trust, Annie would teach her about pole gentling so she could safely approach him from behind.

Annie's phone rang on the way home, and her heart skittered when she saw Midge's name on the screen. *Please, God. Not bad news.*

She answered the phone, and after trading greetings, Midge got right to the point.

"Well, we're a little over halfway through your ninety-day probation . . . I'm afraid we're still getting letters."

Annie winced. "I'm sorry, Midge. I've lightened the tone, and I assure you I give careful thought to my answers. You know there are going to be differing opinions on this kind of thing. It's love—hardly as cut-and-dried as a horse advice column."

"I see your point, Annie, I do. But something has to change. Some of your responses don't receive the negative feedback. I'll e-mail you the ones that readers favor. Maybe that'll help guide you."

After agreeing, Annie hung up the phone. If she didn't turn this around quickly, she was going to lose her job.

Annie pulled up to the house and spotted Sierra's car. Her sister was supposed to be at work, but she must've gotten off early. Weeknights at the diner were often slow.

Annie went to greet Pepper, who was grazing happily in the meadow. When he ambled to the fence, she stroked his speckled nose and rubbed behind his ear where he liked. "Go for a ride tomorrow, big fella? . . . Yeah, I miss you too." She kissed his nose, gave him a final rub, and headed toward the house.

Inside, a cartoon was blaring from the TV, but Ryder was nowhere to be seen. The smell of garlic filled the house, and she heard something sizzling in the kitchen. Maybe she'd have time for a bite or two before she took off again.

"I'm home for a quick shower," she called as she went down the hallway.

"Okay," Sierra called back.

Annie spotted new photos of her and Ryder hanging in the hallway and paused. She recognized them from the Fourth of July, several of Ryder in his new cowboy hat, and a few shots of Annie. A couple of the photos were professional quality.

"Hey, your pictures turned out nice!" she called.

"Thanks. I'll show you the ones of Sawyer later."

Annie showered away the day's dirt and grime and slipped into a comfy pair of jeans and a button-up. She blow dried her hair and slid into the kitchen with a few minutes to spare.

Sierra was standing over the stove when she entered the room. Her sister lifted a full ladle, blew on it, and tasted.

"You're home early," Annie said.

Sierra drained the pasta, her movements quick and proficient. "I tried to call, but you were out of range, I guess."

"Thanks for starting supper. Was the diner slow again?"

Sierra dumped the macaroni into the sauce and stirred. "Um, sort of."

Sierra hadn't looked at her yet. A series of warning signals went off inside Annie.

"What happened?"

Sierra grabbed a towel and wiped her hands, still avoiding eye contact.

"Please tell me you didn't get fired." Not after Mabel and Roy had so graciously taken a chance on her. Not when her own job hung in the balance.

Sierra set the food on the table, looking everywhere but at Annie. "No, I didn't get fired. I—I quit."

"Quit! Sierra, how could you?" Did her sister think jobs grew on trees like pinecones?

"It couldn't be helped. It was—it was the wrong job for me. I'll get a job someplace else, I promise." She folded her arms, more guarded than defiant.

"I don't understand you. We need the money, and the Franklins went out on a limb to offer you that job!"

"I know, but—" Sierra's eyes glossed over. "I just couldn't stay there anymore."

No, not this time. Annie wasn't softening at the first sign of emotion. Her sister needed to learn responsibility. She wasn't a child anymore. She *had* a child, for heaven's sake.

"You barely worked there a week." She crossed the kitchen and looked out the patio door, thinking. Maybe Mabel and Roy would take her back. The diner had been her only job opportunity since she'd been fired from the Mocha Moose.

"Okay." Annie took a deep breath as she turned. "Here's what we're going to do. We'll go to the Tin Roof in the morning and sit down with the Franklins. We'll explain that you made a rash decision and that you realize now it was a—"

"No."

"—bad idea, and we'll beg for your job back."

"No!"

"Yes, Sierra! You have to take responsibility for your decisions—"

"You can't tell me what to do!" Sierra whirled from the room.

Annie followed into the living room where a commercial blared. "There's not another job waiting in the wings! It took weeks to find this, and you can't throw away opportunities like old, holey socks!"

"Leave me alone!" Sierra kept going right out the door.

Annie followed. "I'm working two jobs to keep our heads above water. Don't you think you could at least hold down one? Is that asking too much?"

Sierra spun in the dirt, her auburn hair flying around her

shoulders. "I'm sorry we're such a burden!" She turned toward her clunky car. "Ryder! We're leaving!"

"I didn't mean it like that and you know it."

Ryder came trotting around the house, cowboy hat firmly in place. "Where we going?"

Sierra's shoulders still heaved, but her voice was calm. "Get in, puddin', we're going for a ride."

"Don't, Sierra."

She buckled Ryder's seat belt, then got in and started the car.

"We'll be out of your way now," she said through the cracked window. "And don't worry, *Mom*. I'll be home by curfew." Her tires spun, spewing dirt and gravel.

Annie spun and marched into the house. She passed the television, flipping it off, and kicked Ryder's rope out of her way.

The pasta sat in the center of the table, steam rising toward the ceiling. She wasn't the least bit hungry now. She felt like jumping in her truck and running off too. Must be nice to just pick up and go on a whim, never mind the supper cooling on the table. She glanced across the kitchen. Or the stovetop—still on!

She turned it off and dished the pasta into a Tupperware container, then cleaned the skillet and pot and put them away.

Why did Sierra have to be so flighty, so stubborn! Surely she could understand they needed the money. Couldn't she see how hard Annie was working to keep them on their feet?

Where had she failed? She looked heavenward, envisioning the look on her grandfather's face when he'd begged Annie to look after Sierra, and feeling a familiar stab of guilt.

I'm trying, Gramps. Is this what you went through with Mom? She thought of how distant her mom and grandfather had been with each other during her childhood. Is that where she and Sierra were headed?

Well, she couldn't let that stand in her way. First and foremost was getting the girl on her feet before some cowboy came along and swept her off them. There was time enough to worry about their relationship later.

After refrigerating the pasta Annie hopped in the truck and made the short drive to Dylan's. She looked futilely for Sierra's car on her way through town. Hopefully she'd gone to Bridgett's and not some guy's since she had Ryder in tow.

At the Circle D Annie found Braveheart in his stall, stomping his hooves. He must be so tired. She soothed him with soft words as she approached, making a concerted effort to clear away all thoughts of Sierra.

He raised his head and neighed, looking for her.

"Right here, baby. Annie's right here." She held her fist to his nose, and he tensed up and moved back until he hit the stall.

Annie continued talking. She didn't dare put the horse in the pasture just yet. He was too skittish and distrustful, and now that his sight was completely gone, she was afraid he'd stumble in a rut or run headlong into the fence.

She'd finally gotten him to approach the stall door and was scratching his neck when Dylan entered, leading the bay quarter horse she'd seen in the pasture before.

Dylan's smile lit up the barn. "Evening."

He wore tan chaps, a plaid shirt, and a hat that had been put through the paces.

"Hey."

She worked quietly with Braveheart, aware of Dylan nearby. He moved with efficient motions, unsaddling the bay and brushing him down.

When he was finished, he joined her. "Hey, buddy."

Braveheart tossed his head and neighed.

She felt Dylan's appraisal and put a few inches between them.

"You smell like flowers and sunshine."

She started to say she'd stopped home for a shower, but heaven forbid he think she'd gone to extra measures on his account.

"You smell like horseflesh and sweat."

He laughed. "That's my Annie, always putting me in my place."

Too bad it only seemed to amuse him. "Someone has to."

He stroked Braveheart's neck, his attention still on her. "If you knew how much I enjoyed it, I bet you'd stop." His deep, quiet drawl caused a visceral reaction in her.

She shifted farther away and cleared her throat, willing the heat in her stomach to stay put and not flood into her cheeks.

Braveheart snorted.

"Easy, fellow," Dylan said.

The horse wasn't responding well tonight. No doubt he sensed the leftover tension from her quarrel with Sierra. And it hadn't dissipated since Dylan's arrival.

"He's restless," Dylan said.

Annie was glad to have the focus on the horse. "He's letting us touch him at least. How's he eating? He looks thinner."

"His appetite's down. I'm getting worried. What more can I do for him?" He leaned on the stall door, and his arm brushed hers as he reached out to rub Braveheart's neck.

The horse nickered.

"Just keep loving on him as often as you can. Try not to worry. Time will take care of it. It's like with any sudden loss. You just keep breathing and eventually everything settles into a new normal. He's depended on his sight all his life, but his other senses will pick up the slack. Be patient."

He gave her a lopsided grin. "Not my forte."

She thought of Sierra and sighed. "I know what you mean."

He rubbed and scratched Braveheart while she talked to the horse in soothing tones.

After a few minutes Dylan gave Braveheart a final pat and withdrew his hand. "I need to grab a shower."

"Meet you on the porch in a bit."

"Actually . . . I thought you might be interested in a field trip." He flashed his dimple.

Annie looked away. He was at it again. "The porch suits me fine."

"Did you know your grandpa's childhood home is on my property?"

She met his eyes. Her grandpa had told countless stories about growing up in a cabin, but she'd thought it long gone. "It's not still standing . . . ?"

"It is. Road's kinda rough getting back to it, but my truck can handle it. My grandpa bought up the property way back and used the cabin as a bunk for his cowhands. But the creek floods over the road leading back there, so he stopped using it."

She weighed the exciting proposition of seeing her grandpa's home with the daunting one of extra time with Dylan.

"Whaddaya say? We have enough daylight if we go there first."

She remembered the tales her grandfather had told her. About falling into the creek when he was just a wee thing, about jumping off the roof on a dare from his big brother and breaking his ankle. And he'd told her about the view from his mama's kitchen window.

"I'd love to see it."

"I'll grab a shower and we'll be on our way then."

He was out of the barn before the second thoughts could swarm

over her like bees over a honeycomb. She was going with Dylan to
some remote cabin in the woods? What was she thinking? What
would John think?

Oh, for heaven's sake, it's Grandpa's cabin. She was being ridiculous. It was daylight, after all, and it wasn't a date. Just a . . . field
trip, like he'd said.

She pulled her focus back to Braveheart and worked with him
until she heard Dylan enter the barn.

"Ready?" he asked.

She gave Braveheart a final pat. "Hang in there, baby. I'll be
back soon."

"How far is it?" she asked as Dylan opened the truck door for her.

"Fifteen minutes or so." He rounded the vehicle, tossing his
keys in the air and catching them easily. His spread was larger than
she'd figured if they could drive fifteen minutes and still be on his
property.

She took a deep breath and realized his truck smelled just like
him. Leather and musk. He got in, started the truck, and a country-
and-western tune filled the cab.

"Chilly?" he asked.

The sun had sunk behind the mountains, and clouds had rolled
in across the sky. "A bit."

He flipped on the heat and turned down the drive. She didn't
like being in tight quarters where she could smell him and feel his
body heat. He tapped his fingers to the country jig and hummed
along.

She wished she'd brought her letters so they could make good
use of their time. But she hadn't, so she might as well settle back
and enjoy the scenery. From the corner of her eye she watched his
square fingers thump the steering wheel, then curl around the

wheel as he turned onto a rutted drive. His sleeves were folded up, exposing thick forearms with a sprinkling of black hair.

The mountain scenery, Annie. For heaven's sake.

"Tell me about yourself, Annie. All this time together, and I don't even know what you do in your spare time."

She shrugged, keeping her eyes on the green hills dotted with cattle. "Ride my horse, Pepper, mostly. Read, when I get the chance."

"What do you read?"

She sure wasn't telling him she was a Jane Austen junkie. Didn't want him thinking she had grand illusions of romance. "This and that."

"That's my favorite genre too."

She rolled her eyes.

"How's your nephew? Getting good with that lasso?"

"He's becoming quite the cowboy."

"How come I get the feeling you don't approve?" The smile in his voice was audible.

"Because I don't."

"Come on, now. We're not so bad, are we?"

She humphed.

"Saw your sister flitting around tables at the Tin Roof Monday, chatting up the customers, doing a fine job."

The anxiety she'd felt earlier snaked back up into her throat. "She quit today."

She felt his perusal for several seconds before he turned his attention back to the rutted lane. "Sorry to hear that. Anything I can do?"

She shook her head. "We had words before I came to your place. She took off with Ryder in a huff."

"She'll be back. Any idea why she quit?"

"I'm sure she got tired or bored or something. It's always the same with Sierra. I couldn't count on both hands all the jobs she's had, and with a track record like that, no one will touch her. I don't mean to talk bad about her. She's really a sweet girl, and I love her to bits, but . . . she can be a handful."

She was surprised to find her tongue so loose. He was easy to talk to when he wasn't being all Dylan.

"Maybe I can put in a good word somewhere."

"Thank you, but I wouldn't want you ruining your good word. Besides, I think she's asked around about everywhere. I just hope her car holds out. It's making a funny noise, she said, but we can't afford to get it checked right now."

"Maybe I can help. I'm a mechanic of sorts. Have her bring it over and I'll take a look."

She looked at him, catching his profile. Masculine square jaw, neatly clipped sideburns. "Thanks. That's nice of you."

He turned a smile on her. "Anything for a pretty lady."

She didn't want to know if he was talking about her or Sierra. They crossed a low wooden bridge. Moose Creek was barely a trickle, the water having evaporated under the July sun.

The lane became more rutted and he slowed down, dodging potholes.

"You weren't kidding." She reached for the door to steady herself.

"This area's been flooded so many times, and like I said, no one comes back here anymore."

Her shoulder thumped into the door. "I see why."

"Used to ride over here when I visited my grandpa." He tipped a smile her way, waggling his eyebrows. "Made a great rendezvous spot with the girls."

Brother. "I'll just bet it did." Her grandpa wouldn't have appreciated his use of the place.

They bounced and bumped their way down the lane. The hills leveled and the pine trees grew thicker. The lane became covered with a bed of pine needles.

Awhile later she spotted the cabin nestled in a grove of tall pines. "There it is."

Weeds and overgrown bushes virtually engulfed the front of the one-story cabin. As they drew closer she made out weathered logs separated by lines of chinking. The tiny porch featured broken handrails, and a stone chimney rose from the wooden-shingled roof.

"My grandpa jumped off that roof when he was a boy."

Dylan put the truck in park and shut off the engine. "Oh yeah?"

"Broke his ankle." She got out of the cab. "His brother had to do his chores the rest of the summer for daring him." She took a deep breath of the pine-scented air.

"Sounds like you've heard a tale or two."

She couldn't prevent the smile as she approached the steps.

"Careful of the rotting wood," he said.

On the porch she tried the rusty handle and the door squeaked open. Inside it was dim. Dust motes danced in front of the cabin's tiny windows. Something scurried away in the dark corner, making her jump.

"I'll get a flashlight," Dylan said, and then she was alone. The air in the one-room cabin smelled stale and musty, as if it hadn't been energized by human presence in years. A stone fireplace dominated one wall. The mantel, no more than a rough-hewn beam, slanted across the empty grate like a cocked eyebrow.

Opposite it, a tiny loft nestled near the beamed ceiling, marking the place where her grandpa and great-uncle had slept. The room below was empty from what she could see, save for something that appeared to be a small bed.

She made her way into the kitchen, bumping into an old chair. The window over the sink beckoned. She braced her hands on the cast-iron sink ledge and looked out past the cobwebs and dirty windowpane. Beyond the pine boughs, the Gallatin Range stood in silhouette against the pink evening sky.

She heard the front door squeak open, then Dylan's footsteps as he crossed the wood-plank floor. The flashlight shed a golden glow over the room when he entered.

"Sorry. Forgot how little light these windows let in." His voice seemed deeper in the quiet of the cabin. "Great view," he said, coming nearer.

"My great-grandpa built the house at just the right angle so his wife could see the mountains she loved."

She looked around the room as Dylan shone the light. An old rug hugged the wood floor near the chair she'd bumped. Chunks of chinking were missing, and daylight seeped through the slits.

"I wish these walls could talk," she said. "Imagine the stories . . ." She walked back to the main area and peered up at the loft before stepping onto the ladder.

"Careful, it's old." Dylan grabbed her waist. He probably had ulterior motives, but she was too distracted to put up a fuss. She reached the top and peered into the dark loft.

"Here." Dylan handed her the flashlight, taking hold of the rickety ladder. "Not sure how sturdy the loft is."

She shone the light around the space, disappointed to find it empty except for some debris in the corner. She stepped back down, turning into Dylan's arms at the bottom. Her heart bucked in her chest and gooseflesh raced down her arms.

"Excuse me." It was an effort to keep her voice steady.

He pulled his hands away, letting her by. She approached the big fireplace, shining the light on the old stones.

"They were probably pulled from the creek."

He was probably right. "Chopping firewood was my grandpa's chore. He hated it. He had a fireplace at his house and I was always asking him to light it, but he rarely did. Just turned up the thermostat and covered me with an extra blanket."

"Can you imagine how much firewood they must've gone through on a winter's day?"

"Even in the summer they must've needed it at night."

"I'll bet he never wanted to see another chunk of firewood again."

She smiled. "Probably not."

She shone the light around the room, then checked her watch. She wondered if Sierra and Ryder had returned home. She'd probably stay out till all hours just to prove she could.

Still, it was getting late and they still had to work on the column. "We'd best get back." She handed him the light and started for the door. On the porch she navigated the steps carefully. Darkness was falling fast and the clouds obscured the moon and stars.

"Thanks for bringing me here." She skirted Dylan as he held the passenger door.

"My pleasure." He smiled and touched the brim of his hat in a way that made something flutter in her stomach.

She buckled her seat belt as he rounded the front, taking one last look at the cabin. She'd like to bring Sierra here sometime.

Dylan got in, put the key in the ignition, and turned it. A clicking sound followed. And then . . . nothing.

Dear Regretful,

  The hardest words in the English language are "I'm sorry,"
but it sounds as if you'd better call upon them soon.

17

*A*nnie watched as Dylan turned the key. Nothing. His brows
pulled together as he turned it again and came up empty.

"What's wrong?"

"Not sure." He reached behind the seat and retrieved the
flashlight, then pulled the hood release. "Hang tight," he said as he
got out. A moment later the hood went up, blocking her view.

She looked out the passenger window at the growing darkness.
Only the skies where the sun had set were lit, and that light was
quickly fading.

She heard Dylan tinkering around with the engine. They were
awfully far from civilization. *Relax, Annie. He's good with cars, he
said so himself.* He'd be able to fix whatever it was. And if he
couldn't, they could call for help.

She could call Sierra or Shay or John. She looked around at the deserted cabin, then at Dylan's hands reaching into the engine cavity. No, not John.

The lid fell closed with a quiet thump and Dylan returned. Awesome. He must've fixed it.

But when he got into the cab he wasn't smiling, and he didn't even reach for the keys.

"What's wrong?"

He gripped the bottom of the steering wheel and stared out the windshield. "A belt snapped." He was ominously still.

"Okay. Well . . . I'll call my sister—she may be mad, but she won't leave me stranded in the middle of nowhere." Her laugh sounded nervous even to her.

She pulled out her phone, dialed, and put it to her ear. When nothing happened, she checked the screen.

Oh. She should've figured, way out here. "No signal." She turned to him. "Try yours."

"Can't."

"Why not?"

"Left it in my bathroom."

Dread sank like a lead weight to the bottom of her stomach. "You don't have it?"

He tapped his fingers on the wheel. "Nope."

She couldn't stay out here all alone with Dylan. At the very thought, dread sucked the moisture from her mouth, the air from her lungs. "Well . . . maybe you can fix the belt."

"Nope."

"Let's walk then. It's not that chilly and we have a little daylight left." Very little.

"There are mountain lions and rattlers out there, Annie."

He was right. Their options were evaporating like a mud puddle in August.

She looked out the passenger window, her insides roiling like a tornado. She couldn't stay. Sierra would worry if she didn't come home. And John—what would he think? Heavens, what would *everyone* think if word got around?

But she was getting ahead of herself. Sierra would probably fall asleep and never notice she hadn't come home. *Annie* was the one who waited up.

"We'd best head inside," he said. "I have a lighter in the back. I'll start a fire."

That's what she was afraid of. She remembered the small, dark space. The tiny cot in the corner. Panic wedged its way into her chest. "Wait. There has to be another option."

If only they'd taken her truck. If only he hadn't asked her to come out here to begin with.

But he had asked her . . . and right at dusk . . .

And now the truck conveniently wouldn't start. A belt suddenly "snapped." How did that happen anyway?

She remembered that he'd returned to the truck for the flashlight—or had he? Maybe he'd set this whole thing up. Figured this was his chance to get her alone. It would be just like him to manipulate the situation to suit his whim. Never mind the trouble it would cause.

She peered at him across the darkening cab, the new suspicion sinking in and gaining validity with each passing moment. Hadn't he said he used to bring girls out here? He'd probably used the broken-down vehicle ploy more than once. He was a regular pro. All it took was a pair of scissors and the cost of a new belt—a cheap fix. And she'd worried that Sierra was gullible!

"What?" He stared back at her, all innocence.

Innocent, my fanny. "Is this how you got all the other girls up here?"

"What?"

"I'm not all those other girls, Dylan. I don't want to be here with you. I have a boyfriend. This isn't a three-minute dance you can bribe me into so you can worm your way into my—my affections, or whatever you had planned. This is a whole night, alone, with people worrying where we are, and I have my reputation to think about, you know!"

He turned his upper body toward her. "You think I *planned* this?"

"Like you'd never do such a thing. I'm not as naïve as you think, and I am not staying here with you all night!" She reached for the handle, opening the door. "I'm walking!"

He grabbed her arm. "Don't be ridiculous! It'll be pitch black by the time you reach the creek."

"I'm perfectly capable of finding my way back."

"You perfectly capable of fending off wildlife too?"

She wrested her arm from him, glaring at the unwelcome reminder. Both the animals he'd mentioned hunted at night. The thought of stepping on a rattler was enough to stop her, one leg out the door.

"Contrary to your opinion, Annie, I'm not the dog you think I am. I never coerced any woman into coming with me here or any-where else. Yeah, I like to flirt and have a little fun, so what? Despite rumors to the contrary, I don't sleep around with the ladies—willing or not. I'm a Christian man; that means something to me."

She looked out her open door, unable to meet his gaze any lon-ger. Her breath came fast, keeping pace with her heart. Maybe he was telling the truth.

The darkened cabin drew her eyes, and she imagined nine hours alone with him. She'd barely made it through a three-minute dance. Hadn't actually made it through the whole thing because of what he'd said. And what rankled was, he was right about the chemistry. That's why being trapped here scared the living daylights out of her. Why a hard knot of fear balled in her chest even now. The thought of rattlers was growing more tolerable by the minute.

A drop of rain splashed on the windshield. Then another. Seconds later, a steady patter began.

"Perfect," she said.

Dylan grabbed the flashlight and opened his door.

"Where you going?"

"To gather firewood." He got out, slamming the door behind him.

She didn't like how easily he was accepting this. Surely there must be something else they could do. She saw the keys dangling from the ignition and reached toward them. She wrapped her fingers around them and paused.

Please, God. I know I got myself into this, but please, just let this thing start, and I won't ever go anywhere with him again.

She closed her eyes and turned the key.

Nothing.

She let go and settled back in the seat, releasing a deep breath. Well, there had to be some way to fix this belt. Couldn't he duct tape it or something? She got out and found Dylan at the edge of the pine grove, gathering wood.

"Don't you have some tools or something? Maybe you can find a way to rig something up, just enough to get us back."

"What do you want me to do, Annie, fashion a belt out of branches and pine needles? I'm a mechanic, not a magician."

He'd obviously given up. Maybe she should too. She pulled her phone out and checked for a signal, holding it skyward, turning every which way.

Nothing.

The realization pressed down on her shoulders. She was stuck here with him, all night, like it or not.

She walked into the copse of trees and began gathering wood.

"Get inside before you're soaked through."

"I can help."

He turned and glared, the beam of light making his eyes glitter. "You can help by staying dry. Take this and go." He held out the flashlight.

He wanted to do all the work himself . . . fine. She snatched the light from him and started for the cabin. She crossed her arms against the chill in the air, against the cold droplets falling on her.

She stopped inside the door, using the tail of her shirt to dry her face. She shone the flashlight around the room. It had seemed so much more inviting before. Before the sun had set. Before she'd been trapped.

She wondered if Sierra were home yet and if she'd begun to worry. Doubtful. She might even spend the night with a friend, Ryder and all. Annie would probably make it home before she did.

Annie approached the bed and shone the flashlight on the mattress. Foam peeked from the edges where the seam had ripped. Stains of all shades colored the blue-and-white striped covering. She tried not to think about what they were or about the news segment she'd seen on dust mites and bedbugs.

The floor was starting to seem more appealing. She thought of the animal that had scurried away when they entered and shivered. Maybe not. Besides, she'd probably have to flip a coin for the bed.

The door flew open and Dylan came through, dumping a large load of firewood on the hearth. He went back out and came in again a few minutes later with another load.

She shone the light into the grate as he set two large logs parallel, then stacked more on top, the opposite direction. Next went smaller logs, then the twigs and a pile of dry pine needles he must've dug for.

His shirt clung to his torso and his arms as he worked. A rivulet of water dripped down his nape and beneath the collar of his shirt.

When he finished, he opened the damper. It croaked as debris fell onto the logs.

"What if it's blocked?"

He pulled a lighter from his pocket. "Take our chances."

The room seemed colder since his arrival. Okay, so she'd jumped to the wrong conclusion . . . possibly about more than the truck. She knew she should apologize, but the words stuck in her throat. As uncomfortable as this stony silence was, it was safer than the alternative. His anger was the only barrier between them tonight, and she wasn't about to remove it.

He blew on the wavering flame and the pine needles hissed as the fire spread. The smoke seemed to be going up at least. He blew some more and a twig caught fire.

"You're a regular boy scout," she said, hoping to break the tension. But he said nothing, just lit the other side and tended the flame.

A few minutes later her stomach rumbled loudly. She remembered the pasta she'd so hastily rejected. She wished for a big plateful right now, steaming hot. Her stomach echoed the thought.

The fire began crackling in earnest and the room brightened a bit.

She turned off the flashlight and set it on the hearth. "Wish I'd brought my purse. I had a granola bar in there."

He crossed the room, retrieving a blanket she hadn't seen him carry in. She stepped aside as he pulled the cot closer to the fireplace and spread the woolly blanket over the mattress. "Best get some sleep. We'll want an early start."

She warmed her hands by the fire as he made his way into the corner and lowered himself onto the dirty floor facing the wall. He tucked his arm under his head and went still.

He was going to freeze over there in the shadows, soaked to the skin. She looked at the blanket covering the cot and started to offer it to him. But the memory of his stony silence stopped her.

Dylan turned for the millionth time, propping his head with his arm. He had no way of telling the time, but it had to be one or two. His shirt was dry now, but the cold seeped through his damp jeans, chilling him to the bone.

Across the room the fire snapped and popped. He'd banked it twice, adding more logs. Annie had slept through it, her breaths slow and steady. He'd watched her lying there, her face relaxed in sleep, her dark lashes fanning across her cheeks. Her cheeks had been flushed, with heat, he'd hoped.

He tucked his hand under his torso, looking for heat even as his insides twisted. He'd been excited about showing her this place, knowing how close she'd been with her grandfather. And yeah, he had wanted to spend time with her, so sue him. He wasn't trying to get her alone so he could seduce her or something. Was that the kind of man she took him for?

She'd hinted at it, little barbs here and there, and, true, he'd had every chance to correct her. But he preferred his actions to speak louder than his words—and louder than the embellished rumors that flew around.

He'd thought she might see the real him given time, but it had been—what?—going on two months now, and she still saw him as some playboy. What really rankled, though, was that her low opinion bothered him so much. That he'd been lying here awake for at least three hours, turning it over and over in his head until he felt crazy with it. Why did he care so much? He wasn't even dating her. She was someone else's girlfriend, for crying out loud.

He hated to admit it, but sometime between the broken belt and the cold, hard floor it had become evident he'd developed feelings for the woman. Her negative opinion of him wouldn't needle him so much otherwise.

Only a handful of women had come close since Merilee had taken his heart and stomped all over it. And now he'd reached that point with Annie.

That critical point in the relationship where he broke it off before the feelings sank in too deeply. Before his heart was in danger. Only problem was, he couldn't break it off with Annie because he hadn't so much as taken her on a first date.

And he couldn't stop seeing her—Braveheart still needed her. Who was this woman who had the power to make him fall so effortlessly? And how did he stop the feelings from getting out of control when he couldn't cut her from his life?

Dear Miserable in Missoula,

 The tension between you and your boyfriend means there's an issue that needs working through. Get it out on the table before it grows into something more.

18

$\mathcal{A}$ sound pulled Annie from a deep sleep. She became aware of an ache in her arm.

She stirred, stretching, opening her eyes. The cot, the cabin. She sat up and looked around. Daylight seeped through the dirty windowpanes. The space in the corner where Dylan had slept was empty and the fire was low but warm.

"Dylan?"

She wondered what time it was, then grabbed her phone off the floor and checked: 6:47.

Where could he be?

A rumble outside drew her attention, and she recognized the sound that had pulled her from slumber. An engine!

A moment later a car door slammed, then the cabin door creaked open. Dylan's silhouette filled the space.

"Mornin'." The curve of his lips fell short of a smile. He wore last night's clothes with the addition of a jacket.

She swung her legs over the cot and rubbed the sleep from her eyes. "Someone's here?"

"I walked back and fetched my work truck. Ready to go?" Using a log, he spread out the crumbling wood, then emptied a water bottle over it. The fire sizzled out.

She stood, pulling the blanket from the cot and smoothing her hair. She must be a sight. "You should've woken me."

"You were sound asleep."

She followed him out the door, pulling the blanket closer against the cool morning air. "Well, thanks."

When they were both seated, he put the truck in gear and pulled away from the cabin.

"What about your truck?"

"I'll fix it later."

She hated the lingering tension between them. It would be a good time for that apology she owed him. Despite his detached demeanor, he'd been nothing but gracious since she'd made that accusation. Given her the cot, given up the blanket, and he must've kept the fire banked because she hadn't so much as shivered all night.

Time to eat crow. She opened her mouth.

"Have some bad news," he said before she could produce a word. "Your sister left some frantic voice mails on my phone."

"Oh no. I was hoping she went to bed early."

"No such luck. I called and explained what happened."

At least Sierra knew now. "Thanks."

"That's not all. She got worried around midnight and called

Oakley. He drove over and found your truck in my drive, then left a voice mail that sounded less than happy. Thought I'd better let you handle that one."

Oh no. "He must be worried." She pulled out her phone, but she still had no reception. They hit a rut and she braced herself against the door.

"Try mine." He pulled out his cell and handed it to her as they crossed Moose Creek. "You should know that your boyfriend also called the sheriff. There was a message from him on my voice mail too."

Annie ran her hand over her face. "Oh, man."

"I canceled the all-points bulletin."

She punched in John's number, ignoring Dylan's jibe. She hoped word hadn't spread around town, but it was seven o'clock, and the rumor mill opened at sunrise.

"What's going on, Taylor?" John said in a tone she'd never heard from him. "Where's Annie?"

"It's me. I'm so sorry for the worry."

"Annie! Where have you been?" She was taken aback by the anger in his voice. He'd been worried though. She should cut him some slack.

"I went to see my grandfather's cabin last evening and the truck broke down. I was stuck there all night."

"With *Taylor*?"

"Right. There was no cell reception and it was dark, so we had no choice but to stay the night."

"What did he do? Did he lay a hand on you, Annie? Because if he did, I'll sue his sorry rear end!"

"No." She glanced at Dylan. "No, he was—nothing happened. Really. I'm fine. Everything's fine."

A shadow moved across Dylan's face as he clenched his jaw.

"Where are you now?"

"On my way back." She purposely left Dylan out of the mix.

"Well, thank heavens for that. I was very worried about you, Annie. I called the sheriff when I couldn't reach you. I'd better let him know you're safe."

"Already done. And thank you for your concern." She nailed Dylan with a look. Regardless of his sarcasm, it was nice to have someone who cared.

"Are you sure you're okay? There was no trouble with Taylor? Because he has a reputation, Annie, and it would be just like him to take advantage."

"No, not at all. I'm right as rain, just a bit hungry." They hit a rut and Annie grabbed for the handle.

"Well, I'll bring you something from the café then."

She desperately needed a reprieve from human company. "No, no, you must be exhausted. Besides, I have a full schedule today. I'll just grab something from the cupboard. But thank you. It's sweet of you to offer."

"If you're sure."

"I am, but I'll see you tonight. Have a good day, John."

They said good-bye, and she pushed End just as Dylan turned onto the main drive.

She held out the phone. "Thanks."

"I see Oakley also has a high opinion of me."

She felt the barb down to her heart. "Dylan, I'm really—"

Her phone rang, apparently in range now. It was Sierra, probably needing to hear her voice. The apology would have to wait a few minutes. She answered the phone.

"Annie! I'm so glad you're all right!"

"I'm sorry for worrying you."

"It's not your fault. Dylan explained everything, and I'm so sorry for everything I said last night—I didn't mean it." Her sister's voice wobbled.

"I'm sorry too. I love you and Ryder so much. I just want you both to have the best opportunities."

"I know you do. I know."

Dylan pulled up to the barn and shut off the engine. He motioned toward the barn. "Gotta run," he said quietly.

Annie covered the mouthpiece. "Thanks, Dylan."

He nodded once and offered a smile that didn't reach his eyes or call on his dimple.

She wanted to say so much more, but he was leaving the truck and heading into the barn. Annie walked to her truck, still comforting Sierra. She wanted to stick around and finish the apology she'd barely started. But it was after seven and she had to grab a shower and a bite to eat and be at the mayor's ranch by eight. As she pulled down the drive, she realized they'd never even discussed the letters for this week's column.

Dear Uncertain,

   Trust is the bedrock of a relationship. If it's absent, the whole foundation will be shaky.

19

Annie checked her watch for the dozenth time, then glanced toward the stage where the Silver Spurs blasted their most popular country-and-western tune. John was late, but he'd texted to let her know.

Brenda Peterson appeared tableside, pink lips tipped sideways, eyes sparkling under her long bangs. "So, you and Dylan, all night at the old Mahoney cabin, huh?"

Annie sighed. Fending off rumors had been a full-time job today. "His truck broke down, that's all. I'm dating John Oakley, you know."

Brenda Peterson winked. "Yeah, but come on . . . Dylan Taylor . . . Don't tell me there weren't sparks, and I'm not talking about that fire he built you."

"Good grief, did somebody bug the place?"

Brenda's smile widened. "I knew it!"

"No. There were no sparks." Oh, for pity's sake. She was wasting her breath. "I'd like a Diet Coke, and *John* will have iced tea with extra lemon."

Brenda shrugged, hopes apparently dashed, then sashayed away.

Annie's gaze fanned the room and caught Marla Jenkins's eyes. The woman quickly looked away. There were others darting glances her way too. Bridgett Garvin, Wade Ryan, even Mrs. Wadell. Good grief. She was never going to live this down.

She slumped in her chair and propped the menu high on the table, wishing they'd turn up the air-conditioning. No, what she really wanted was to go home and curl up in bed with her book. But that wasn't fair to John.

At least Dylan wasn't here tonight. Maybe he'd thought it best to lie low. No doubt he'd heard the rumors too, though they probably didn't bother him one bit.

When he'd called that morning, she'd let it go to voice mail. He'd invited her over the next day to work on the column. He hadn't sounded as friendly as usual. But could she blame him?

"Sorry I'm late, Annie."

She lowered the menu and smiled as John sat across from her. He wore his work clothes and a stilted smile.

She was relieved to see a friendly face. "Hi, there. I ordered you an iced tea."

"After the day I've had, something stronger may be in order."

She gave him a sympathetic grin. "I'm sorry. Rough day at work?"

He nailed her with a look. "It wasn't work, Annie."

So he'd heard the rumors. Of course he had. John's job as

moneylender made him less than popular. She imagined he'd probably taken a few barbs.

Guilt wedged between the walls of her ribs. "I'm sorry. It'll pass, I'm sure . . ."

John leaned forward, folding his hands on the white paper place mat. "Annie, you know I trust you implicitly, but I need to know what happened."

Annie squeezed the napkin in her lap. "Nothing happened, John. I already told you that."

He looked down, then back at her, a glare flashing off his glasses. "I believe you. What I meant was . . . what did *he* do? You can't tell me he got you out there all alone, a pretty girl like you, and didn't . . . try and take advantage of the situation."

"Well, he didn't."

"In fact, the more I've thought about this, the more sure I am that he lured you there on purpose."

His unwarranted judgment hit her in the gut, mostly because it echoed her own accusation. "That's not true."

"It's just the sort of thing he'd do, and you're naïve to think—"

"I'm not naïve, and he didn't do anything, John." She tossed her napkin on the table. "I think I'd know if someone came on to me."

His eyes widened, whether at her action or her words, she didn't know. "He's got you defending him."

"He hasn't 'got me' doing anything. He's innocent. Look, I know he has a reputation, but you don't even know him. I told you nothing happened, and it's a little disconcerting that you can't seem to believe me."

Brenda appeared and set the drinks down. She glanced between them and seemed to realize she'd interrupted something. "Need a few more minutes?"

"Yes, please," John said.

Annie took a deep breath as Brenda retreated. Her heart pummeled her ribs. She was bone tired and sick of being on the defense. Defending Dylan Taylor—now there was a spot she'd never expected to be in.

The Spurs belted out the chorus, the music too loud and boisterous. She didn't want to be here anymore. In public or with John. Annie gathered her purse and pulled out a few dollars. "I think we'd better call it a night."

John set his hand on her wrist. "No, Annie. I'm sorry. I had a bad day, and I'm taking it out on you. Stay."

She paused, took a breath. "I appreciate that. But I really am tired, and I just want to go home." She stood.

John popped up. "Let me come with you."

"I won't be good company tonight, John. Maybe I'll see you tomorrow."

"For lunch?"

She was working with Dylan on the column then. "I have to work. Maybe dinner."

"I'll call you."

She nodded once and made for the door.

Dear Can't Help Myself,

You need to stay far, far away from Too Tempting. Don't call,
don't visit, and whatever you do, don't end up in his arms again.

20

*D*ylan set the bucket of water by the dirty rims of his truck.
He'd replaced the belt yesterday, but the muddy drive home
had left it a filthy mess.

He wondered if Annie would come. She hadn't responded to
his voice mail. Did she need his help badly enough to see him
again? Apparently he was a pain in the backside. And if she'd faced
half the barbs he had yesterday, she wasn't going to be any happier
to see him today.

The innuendos had worn fast, even on him. Had only reminded
him of how little Annie thought of him. He'd done his best to put
out the fires, for her sake, but sometimes people preferred to
believe the worst.

He hooked up the hose to the barn spigot and was unwinding it when a car rumbled down the drive. His heart did a Western shuffle as Annie's truck came into view. He dropped the hose, turned off the flow of water, and met her as she pulled to a stop.

"You made it," he said, careful to keep his tone friendly. Regardless of his hurt feelings, there was no need to scare her away. Braveheart still needed her, after all.

Annie stepped from the car, looking fresh as a daisy in her grass-green T-shirt and worn jeans. "Now a good time?"

"Good as any. Have a seat on the porch and I'll put on some coffee." He knew better than to invite her in, and frankly, he was seeing the need for caution.

He returned a few minutes later and handed her the mug, careful that their fingers didn't touch. He settled onto the swing with his own coffee and took a sip.

"Your sister all settled down?"

Annie nodded once. "She is; thanks for asking."

"I guess John told you he called." The man had made all kinds of accusations, no doubt sore about the rumors.

Annie's mouth went slack, then pressed into a tight line. "When?"

Whoops. "Thought he told you. Everything's fine now, I'm sure." He lightened the mood with a smile. "So what've you got for me today?"

After a moment she reached into her bag for a letter.

He leaned back and read.

Dear Annie,

There's a man I work with who has a certain reputation with the ladies. I recently found out that his reputation is unwarranted, but not before putting my foot in my mouth and making a nasty accusation.

I tried to apologize, but the words got stuck in my throat, and now I have this awful ache in my gut every time I remember what I said.

What can I do or say to make it up to him?

Signed,

Remorseful in Moose Creek

Dylan bit back a smile. He read the note again, relishing the part where she admitted his reputation was unwarranted. That said something, especially coming on the heels of all the gossip. The ache he'd felt since Thursday night vanished.

He looked up from the letter, smiling. "Cute."

"So . . ." Annie's hands trembled in her lap, and she pressed them together. "What do you think she should do?"

"Remorseful in Moose Creek?"

She nodded.

He wanted to say all was forgiven, especially when she bit her lower lip. Her full lower lip, just the right shade of pink, and as ripe as a huckleberry in late August.

"They should probably kiss and make up," he said.

Annie snorted. But a smile lifted her lips. "How about a handshake."

"Take what I can get." He closed his hand around hers, squeezing gently, and thought a touch had never felt so good.

Since Annie's job was riding on Dylan's answers, she confided in him about the negative feedback. He suggested she use letters that had a more obvious solution. Maybe that was the key to gaining reader support. After their talk she felt more hopeful about the future of the column.

When they finished discussing a letter about a noncommittal boyfriend, Annie packed her bag. It was getting hot as the sun hit its pinnacle in the blue sky, even under the shade of the porch. A magpie called from a nearby tree, and a hot breeze rustled through the long grass in the pasture.

She was relieved to have her apology over with and glad he didn't carry a grudge. If he'd been subjected to innuendos and speculations, he hadn't said so.

Dylan set the swing in motion. "Any job prospects for your sister?"

"Not yet. I don't know, school starts in a month—might be hopeless. How's Braveheart doing?"

"Wanna see him? If you don't have plans with Spreadshee—I mean Oakley."

She tossed him a look. "Sure."

The barn was dim and pleasantly cool. The smell of horseflesh and fresh hay assaulted her senses.

"Hey, buddy," Dylan said as he approached the horse. "Got a visitor."

"Hi, Braveheart."

The horse tossed his head and neighed, looking for them.

He wasn't so bronc-y today. His ears flicked and his nose worked. "His other senses are kicking in."

"I noticed." Dylan stretched out his hand, letting Braveheart smell his fist, then he rubbed the horse's neck. "You'll be all right, fellow."

Braveheart's eyelids drooped, even as Dylan rubbed him down.

"How's he sleeping?"

Dylan shrugged. "I catch him snoozing on his feet sometimes, but I was wondering the same thing. Think he needs a sedative?"

"Why don't you stable a couple of horses near him—horses he trusts. He'll be more relaxed with them standing guard."

"I'll try that tonight." His shoulder brushed hers as he leaned on the stable door.

She knew she should move, but she checked her instinct. His solidness was reassuring, the smell of him familiar and pleasant.

"Can we let him out?"

"I'd rather wait till next week. You should fill any new holes in the pasture—you'll need to do that regularly because of gophers and such. And put a ring of gravel or sand around the trees."

"I'll do that Monday." His voice, so deep and close, sent a shiver up her spine.

"I'll work with him next week on navigating with his other senses." She gave Braveheart a final pat. "I should go."

"Wait. Stay for lunch. You must be hungry."

She was sorely tempted, and that alone was grounds for refusal. "I already ate. Besides, you were getting ready to wash your truck— for your date *du jour*, no doubt."

He followed her out of the barn. "You should probably help me with that, you know."

"Your date *du jour*?"

"Sugar, you can *be* my date *du jour*."

"Oh, lucky day."

He laughed. "Fine. I was talking about the truck anyway."

"Now why should I help with that?"

"Well, it did get dirty on the way to your grandpa's cabin." The sunlight sparkled in his dark eyes, and a shadow pooled in his dimple. He tugged his hat lower.

"Are you saying I owe you or something?"

He shrugged dramatically. "Well, *I* wouldn't put it like that, but . . ."

She laughed, drawn in despite herself. He had forgiven her so nicely. The real kind of forgiveness, without a side of sulking like she sometimes got from Sierra. Besides, it wasn't as if she had anywhere to be. Sierra had taken Ryder to a nearby fair, and John was helping his mother move to an apartment in Bozeman.

"All right," she said. "But only because I feel sorry for your date. Bad enough she has to be stuck with you."

"Ouch," he said, but his eyes danced.

She put her things in her truck, then rolled up her sleeves while he turned on the spigot. When Dylan returned, he sprayed down the vehicle and fetched another sponge from the barn. They set to work on opposite sides of the truck, and he began whistling "I'll Fly Away."

"So the truck runs fine now that you replaced the doohickey?" she asked a few minutes later.

He tossed her a smile over the hood. "Yeah, the new doohickey did the trick."

She rubbed in circles, covertly watching his movements. Dark hairs glistened on his tanned arms, and the corded muscles shifted with his motions. She studied his hands, long fingers, tapering down to squared fingertips.

"You tell your sister to call me about her car?"

"Not yet." She hadn't been sure his offer was still good. "But I will. We're grateful." She dipped the sponge into the soapy water and wrung it out. "This thing's a mess," she said. "Who am I rescuing from a dirty carriage anyway?"

Now why'd she go and ask about his date?

He winked over the hood. "I'm saving the seat for you, sugar."

She felt a shiver run down her arm and make her fingers tingle.
"You can turn it off, Romeo. I'm taken, remember?"

"So you keep saying."

She shook her head and he chuckled. He had a nice laugh.
Deep and mellow, the kind that warmed you straight through like a
mug of cocoa on a cold winter's night.

"Actually, my little brother's coming for a week. He'd rake me
over the coals if he saw my truck like this."

"He's a neat freak?"

"Not really. But I may have nagged him about keeping his own
truck neat and clean."

"May have?"

"Don't forget, I've seen you with your little sister."

"Touché."

She moved to the side, glad when the cab blocked him from her
sight. She just needed to finish her penance and be gone. Surprisingly, she was enjoying his company. Once she realized how
meaningless his flirtation was, it was easy to write him off. As long as
she didn't think about the way she'd felt in his arms when they'd
danced. Or the way he'd looked with a baby in his arms.

Besides, there was John. She'd tried not to think too much
about him since their date had ended so badly. He'd called this
morning, but conversation had been stilted. She got the feeling he
was punishing her for defending Dylan. Still, she hadn't liked the
way he'd behaved, and she really didn't like that he'd called Dylan
after she'd insisted nothing had happened. It reeked of distrust,
regardless of what he'd said.

A splatter of water hit the top of her head. "Hey . . . watch it."

"Sorry 'bout that."

She heard the smile in his voice. "I'll bet you are."

The sun beat down overhead, and the cool water had actually felt good, though she wasn't about to say so.

Dylan's phone rang, and he answered. "Hey there, sweetie."

Oh brother. Probably his date. Maybe the woman had come to her senses and was calling to cancel.

"How's my Maddy?"

Nope, not his date after all. Just a little girl.

"Yeah?" He laughed, then went into listening mode, punctuating the silences with *uh-huhs* and *reallys*, his sponge making squeaky circles on the other side of the truck.

Annie returned to the bucket. She dumped the mucky water and refilled it, squeezing in some soap from a container lying in the grass.

"Who is it? . . . Well, why not?" He laughed. "I would not. Well, maybe I would."

Annie wet her sponge and wrung it out. She finished the side, leaving the wheels for last. She paused, wiping the sweat from the back of her neck. She wished she'd worn a hat, but she hadn't expected to be outdoors. Her cheeks were probably already pink.

"He definitely likes you . . . Well, that's what boys do."

Annie squatted down, smiling, and washed the rims.

"Yeah, you could do that . . . Well, sure, that too, but you don't want to be too obvious, you know. Boys like a challenge."

She rolled her eyes and scrubbed hard at the wheel well. The sun ducked behind a huge cloud, offering a reprieve.

"All right. You're welcome, sweetie. See ya at church."

He hung up the phone and appeared at the bucket the same time she did.

He smiled. "Girls."

She wrung out her sponge, leaving the bucket to him, and went to finish the wheels. "She call often?"

"Now and then."

"Sounds like she's got a boyfriend."

"Boy better treat her right, or he'll have me to reckon with."

"Between you and Wade, the kid'll be lucky to get within a mile of her."

"So long as he knows that."

Annie finished the second rim and went to scrub a spot she'd missed by the door handle. "Poor girl won't have a boyfriend till she's twenty."

"All the better."

She shook her head. "Oh brother. No double standards there, Mr. Date *du Jour*."

On the other side of the cab his squeaky circles stopped. "You saying I have double standards?"

"That's what I'm saying."

"What I thought."

A quick spray of water hit the top of her head.

"Hey!" She looked through the windows at Dylan's smirk.

He hiked a brow as another spray arced over the cab.

"You better watch yourself, buster."

His smile widened. "Or else . . . ?"

"I have a bucket over here, and I'm not afraid to use it."

Another spray of water hit the top of her head. She sucked in a breath at his nerve, wiping the drizzle from her face.

"You asked for it, buddy." Tossing the sponge, she raced for the bucket. It was heavy and awkward. Water sloshed with each step.

Dylan waited on the other side, leaning casually against the truck. He was pointing the nozzle at her, all John Wayne.

She froze, panting, the bucket at the ready.

"Mine reaches farther . . . ," he said.

"Mine's dirty."

"Take my chances." He let loose a spray of water that caught her on the stomach.

She released a squeal.

Just as quickly, the spray ended. Her shirt stuck to her stomach. She stood stock still, dripping.

She fixed her eyes on him, then she sprang forward, heaving the bucket.

Time slowed. His eyes widened, his mouth went slack. He closed his eyes as the wall of water hit him with a satisfying slosh, knocking his hat from his head.

Laughter bubbled up inside her, but before it found release, he bounded toward her, extending the nozzle. She turned and yelped as a burst of water hit her square in the back.

Rounding the truck, she sought shelter from the assault, but he followed, spraying. "No fair! I'm defenseless—"

"Shoulda thought about that before you dumped that bucket on me, woman." He caught her around the waist.

The water off, she didn't fight him. She turned, stepping away, wiping her face with her wet sleeve. Dylan's hair was plastered to his head, his hat replaced by a cap of suds.

The laugh that had bubbled in her belly moments earlier found release.

He smoothed his hair back, removing the bubbles as his eyes narrowed. "Something funny, missy?"

Prince Charming, soaked and sudsed. Hilarious. A stick of grass was plastered to his cheek, and rivulets of water trickled down his temples.

He calmly cocked his head and raised the spray gun.

"Don't." She took a step back, sobering, except for a tiny gurgle that slipped out.

He stepped forward, mischief in his eyes.

She stepped back, one step, two. Then she hit the truck. "Dylan . . ."

He continued advancing until the nozzle was inches from her belly. His eyes danced. "Say uncle, Annie."

She bit back her laughter. "Uncle Annie."

"Come on now . . . no escaping me this time." His gaze skimmed over her face. His eyes danced over her cheeks, her nose, her lips.

His appraisal was like a touch. Gooseflesh rippled down her arm. Suddenly aware of his nearness, she couldn't seem to draw breath into her frozen lungs.

By the time his eyes returned to hers, the twinkle had dismounted, the easy laughter now galloping into the sunset. The corners of his lips gave in to gravity, erasing his dimple.

Oxygen-deprived, she sucked in a deep breath, filling her lungs with air, her nostrils with his musky scent. The heat of his body, so close, made her tremble.

His eyes. She couldn't look away from them. Brown pools of melting chocolate. Warm. Serious. Fastened on her.

He framed her face with his strong hands and lowered his mouth to hers.

She stretched toward him like a flower toward the sun and was rewarded with a surge of something pleasant and exhilarating. His lips moved over hers with unbearable tenderness. His ministrations were unhurried, as if savoring the taste of her. Inside, a quake started in the vicinity of her heart, spreading through her limbs and turning her legs to jelly.

He jerked back suddenly, emptying the space between them.

His eyes widened. His hands lifted slowly in surrender. "Annie . . . I'm sorry."

She couldn't think past the pleasant chemicals surging through her, past his intoxicating touch. She wanted it back. Now.

She latched onto his shirt, tugging, and pressed her mouth to his.

His groan sent a tremor of pleasure through her. His arms came around her, and he deepened the kiss, taking her someplace far away, a place from which she never wanted to return.

He forked his fingers through her wet hair, and she heard a low, throaty moan. Hers?

What kind of man was this whose touch made her feel so much? No one, ever, had turned her upside down, inside out, and made her desperate for more. Certainly not John and his tepid kisses.

The fuzzy thought took shape, growing slowly into focus.

John.

Her boyfriend.

He wasn't the man kissing her now. The man *she* had brazenly pulled into her arms.

She let loose of the material wadded in her fists and pushed. Dylan's lips left hers, and she swallowed the whimper that rose in her throat.

"I'm sorry." Her words sounded rushed and breathless.

She jerked her hands from his chest. No more touching. None whatsoever. She smoothed her hair, turning her back to him, afraid of what he'd see in her eyes. Afraid even more of what she'd see in his. Like humor or teasing.

She couldn't bear it if he teased her now. Not when she'd so foolishly laid it all out there like that.

God, what have I done? He'll never let me live this down.

Prince Charming had worked his magic on her, and she'd

fallen under his spell, just like all the others. Worse, she knew it was more than physical. She couldn't believe she'd fallen so quickly. So hard.

She had to get out of there. Far away. Out of sight, out of mind, or so she hoped. "I should go. I have to go." She started toward her truck.

"Annie, wait."

Hearing his footsteps, she quickened her own. "Don't, Dylan."

She dug for her keys and had them at the ready by the time she entered her truck. Without a second look she started the engine and drove past him, a still, lone figure in her peripheral vision.

Dear Fearful in Great Falls,

Don't be anxious about the feelings stirring inside. Sure, love can hurt, but what's life without love?

21

Dylan retrieved the hose and pointed the nozzle at the truck, his mind spinning, his hands shaking. What in the blue blazes just happened?

You kissed her, idiot, that's what happened. And she kissed you back.

He'd been headlong into that first kiss when he'd come to his senses. He was kissing Annie Wilkerson. Kissing someone else's girl.

When he'd pulled away, he'd half expected her hand to come cracking across his jaw. What he hadn't expected was her reeling him back in for take two.

Have mercy.

I'm in deep trouble here, God. Deep, deep trouble.

A magpie chattered from a nearby branch. The spray of water was hitting the truck's hood and hadn't moved since he'd begun.

It was just a kiss, right?

He pocketed his trembling hand, spraying down the soapy side of the truck. His thoughts replayed the kiss, lingering over it until he was torn up inside all over again. Despite all of Annie's rebuffs, despite her supposed exasperation with him, despite the fact that she was taken . . .

She'd kissed him back.

And initiated the second kiss. He couldn't stop the little thrill that passed through him, felt heady with it. But what did it mean? Had he just caught her off guard? Was it only because she was used to Oakley and his—he could only imagine—lame kisses?

Who was he kidding? That kiss, *those* kisses, had been more than a surprise. More than your everyday, run-of-the-mill kisses. More than he'd ever felt with any woman. Had Annie felt the same thing?

He was half tempted to chase her down and pick up where they'd left off. He let loose of the trigger, shutting off the flow of water.

But therein lay the trouble. Annie had already reached in somehow, gotten through his walls. For the first time he was tempted to lower them. Maybe he could love again. Maybe it wouldn't hurt this time.

He dropped the hose, retrieved his hat, and headed toward the house, shaking water from the brim. Maybe he could move past his pain with the right woman. Wade had managed it after losing his wife, his rodeo career. Took him awhile, took the right woman, but he'd done it.

The thought of putting himself out there again made his legs shake. He sank onto the porch steps. He felt like a coward. But Merilee had done a job on him, and what kind of fool signed up for that kind of pain twice?

He'd been head over heels for the girl. They met after a rodeo in Waco. He was high on a win, and he was smitten with her from the moment he saw her across the room at El Charro.

She said yes when he asked her out, and they talked for hours in his truck afterward, both of them reluctant to say good night. Originally from Oklahoma, she'd moved to Waco to attend Baylor and was set to graduate with a teaching degree the following year.

They became exclusive almost immediately. For the first time Dylan didn't miss other girls. Didn't want to flirt with anyone else. He spent his days working a ranch and his evenings with Merilee. She was passionate about her faith, could talk intelligently about any subject, and she was a great listener.

When he told her he loved her one night, tears had filled her eyes and she'd returned the words. After that their good night kisses became longer, and his resolve to wait for marriage was sorely tested.

She was a couple weeks from graduation when they slipped over the line, and once they did, it seemed impossible to return to mere kisses, especially when she was going back home for a couple of months following graduation.

Dylan wanted to go with her, but he couldn't afford to leave his job. Besides, the two months would go quickly, she promised.

The one thing her absence taught him was that he never wanted to be separated again. The phone calls were too short and e-mail too distant. He wanted her with him every day, every night. He wanted to share her life.

When she'd been gone a month, he made up his mind. He was

going to ask her to marry him. He'd have to move from his bunk-
house, but with both their incomes they could afford an apartment
or even a starter house.

His winnings from his last rodeo long gone, he made the difficult decision to sell his horse. Merilee deserved a nice ring, not
some flimsy piece of tin with a flea-sized diamond. By the time she
returned, he had it all planned out. With the little left over from the
sale of Fritz, he took her to her favorite restaurant.

She seemed distracted during the meal, so he suggested the
River Walk afterward. Pretty and free, it had become one of their
favorite things to do.

His hand became sweaty in hers as they walked the long, curv-
ing path, but he wasn't nervous, only excited. Excited to be with
Merilee again, excited at the thought of their future.

Just when he thought he couldn't contain himself a minute
longer, she spoke.

"I'm glad you suggested a walk, Dylan. I—we really need to talk."

He frowned at her serious tone, but his Merilee was a deep
thinker, always pondering something.

She tugged him to a stop. In the waning light her blue eyes
looked like midnight.

"What is it, darlin'?"

She looked at the river, at the darkening sky, at everything
but him.

He felt something like dread leaking into his veins, but he
squeezed her hand. "You worried about your job?" She started on
Monday at Parkdale Elementary, though the kids wouldn't be in
session for several weeks.

"No, Dylan. I don't know how to—"

"Just say it, hon, whatever it is."

"I'm pregnant."

The word hit him hard, then sort of sank in slowly.

Okay. It wasn't what they'd planned. He thought immediately of his parents. They'd be disappointed. Hers too. It wasn't the start he'd hoped for. But he loved her. The idea of a baby—his child—would grow on him. It was growing on him already.

He wondered how long she'd been carrying this alone. No wonder she'd sounded distracted lately.

He pulled her into his arms. "Oh, Mer. It's all right. We'll get through this. I love you, you know that."

She pulled away, and he framed her pixie face before she got too far.

"You're not in this alone. In fact—the timing . . ." He laughed nervously, pulling the box from his suit coat pocket. "I want to marry you, darlin'."

She looked down at the jewelry box. He wished he could see her expression, but the River Walk lights hadn't kicked on.

"Oh, Dylan . . ." She turned away, crossed her arms.

It wasn't the reaction he'd expected—hoped for. Was she worried about working during her pregnancy? What the folks at church would think? About their finances? He didn't make as much money as he'd like, but with both their incomes . . .

He pocketed the box, put his hands on her shoulders. "We'll get through this, Mer, I promise. Marry me. I want to spend the rest of my—"

"I'm four weeks pregnant."

Four weeks? The words reverberated in his head. Numbers weren't his strong suit, but the math wasn't that complicated. Dread seeped into his bones.

"That can't be right."

"Dylan . . . ," she whispered. "The baby isn't yours."

Her words hit him like the force of a two-by-four slammed right into his gut. How could she be— She'd been a virgin, just like him. How could this—

His hands dropped from her shoulders.

She turned, and he was glad now that he couldn't see her eyes. "I'm so sorry, Dylan. I didn't plan for this to happen."

Anger rose, hot and heavy. His ears burned with it. "For what to happen? What happened, Mer?"

"I—I didn't know he was back in town, didn't expect to see him."

"*Who?*" And then it dawned on him. Jeremy. Her high school sweetheart.

"It just happened. I tried not to let it, and I wanted to tell you, but I couldn't do it over the phone."

"So you just—you just slept with him? After all we've shared? After all we mean to each other?"

"I'm so sorry."

He heard the tears in her voice, but he couldn't bring himself to care. The betrayal hurt too much. She tried to say more, but he didn't want to hear it. They headed back to his truck for a short, silent ride to her apartment.

By the next day reality had set in. Merilee had done a terrible thing. He was angry and hurt. But did he really want to lose her over it? He couldn't bear the thought. He had to adjust to the new reality. He still loved her, and they still had the rest of their lives ahead of them.

He drove to her apartment with the ring in his jeans pocket. He would marry her and raise the child as his own. It would be hard at first, but the thought of losing Merilee was much worse.

But when he arrived at her apartment, he discovered Merilee had other plans. Jeremy already knew about the baby and wanted to marry her. She wanted to marry him. His happily-ever-after had been stolen in the space of two months, but it had taken far longer than that to get beyond the betrayal, to stop feeling sick at the thought of Merilee.

Now he ran his hand through his damp hair. He didn't want to think about Merilee, and he didn't want to think about Annie anymore either. There was a reason he kept that wall in place. How could one kiss have made him forget so quickly?

He put on his hat and headed toward the barn. He had salt blocks to put out, a circle to ride, and a woman to put from his mind.

Dear Regretful,

A kiss is just a kiss. Except when it isn't.

22

*A*nnie drove through town, turned around, and drove back through. She should go home. But she was too wired to face an empty house.

That kiss.

Annie, Annie . . . She shook her head.

What had she been thinking? She hadn't been, that's all there was to it. Dylan Taylor addled her brain. One second he vexed her, the next she was in his arms kissing him—and her with a boyfriend.

She looked up and saw the brick storefront of Miss Lucy's doll shop. She hadn't realized she'd turned into the diagonal parking space. Through the picture window she saw Miss Lucy dusting a shelf, her ample frame making the stepladder wobble.

Annie exited her truck and went inside. The bell over the door tinkled loudly.

"Annie!" Miss Lucy stepped down and waddled forward for a hug.

Annie sank into Miss Lucy's arms. The woman's warmth drew her feelings to the surface and a knot formed in her throat. "Hi, Miss Lucy."

When the woman drew back, her eyes narrowed behind her Coke-bottle glasses. "What's wrong, child?"

She didn't want to think about it anymore. Annie took the duster from Miss Lucy, tapped her shoulder with it, and ascended the ladder. "I saw you tottering on your rickety ladder. Call me next time. You shouldn't be up on this thing."

"You're changing the subject. And you didn't even say hello to the girls."

Annie looked around the room at the dozens of blank smiling faces. "Hello, girls." She lifted a prairie doll and dusted beneath her. "Hello, uh . . ."

"Rosalie."

"That's a very pretty calico dress you're wearing, Rosalie. How's business, Miss Lucy? Lots of tourists coming through this summer?"

"Let's say we skip the nonsense and talk about why your hands are shaking instead."

Annie slowly set Rosalie back on the shelf and lowered the duster. They were shaking. Even the ladder quaked under her.

Miss Lucy took her hand. "Heaven's sakes, get down off there before you break an ankle."

Reality setting in, Annie stepped down. Miss Lucy took the duster from her hand, tossed it on the counter, and led Annie to her rocking chair. "Sit."

Annie obeyed.

Miss Lucy pulled up a chair, gathered her cotton skirt, and sank into it. "Now what's got you so worked up on a beautiful Saturday afternoon? Your sister? Mabel told me she quit. Or that silly rumor floating around about you and the Taylor boy out at your grandpa's cabin? I 'bout smacked Priscilla Teasley upside the head yesterday when I heard her spreading that one."

Annie gave her a weak smile. "Thanks."

The night at the cabin seemed like a lifetime ago. Had it only been the night before last? She'd been so angry with John yesterday for not trusting her.

Look what I've done now, God. I've gone and proven him right. How did this happen? When did I become such an awful person?

Annie groaned, palming her forehead.

"Child, what is it?"

"I'm so ashamed." She dropped her hand.

Miss Lucy narrowed her eyes. "Those rumors better not have been true, young lady."

"No. No, they weren't. I mean, we did get stuck at the cabin, but nothing happened. It's just . . . I just left Dylan's place. I'm working with—"

"His horse. Yes, I know. But what's got you so unsettled?"

Annie cringed. "He kissed me."

Miss Lucy smiled. "You don't say."

Just admitting it made her relive the kiss in its full glory. The slow, deliberate way his lips moved over hers, the aching tenderness. Her cheeks warmed, no doubt displaying twin splotches of pink, just like Miss Lucy's dolls.

"And I kissed him back." She skipped the part about her hauling him back into her arms.

"Well, fancy that." Miss Lucy tilted her head.

"Didn't you hear me? I kissed him back."

"My ears work just fine."

"Well, what kind of awful person am I? I'm dating John. Besides, I don't even like Dylan. He's a—a cowboy, for pity's sake. And he parades all over town with a different woman every week. He just lives to make the ladies swoon."

"And now you're one of them."

"Don't be ridiculous!"

Miss Lucy's thin brows rose over her thick-framed glasses.

"I'm not swooning. Not even close. I'm just—" She straightened, lifted her chin. "He's had a lot of practice, that's all. I guess it paid off."

"Come now, child."

"I don't even like him."

"Is that so."

"Yes, that's so. He's annoying and arrogant and—and entirely too . . . cowboyish."

Miss Lucy's lips twitched. "Well, dear, he is a cowboy."

"And you know how I feel about *them*."

"Yes, I do."

"What's really bothering me is that I betrayed John. I was so upset with him for not trusting me with Dylan, and then I went and proved him right."

"Now, that is ironic."

Miss Lucy wasn't helping at all. Annie needed someone to tell her how to fix this. What to do with her feelings for Dylan. Though she hadn't exactly admitted to feelings. And deep down she knew what she had to do with her feelings for Dylan. Stuff them deep inside. Way down deep.

"I have to tell John. I mean, that's the honest thing to do, right?"

"And then what?"

She didn't even want to think about what John would say.

"He'll be upset, but I think he'll forgive me." It would be pretty tricky working with Dylan from here on out. John wouldn't like it, but it couldn't be helped. She wasn't deserting Braveheart.

"What of your feelings for Dylan?"

Annie's laugh sounded nervous, even to her own ears. "They're not feelings, exactly. He has a way with women, and I got sucked in somehow, that's all."

"Is it?"

"Oh, Miss Lucy. You know how he is. He leaves a trail of broken hearts wherever he goes, and I sure don't plan on being one of them."

Miss Lucy patted her trembling hand. "Sometimes, Annie, there's more to a person than meets the eye."

Annie frowned. "What are you saying . . . that I should break up with John? That I should pursue a relationship with Dylan?" Annie gave a wry laugh. "He's probably forgotten about the kiss by now. Probably having a good laugh about how easy it was to get Annie Wilkerson in his arms."

The notion caught her right between the ribs, and her eyes stung. "I can hardly wait to hear him mocking me."

Miss Lucy gave a sad smile. "Have you ever thought that maybe the kiss meant something to him too?"

Annie snorted. And yet, she couldn't forget the look he gave her right before the kiss. It was lasered into her memory, those warm, melty eyes, so somber and focused on her.

She shook the image away. She had to stop this. She was only fooling herself.

"I've seen the way he looks at you, Annie."

"He looks at every woman that way."

"No." Miss Lucy shook her head. "No, he doesn't."

The older woman had never looked more serious. Despite her eccentricities, Miss Lucy was grounded in the important things. But this . . . She was so wrong.

Even so, Annie longed to hear more. "When? When did he look at me like that?"

"At Founders Day, during the wedding ceremony. On the Fourth, when you danced with him—yes, I saw you dancing. Not to mention every Sunday at church. I may be old and slightly batty, dear, but I know love when I see it."

"*Love?*" Good grief! Maybe Miss Lucy was more unstable than she realized. "Dylan does not love me, Miss Lucy."

"No?"

"No!" Annie popped to her feet, squeezing past the woman. For pity's sake, she was more confused now than when she walked in. Love had never entered her mind.

Nor should it!

Love. Good grief. Dylan didn't know the first thing about love. But then, hadn't she sought him out to help her with the lovelorn column?

She was so confused. No sooner did she think he was nothing more than a big flirt than she glimpsed a deeper side of him. And then, before she could say Casanova, he was back at it again. Was it any wonder she was confused?

She rubbed her throbbing temple.

"Keep the door of your heart open, that's all I'm saying. You never know what God has in store."

"God knows how I feel about cowboys."

"Yes, He does."

Annie's mind whirled as she paced. She needed a nice long

bath and her favorite book, not crazy conjectures about Dylan's feelings or ridiculous suppositions about God's plan for her life.

The bell tinkled over the door as a customer entered.

Relieved, Annie gave Miss Lucy a hug and promised to come back to dust the high shelves next week. She went home and drew a bath, but by the time she was finished, her head still throbbed. When Sierra and Ryder returned, loud and wired from a day at the fair, Annie knew she was on her way to a full-blown migraine. She retreated to her room with a pain med and a tall glass of water.

Dear In Denial,

You can pretend it didn't happen, you can refuse to give it a thought, and you can avoid the man at every turn. But here's the thing: it did, in fact, happen.

23

Annie overslept the next morning, missing church. The medicine had knocked her out, but at least her migraine was gone.

She missed the weekly fellowship but was relieved to put off seeing Dylan. She had her own quiet devotions, meditating on Psalm 1 and then spending time in prayer. She had a lot to talk to God about today, but even after she closed her Bible she felt confused and unsettled.

After her shower she took Pepper for a long ride. She savored the wind in her hair, the creak of the saddle, the way they moved in tandem as they galloped across the pasture. She'd hoped to clear her head of Dylan and the kiss, but the memory lingered long after Pepper was unsaddled and brushed down.

Unwilling to dither away the day, she headed to the market to stock up on healthy food. Ryder had come home the day before on a sugar buzz, and Sierra only ate vegetables if they were set down in front of her.

Annie strolled her empty cart straight to the produce department, checking her list, then scanned the bin for some fresh leaf lettuce. She'd fix a nice salad for supper.

In the front of the store she heard Marla Jenkins chatting with Brenda Peterson as she rang up the waitress's groceries. Annie put the lettuce in the cart, strolled forward, and picked up a nice, juicy-looking tomato.

When a male voice floated her way, she recognized Dylan's low, familiar drawl.

Oh no. He was the last person she wanted to see. Thank goodness she wasn't at the front of the store, checking out.

She hadn't put on a stitch of makeup. Had she even combed her hair before she'd scooped it into a ponytail? Her heart pounded as she listened to him greeting Brenda and Marla. She hoped he'd only stopped in to chat and not stock up on groceries.

Please, God. I'm not ready to see him yet. I haven't had a chance to digest that kiss or decide what to do. What would I even say?

She closed her eyes. Maybe this was her penance for missing church. How come Sierra got away with it week after week, and the one time she overslept . . .

Dylan's low chuckle mingled with Marla's and Brenda's. She recognized another male voice and heard Dylan introduce his brother, Luke. They were just having a good old time. Dylan's tone was flirtatious, and the women were giggling in response.

Of course he was flirting; that's what Dylan did. He'd no doubt kept his date last night, possibly with Marla, and probably ended it with a long good-night kiss. The thought opened a gaping hole in her gut. While she'd been stewing over her confused feelings, he'd no doubt moved on.

So much for Miss Lucy's crazy conjecture. Love. Hah! Dylan's feelings ran about as deep as a mud puddle.

She tightened her fingers around the tomato. She didn't care about the groceries anymore. She just wanted out of there without being spotted.

They were still talking, rambling about a concert coming to Billings. *Leave, Dylan.* Why did he have to be so social? She leaned forward ever so slightly, peeking around a giant cardboard banana.

Dylan perched on the low counter across from Marla, his back to Annie. He wore his white shirt and black vest with a pair of worn jeans. She wondered if he'd noticed her absence from church. She hoped he didn't think it had anything to do with him and that kiss.

Brenda picked up her two sacks. "All right, I gotta run. See you around, guys."

"I'll carry those," Dylan said.

Yes!

"No, I got it." Brenda gave a final wave and slipped out the door.

After she left, Dylan said something, and Marla smacked him on the chest, producing another chuckle from him. Dylan's brother was checking out the community bulletin board.

A minute later Dylan lifted his hand and leaned over the counter. Annie couldn't see what he was doing. He said something. She said something.

He leaned closer.

Annie jerked back before Marla saw her. Was he kissing her? She felt her lunch turn sour in her stomach, and a burn started behind her eyes. She supposed Marla wasn't likely to see her, what with her eyes closed and all, but she couldn't bring herself to look again. It got quiet. Very quiet. Annie swallowed against the lump in her throat.

Moved on wasn't even the word.

She was such a ninny. Pondering the meaning of his kiss, imagining there might be something between them, like he was Mr. Darcy and she Elizabeth Bennet. He was no Mr. Darcy. He was Dylan Taylor, stomping on hearts all over Big Sky Country without a second thought.

Laughter sounded. At least the kiss, if that's what it was, was over now—and much shorter than hers had been. She chided herself for the comparison.

"Yes, we do," Marla was saying. "They're right by the brussels sprouts."

At the mention of produce Annie's head snapped their way.

"No, they aren't."

"Men. You might have to actually open your eyes. Come on, I'll show you."

No, no, no! Annie looked for cover. The cardboard banana was tall enough, but once they were on this side, she'd be in plain sight. The produce bins were only waist high.

Where?

"What do you want with asparagus anyway?" Luke asked. So close.

"Hey, I cook."

Quick, Annie!

"Sure you do," Marla said.

She ducked down by the tomato bin, her heart pounding. The tomato in her hand flattened against the glossy concrete floor.

"See, I told you. Right by the brussels sprouts."

"Well, it's practically hidden behind that leafy stuff."

"It's called kale, Dylan," Marla said.

Their footsteps passed, stopping at the long display along the wall. She could see their feet beneath the potato stand, two sets of brown boots and Marla's white Sketchers.

Someone ripped a produce bag off the roll. "Think I'll take some kale while I'm at it."

"Like you'd know what to do with it," Luke said.

Annie's heart pounded so hard it shook her whole body. She remembered her cart behind her, her purse in the seat, and prayed they wouldn't notice.

She realized it had gotten quiet over by the brussels sprouts. Then she watched a pair of boots move around the potato bin toward her.

No. Please, God, no. Don't let him see me.

She ducked her head, her hair swinging forward like a curtain. She closed her eyes for good measure.

"Annie?"

She opened her eyes, lifted her head.

Dylan's brows pulled together.

She straightened slowly, her face no doubt going the color of the tomato in her hand.

"Annie, you okay?" Marla asked.

"I'm fine—I—" She held up the tomato, hoping they'd draw their own conclusion. Preferably something that explained why she'd been huddled on the floor for the last twenty seconds.

She shrugged and tried for a smile as she set the tomato in her cart.

Marla stepped forward. "Oh, honey, you don't want that, it's been on the floor." She snatched the tomato, then wrinkled her nose. "And it's gushy." She walked away, presumably to throw out the ruined tomato.

Annie dared a look at Dylan.

One brow was cocked now. His lips tilted in a wry grin. "Annie, meet my brother, Luke. Luke, Annie."

"Nice to meet you." Luke shook her hand. Wearing a cowboy hat, he was a younger, curly-haired version of Dylan, minus the dimple.

"Uh, I'll wait in the truck," he said.

Annie watched him flee the scene, wishing she could go with him.

If Dylan realized she'd witnessed him kissing Marla, he didn't seem to care. "Hiding, Annie?"

She wanted to deny it, to say she'd dropped the tomato or that it had fallen, but she wasn't going to stoop to his level.

She lifted her chin. Her dignity was gone, but she could fake it. She stared him down and he stared right back. When his eyes dropped to her lips, her pulse kicked into overdrive.

Say something, Annie.

"How was church? I overslept." She clamped her lips shut. She owed him no explanation.

A glimmer of amusement touched his eyes. "We just pretending that kiss didn't happen, then?"

Annie's stomach dropped to the floor. Leave it to Dylan, she thought, feeling her face go five degrees hotter. She knew he wouldn't let her live it down.

Annie tilted her head. "What kiss?"

She strolled to her cart, trying for casual—no easy feat on her quaking legs. "I have to be going."

As she wheeled the lone head of lettuce past him, she felt his eyes on her, felt the back of her neck prickle with heat.

"Oh, Annie . . . ," he called, just when she thought she'd gotten away.

She stopped, turning, as something came flying through the air. She reached out just in time, catching it against her chest.

"Don't forget your tomato." His eyes twinkled, and the other side of his lips rose, bringing out his dimple.

Annie proceeded to the counter where Pappy rang up her two items, then she scurried out the door.

Dear Worried in Whitefish,

The winds of change are blowing. You don't have to like it, but maybe you should buy a windbreaker.

24

Dylan entered his house and closed the door. His brother waited in Dylan's favorite recliner, a copy of *Montana Living* spread open in his lap.

"Sorry I'm late. Had to help Wade with a mechanical problem and it took longer than I thought."

"No problem," Luke said. "I kept myself busy."

"Ready? Thought we'd hit the diner for supper."

"Sounds good." Luke set the paper on the table and followed Dylan out the door. "You have a columnist here in town. Annie Wilkerson?"

Dylan scowled. "You must be bored silly if you're reading a lovelorn column." Dylan felt a surge of pride in Annie that belied his words. Wasn't about to admit helping her on the column though. He'd never hear the end of it.

"So she does live here?" Luke said after they were in the truck.

"Annie? You met her yesterday at the market."

Luke frowned, then his eyes widened. "The tomato lady?"

Dylan smiled at the memory. "Exactly. She's helping me with Braveheart. She's a horse trainer, actually. Goes to my church."

"I got the feeling there was something going on between you two."

Dylan recalled the kiss, her response, and all humor fled. He clenched his jaw. "She has a boyfriend."

Luke smiled teasingly, something gleaming in his eyes. "She got a younger sister?"

Dylan pulled down the drive. "Actually, she does."

Something flickered in his brother's eyes, but he looked out the window before Dylan could figure it out.

"But you stay away from Sierra," he continued, remembering the last time he'd introduced her to someone. "You'll only be here long enough to cause trouble, and things are complicated enough between Annie and me."

"Complicated?"

"Huh." That wasn't even the word. Last thing he needed was his brother making moves on Sierra. Annie'd have his throat.

Dylan turned onto the main road and toward town. His stomach let out a loud rumble. He'd worked right through lunch. He could almost smell Mabel's roast beef and mashed potatoes.

Several minutes later they pulled up to the diner.

"You know," Luke said as they got out of the truck, "I wouldn't mind staying longer than I'd planned—if you wouldn't mind, of course."

Dylan shrugged. "Stay as long as you like. I could use your help. Can you miss that much work?" His brother was a hand at one of the biggest ranches in Dallas.

"Pretty sure I can get it cleared. Haven't had a vacation since I took the job over three years ago."

Dylan nodded as they entered the Tin Roof. "It'd be great to have you around awhile."

"Awesome." Luke grinned. "I forgot how much I like it here."

Dear Cautious in Clancy,

    Secrets are like poison to a relationship. If you don't want yours to die a slow death, you need to confess everything.

25

Annie chatted with Shay at the back of the vestibule before church, listening to her baby stories. Shay had her in stitches, explaining Travis's method for changing diapers those first few weeks of fatherhood.

Annie looked across the vestibule at John and found herself thinking about her own future. She wondered if he knew how to change a diaper. He'd be willing to learn, she was sure of that. Her thoughts turned to the part before the baby, when their post-wedding kisses would go further and further until it was just the two of them under his mother's wedding ring quilt. She swallowed hard.

Shay was inviting her over for coffee when Sierra appeared out of nowhere, clamping her arms in a tight grip and pulling her aside.

"Excuse me, Shay," Annie said, then turned to her sister.

Sierra's face was pinched, her eyes wide. "We have to go. We have to go *now*." She pulled Annie down the hall toward the children's classrooms.

"It's almost time for church," Annie said, dragging her feet. It was hard enough just *getting* Sierra to church, now she had to fight to keep her there?

"Hurry!"

"Sierra." Annie pulled her arm from her sister's grip. "What is going on?"

She looked over Annie's shoulder. "I'll explain later. *Please*."

She couldn't refuse Sierra's plea. "Okay. But let me tell John first."

"Text him. This can't wait." Sierra pulled her down the hall, where they collected Ryder from his class, confusing him and his teacher.

"I just got here," Ryder said. "I don't wanna go."

"I know, Bed Head, but it can't be helped." Annie spared Sierra a frown as they rushed out the back door and to Annie's truck.

Sierra's hands knotted and released in her lap on the drive home. As curious as Annie was, she couldn't ask with Ryder squeezed between them.

At home Sierra sent Ryder to change from his Sunday clothes.

Annie stopped her sister in the hallway before she could escape. "What was that all about?"

She'd never seen Sierra so shaken. Even now her hands flew aimlessly around her body, seeking a place to land and not finding it.

"Tell me. Are you in trouble?"

"No, no, nothing like that." Sierra's eyes darted around.

Annie grabbed her shoulders. "Calm down. Whatever this is, we'll deal with it."

Sierra's hand settled at her throat. She took several deep breaths, then turned toward the kitchen.

Annie watched her go, frowning, then followed.

Sierra loaded the cereal bowls into the dishwasher. Her hands still shook, but when she turned to wipe the table, the frantic look in her eyes was gone.

"Talk to me, Sierra."

She shook her head, giving a wry laugh. A pretty flush had bloomed on her cheeks. "Sorry, sis. I guess I just overreacted—big surprise, huh?"

Something about her reaction didn't ring true. "Overreacted to what?"

Sierra scrubbed at a spot of dried orange juice on the table. She shrugged. "Nothing, I just— There was someone at church I didn't want to see, that's all." She tried for a grin. "Sorry I dragged you out of there like that. You should go back. No need for you to miss church. Did you text John?"

"Yes."

Sierra seemed almost normal now. What had all that been about? Who could have rattled her so? It didn't make sense. Sierra didn't have any enemies. At least, she didn't think so. But Sierra had been taking her own path lately. Maybe she'd gotten mixed up with something dangerous.

"You're not in trouble with the law, are you?"

Sierra looked up from the table. "Of course not!"

Annie raised her hands. "Just asking. Honestly, I don't know what to expect from you these days."

"Well, I'm no crook!"

"I know, hon. I just thought you might've somehow fallen into—" This wasn't coming out right. "I'm concerned about you. You've changed. You used to be so passionate about godly things, but lately—"

Sierra's brows drew tight.

"Well, never mind." Annie wished her sister weren't so defensive, but maybe now wasn't the time to address her spiritual walk.

When Ryder appeared in his play clothes, Annie sent him out to the backyard, But she couldn't forget the alarm in Sierra's eyes earlier. Maybe the problem wasn't external but internal. Could her frenzy have been a panic attack or another medical problem?

She set her hand on Sierra's arm, stopping the frantic scrubbing. "Are you feeling all right, hon?"

Sierra waved her worry away, but her hand trembled. "Right as rain. Really." Her laugh sounded like a gurgle. "I don't know what came over me. Go on to church. I'll have dinner waiting when you get home. How about if I grill out hot dogs? I can stick some of that fresh corn on the grill too. Doesn't that sound yummy?"

"Sierra, sit down. Talk to me."

Her sister stopped in her tracks, her face falling.

Annie felt dread bubble up from the deepest recesses. She put her hands on Sierra's drooping shoulders, stabilizing her. "It'll be okay. Whatever it is."

Sierra's eyes were wide and frantic again. They filled as her mouth opened.

"Talk to me, honey. You're scaring me."

Her lip trembled. "It's—Ryder's father. He was at church."

"Ryder's father? Why would he be here? Are you sure? It's been four years, maybe—"

Sierra shook her head frantically. "His name is Luke. I'm sure it was him." She covered her face. "What am I going to do?"

"Luke?" Annie asked. "Luke Taylor is Ryder's father?"

"How do you know his name?"

She grabbed Sierra's shoulders. "Honey, he's Dylan's younger brother."

Luke Taylor. He was cut from the same cloth as his brother. Of course he had run from his responsibility after he'd gotten her sister pregnant. Annie wanted to wrap her hands around both their necks and give them a few hard shakes, never mind that he'd probably not told his family anything about the small matter of fathering a child.

She watched the truth register on Sierra's face.

"Luke *Taylor*. I never even—"

"It's a common name. And Luke was miles from here when you met him."

Sierra had begged to go to that summer mission trip near Missoula. She'd been growing spiritually, and Annie had convinced their grandfather it would be good for her.

She wasn't supposed to come home pregnant. Wasn't supposed to have her first love reject her, then disappear without a trace.

"He'll be leaving any day; he's just visiting. But I'll tell you what," Annie said. "I have a few things I'd like to say to that man."

"No, you can't!"

"Watch me!"

Sierra grabbed her arm. "Please! He can't know I'm here. He's . . . he's a cowboy, Annie. Do you really think he'd be a good role model for Ryder? You're always saying they're only good for leaving—do you think Ryder needs that kind of rejection? The kind we got from our father?"

Everything she said was true. But Annie had worked so hard to support them alone. It was unfair that Luke got off scot-free.

"We have to think about what's best for Ryder," Sierra said. "And you know what that is, Annie. You *know*." Sierra swiped the tears from her face. "I'm so close to graduating, we're almost there. Please. Please don't say anything. I'll just hide out until I know he's gone, and he'll be none the wiser."

Annie studied her sister's tearstained face. She took a few deep breaths. She didn't like it one bit, but Sierra was right. They had to put Ryder first. Clearly Luke didn't want anything to do with the boy, and exposing him as the father would only hurt Ryder in the long run.

Besides, they were surviving. It hadn't been easy, but God had always provided for their needs.

"You're right." Annie pulled her into her arms and rubbed her back. "It'll be okay. You'll stay home until he's gone. He'll never even know you were here."

"You can't tell Dylan. Or anyone else, even Shay."

That would be tough . . . but she'd do almost anything for her sister. "Of course not. Everything will be fine. I promise."

Dear Baffled,

Your friend is trying to tell you she's not interested. True, a straightforward answer would be more convenient, but she's chosen a roundabout way of saying "No thanks."

26

Annie pulled the truck into her drive and met Pepper at the fence. Her foot ached as she walked toward the corral. She'd been working with a quarter horse that wouldn't load into a trailer.

Maisy had bumped her head on the trailer last fall, and then, when she wouldn't load in the spring, Frank Peterson had decided she needed a whip to the hindquarters. This had only exacerbated the problem.

Unfortunately he'd been using the same method ever since, and now the mare bucked upon approaching the trailer. Annie had only made progress with Maisy when she'd removed Frank from the premises—a request he hadn't taken kindly to. She'd gotten the horse loaded but not before Maisy's hoof had come down on Annie's boot.

The man had no business working with horses. If people treated
them right, 99 percent of problems would never materialize.

"Isn't that right, Pepper?" Annie rubbed the horse's neck as he
nickered hello.

She'd run into John at the market, where she'd gone for a bag
of ice, and they'd had words over her injury. She wished he understood she wasn't some hothouse flower. Working with horses
carried risks, and he needed to accept that going forward. They'd
finally made up and parted with strained smiles.

She gave Pepper a final pat. "See you later, big guy."

Annie limped toward the house, her foot still smarting. Inside,
a yeast and garlic aroma wafted in the air. Pizza. Not her first choice,
but she'd take it.

"What happened to you?" Sierra asked.

"Minor accident."

Ryder came sliding around the corner for a hug. "Yum, pizza!"

"You're just in time." Sierra set the hot pie in the center of the
table while Annie sank into her chair. The swelling in her foot had
gone down, but the words she'd exchanged with John still lingered
in her mind.

"My turn!" Ryder folded his hands and bowed his head.
"Thanks, God, for the pizza and for letting me beat Mom at Chutes
and Ladders today. Amen."

"You cheated," Sierra teased.

"Did not. Mom doesn't like to lose," he said to Annie.

"She was the same way when we were kids," Annie whispered.

"Hmph." Sierra sliced the pizza and set a piece on Ryder's
plate.

As hard as it had been to make do without Sierra's income over
the summer, she knew Ryder had enjoyed having his mom home.

Only a few more weeks and she'd be back in class. After hiding away the past two days, Sierra was getting antsy. By the end of the week, she'd be happy to go anywhere, even college.

"You got your classes scheduled online, right?" Annie asked.

Sierra wiped her mouth. "Not yet."

Annie squeezed her napkin in her lap. "School starts in less than a month. I know you've been . . . distracted the last few days, but you only have five classes left. What if they fill up?"

"Don't worry, I'll handle it."

"If you miss even one class, you won't graduate in the—"

"I said I'll handle it, Annie."

"And you need to make sure Martha still wants to babysit—"

The phone rang and Annie scooted her chair back, glad for the distraction.

Sierra looked up, wide-eyed. "Don't answer."

Annie frowned as it rang again. "Why not?"

"Just don't, okay?" She gave Ryder a stilted smile. "Let's just enjoy our pizza, huh, buddy? No sense letting it get cold." Her cheery voice wobbled.

"It's yummy, Mommy."

Annie sank into her chair. They'd had to drop voice mail, so the phone rang a few more times. Sierra sat rigidly until it stopped, chewing her food, but Annie didn't think she even tasted it. Had Luke somehow found out she was here? But why would he call when he'd wanted nothing to do with her or Ryder? It must be someone else.

After supper Annie loaded their plates into the dishwasher while Sierra washed the pizza pan.

"Okay, what gives?" Annie whispered.

"What do you mean?"

"Who are you avoiding? Besides Luke, I mean."

Sierra breathed a laugh. "Just some . . . guy. You know." She shrugged, her auburn hair bouncing on her shoulder. "I'm not interested, that's all."

"Have you told him that? It's always best to be direct."

Sierra faced her, blew out a long sigh. "I can handle it, Annie, okay? It's my school schedule, my social life, and I can handle it all just fine." She tossed the towel on the counter and left the room.

Annie could only pray Sierra was right.

Later that night the phone rang again. Annie squinted at the glowing hands on her alarm clock. After one. She automatically reached for her cell, then realized it was the landline ringing. She remembered the phone call at supper. Sierra and Ryder were safe in bed, so it wouldn't be them. If it were a work emergency, whoever it was would've called her cell.

She jumped from bed anyway. She had to know what was going on. If it were some pushy guy, Annie would happily clue him in. But by the time she reached the kitchen, the ringing had stopped.

Sighing, she returned to her room, checking on Ryder on her way past. He was sleeping soundly, his legs in a tussle with the thrift-store cowboy sheets Sierra had found.

She climbed back into bed, worry tickling at the frayed edges of her mind at the thought of those phone calls. If Sierra was going to handle her own life, she wished the girl would do a better job.

Dear Uncertain,

Chemistry isn't everything. But it's something.

27

Annie stirred the green beans and checked the meat loaf. She'd needed someplace quiet to confess her moment of indiscretion to John, so she'd invited him for supper. She'd meant to do it sooner, but with the distraction of Luke being in town, it had taken all her energy to keep Sierra calm. Her sister had been even more upset when Annie had returned from Dylan's the night before with bad news.

"Luke's still in town, Sierra, and I'm afraid that's not the worst of it . . . He's staying three more weeks."

"You said he was leaving any day, and that was five days ago!"

"Dylan said he changed his mind. You just have to hang in there a little while longer."

"Three weeks!"

It was a blessing in disguise that Sierra didn't have a job at the moment.

Her sister had fretted all night, and now she scurried around the house trying to get Ryder ready. They'd decided it would be safe for Sierra to go down the street to Bridgett's house for the evening.

Annie gave the beans another stir. She had to put aside Sierra's problems and focus on her own tonight. *Help me find the words, Lord. I don't want to hurt him.*

She'd had a busy day and had to squeeze in a second run to the market, since the first had been a bust. She only hoped preparing John's favorite meal would help wash down the bad news.

Annie checked the time. "John'll be here any minute."

"Ryder can't find his hat."

Annie fussed over the plates and settings, then chided herself. It wasn't like the perfectly laid table would make the truth go down easier. Since seeing Dylan at the market and realizing Luke was his brother, Annie felt less confused about John. She had to stop comparing him to Dylan. Sure, Dylan made her heart patter, but Luke's tie to Ryder made the relationship impossible—even if he was capable of commitment, which she doubted.

There was no future with a man like Dylan. He was never going to settle down, and—passionate kisses aside—there was no point in riding down that path.

John was her boyfriend. She liked him a lot, respected him, and she could learn to love him. He was everything she needed for a secure future. He'd be a good father, partner, and provider. Her children would have everything she'd lacked, and that was the important thing. So what if he was a little short on passion. Maybe that would grow with time too.

Seeing Dylan that week had only confirmed her thoughts. After working with Braveheart, she'd rushed through her letters with Dylan, hadn't even argued when his opinion was contrary to hers. He hadn't mentioned the kiss, but there'd been plenty of hiked brows and smug grins.

Yes, it was time to forget her silly crush and focus on the man who was serious about her and their future. All she had to do was own up to her mistake and ask his forgiveness. If they managed to survive this conflict, it would set the tone for future problems.

"You seen my hat, Aunt Annie?" Ryder appeared in the doorway, his rope looped in his chubby hands.

"Have you checked your toy box?"

"Nope." Ryder dashed from the room, his bare feet padding across the wood floor. No shoes and socks yet. She glanced at the stove clock.

"Sierra . . . !"

"I know, I know."

"Found it," Ryder called.

Thank goodness.

A knock sounded on the door.

She pushed down her irritation with Sierra and answered the door with a smile.

John looked nice in a short-sleeved dress shirt and navy tie. "Annie. You're a sight for sore eyes." He handed her a bouquet of colorful flowers.

They'd both been so busy the past couple of weeks, they'd barely seen each other. And maybe he felt bad about the squabble over her foot.

"They're beautiful, thank you. Come on in."

He gave her a quick kiss as he passed, and she found herself comparing the kiss to Dylan's.

Stop that, Annie.

"How's your foot?"

"Just fine. Not even limping, see?"

"Good, good. Mmm, something smells delicious."

"Hi, Mr. Oakley." Ryder skidded to a halt in the foyer and plopped on the floor to put on his shoes.

"Hello there, Ryder. What have you been up to this week?"

"Practicing my ropin'! I'm a cowboy."

"You don't say."

"Where's your mom?" Annie asked.

"In the bathroom."

She wished Sierra would hurry. This wasn't how she'd wanted the night to begin.

The oven timer dinged. "Excuse me."

In the kitchen she turned off the timer and pulled the meat loaf from the oven. She found a vase, filled it with water, then spread the blooms and placed the arrangement on the table.

In the other room she heard Ryder calling for Sierra to tie his shoes.

"Here," she heard John say. "I can help with that."

She set the meat loaf on the table and retrieved the green beans, listening to John's quiet instruction.

"Build a teepee, come inside . . . close it tight so we can hide. Over the mountain, and around we go . . . Here's my arrow, and here's my bow."

"Mommy does that too!"

"Does she? Well, it's how I learned to tie my own shoes."

Annie liked listening to him with Ryder. He was good with kids, a wonderful quality in a man. She had a sudden image of Dylan teaching Ryder to rope the fence, of him setting the new cowboy hat on the boy's head. She pushed the images from her mind.

Sierra peeked into the kitchen. "Sorry! We're leaving now. Have fun."

Not likely. Annie said good-bye, suddenly nervous when their departure left the house too quiet.

"Well, supper's ready," she told John.

As he entered the kitchen, she set the basket of bread on the table. John pulled out her chair.

"Thank you. And thanks again for the flowers." They looked cheery in the center of the table.

"Shall I?" John asked, taking her hand.

Annie acquiesced with a smile.

"Heavenly Father, we thank You for this food and for the lovely hands that prepared it. We ask Your blessing on our evening, on our lives. Amen." He squeezed her hand.

"Amen."

John caught her up on his mom's move while they ate. He'd gotten her settled into her apartment, and she was already making friends with her new neighbors and planning to start a book club. His love for his mother was apparent in his tone. Another good quality.

Annie told him about the stubborn stallion she'd worked with that day, quieting when she sensed his worry. He complimented her on the meal and ate two portions of everything, then he helped her tidy the kitchen.

"Would you like to sit on the porch?" Annie asked after the last dish was washed and put away.

"Sounds perfect."

The sun had disappeared behind the mountains, ushering in that golden hour of light. She sat in the swing, and John put his arm around her, then pushed off. The sweet smell of her favorite lilac bush competed with his cologne.

For a few minutes there was only the rhythmic creaking and the hard thumping of her heart. She had to tell him now. The guilt was eating her alive.

"John, I—"

"Annie, I—"

They smiled at their timing.

"You first," she said, suddenly eager for a reprieve, no matter how brief.

He turned toward her, an intent look on his face. The waning daylight reflected in his glasses, blocking his eyes.

He took her hand. "I just wanted to say I'm really sorry about my . . . behavior a couple of weeks ago. I shouldn't have pressed you so hard about that night at the cabin. I should've trusted you."

Guilt weighted her shoulders. "That's not necessary, John, I—"

"Wait, Annie. Please. Just let me get this out."

Hers could wait. She smiled and nodded for him to proceed.

He pushed his glasses up with his index finger, and she could see his eyes again. They were olive green in the golden light and sparkled with purpose.

"I was jealous, pure and simple."

Her heart twisted painfully. He wasn't going to make this easy.

"The fact is, I can't stand the thought of you with another man. I've come to care deeply for you—I've come to love you, Annie."

Her lips parted in surprise.

He laid two fingers against her mouth. "No, don't say anything yet." He lowered his hand to hers. "I know we haven't been together all that long, but that unfortunate incident opened my eyes. I've spent these last couple of weeks thinking hard about us, and I realized . . ."

In one fluid motion he was down on his knee, staring up at her with earnest eyes.

Everything in Annie froze, except her thoughts, which raced ahead like a runaway mustang. She hadn't seen this coming. How had she not seen this coming?

"Annie Wilkerson, I want to spend the rest of my life with you. I want to love you, protect you, partner with you. I want to share morning coffee with you at sunrise, and I want your lovely face to be the last thing I see before I go to sleep at night. I want to raise children together, solve problems together, and grow old together." He squeezed her numb hands. "Will you marry me?"

She opened her mouth and wished he'd put his fingers over it again because nothing came out.

"This might seem sudden, but I've never been more certain of anything in my life. We can have a long engagement if you like. Or not. It's up to you. I just know I love you, and I want you to be mine forever."

His warm words loosened her tongue. "I didn't expect this . . ."

"If you need time, you have it. I won't be offended. But I hope you'll say yes, Annie."

He reached into his pocket and pulled out a ring. The stunning emerald-cut diamond glimmered back at her.

"I admire you so much. You've taken care of your sister and your nephew, and now I want to take care of you. You deserve it."

She wanted to say she could take care of herself, but there were so many other thoughts spinning through her head. Sierra wouldn't be here much longer. She'd graduate this winter, find a job, and she and Ryder would be on their own. She did need to move on with her own life. She wasn't getting any younger, and she wanted a family of her own someday soon.

But you don't love him, Annie.

"It's time for you to have your life," he said, echoing her

thoughts. "I know you want children, and I want them too. I can provide whatever you need—whatever they need."

She didn't doubt that. She looked at the substantial stone shimmering in the waning light. He was the kind of husband her mom had needed and never had. The kind of father she and Sierra had needed. John was security personified. He was everything she'd been looking for in a mate.

Not everything, Annie.

Dylan's kiss flooded through her mind, his electrifying touch, his tenderness. She forced out the memory, replacing it with the image of him pulling Marla into his arms the day after their kiss. Replacing it with the image of his brother, who had abandoned Sierra and Ryder both.

She had put that stupid kiss behind her. Dylan was an impossibility. Besides, she couldn't imagine a man less suited for her. He wasn't husband or father material.

John seemed to be exactly what she needed. So why didn't she love him? Why couldn't there be passion between them?

Life isn't a Jane Austen novel, Annie, all romance and flights of fancy. It's hard, and you need a partner you can count on to be there when the going gets tough—because it will.

But she wanted those other things. She wanted security *and* love. Commitment *and* chemistry. Was that too much to ask? It wasn't Dylan, but maybe God would send her someone else. Someday . . .

"Annie . . . ?" Uncertainty dimmed John's eyes.

Maybe she didn't love him, but she did care for him. Didn't he deserve a partner who loved him? Who longed for his kisses and anticipated their time together?

She suddenly knew the right thing to do. It hit her with a certainty she'd never felt before. "I'm so sorry, John. I can't."

His eyes went flat, his lips parted. She read the surprise on his face and felt like the slime at the bottom of a barrel. He'd expected them to become engaged tonight. She didn't deserve his love, his devotion.

"You're a wonderful man, truly. And you deserve—"

"It's Taylor, isn't it?" His lips pressed together.

"No, it's not." She was relieved she could say that honestly. Maybe Dylan had helped her see what their relationship lacked, but it could never be Dylan. Not now.

She laid her hand on his. "I didn't mean to lead you on, John. I care for you a great deal, but I . . . I realize now that we don't have what it takes to last forever. And you deserve that. You deserve a woman who loves you like that."

He looked down at the ring, awkwardly pocketed it, breaking their connection. "Well. I don't know what to say."

He didn't have to say anything. It was all written on his face.

"I'm so sorry."

He cleared his throat and poked his glasses into place.

If she'd thought telling him about the kiss was going to be hard . . .

When he stood to leave a long moment later, she breathed a deep sigh. They hugged uneasily, then she watched him slip into his shiny blue Buick.

As he pulled down her drive, she remembered her mom, remembered the uncertainty, the instability, and hoped she wasn't holding out for the impossible.

Dear Certain,

Swallow your pride. Like spinach, it won't taste so great, but it's good for you.

28

Annie put her truck in gear and pulled down the drive, something stirring in her belly at the thought of time alone with Dylan. In the week since the breakup, word had circulated through town. Their greeting at church had been stilted, and she hadn't missed all the glances when she'd passed John's pew and sat with Shay and Travis instead.

She hoped Dylan wouldn't broach the subject. Hoped her sudden availability wouldn't make their time together even more challenging.

She sighed as she turned out of her drive. Why was it so hard to find Mr. Right? John was reliable and ready to settle down, but she didn't love him. Dylan stirred her mind and body, but he was like a wispy cloud that disappeared as soon as you moved your fingers through it.

Despite all that, despite his relationship to Luke, she shook with anticipation at the thought of being together. *This isn't good, God. I know he's bad for me, impossible even, so why do I feel this way?*

She brushed her damp hair off her face, making a decision. She had to cut back on the time she spent with him. She'd just have to handle the column on her own. She'd tell him tonight.

But she couldn't turn her back on Braveheart. The horse was finally coming along, and Annie felt Dylan would be able to ride him eventually. Maybe even soon. It would be healthy for Braveheart to have a purpose.

And then that was it. No more time with Dylan. No more fighting the attraction, no more feeling guilty for the secret she kept.

Her cell phone rang and the name on the caller ID made her tense.

"Midge, hello, how are you?"

"Hi, Annie. I hope I'm not calling at a bad time."

"I'm just driving. I haven't heard from you in a few weeks. How are things in Bozeman?"

"Well . . . that's why I'm calling."

A weight settled in Annie's midsection at Midge's cautious tone.

"I'm afraid we've had more negative feedback on your answers, Annie. Quite a bit, actually. It pains me to say this—you're a terrific writer and such a reliable worker, but . . . your probation period is almost up, and my boss asked me to let you go. I'm so sorry."

Annie blinked slowly. "Let me go? But my recent answers were clearly right, don't you think?"

"Honestly, the solutions were so obvious, they were a little, well, boring. Honey, I just don't think a lovelorn column is your thing."

Dylan. Annie squeezed the bridge of her nose. Why had she let him convince her to use the obvious letters? Why hadn't she trusted her own common sense rather than depend on his supposed expertise?

"Give me another chance, Midge. I was getting some—bad advice."

"I'm sorry, honey. My boss has already approached that columnist in Wyoming about taking your place."

"Another column, then . . . something related to my area of expertise. I'll come up with some ideas and send a—"

"I'm really sorry, Annie." Midge sounded miserable.

Annie knew she needed to let the woman off the hook. She drew a deep breath, sucking in courage, and swallowed her pride. "I understand. I'm sorry I let you down, Midge."

When Annie closed her phone, her hands were shaking. She'd never been fired—what an ugly word. Not from the Dairy Freeze, not from the ranch jobs . . . She felt like a failure. She wondered if Sierra felt this way each time she was fired.

And now she'd ruined her reputation at the paper. How could she hope they'd hire Sierra after graduation when she'd let them down so badly?

She pounded her fist on the steering wheel. Dylan. She'd known those answers weren't right. She should've trusted her instincts, but she'd believed Mr. Suave. Had trusted that if he could make half the county fall in love with him, he must know what he was doing.

Ha! She would've been better off using the insight she'd gleaned from romance novels.

But as much as she'd like to blame it all on Dylan, she couldn't. She was the one who'd handed him the reins. She was the one who'd written the answers. Ultimately it was her name on the column.

She wondered if everyone in Moose Creek knew how wrong her answers were. If they thought she was dumb as a doorknob when it came to real love. Maybe she was.

Enough of your pride, Annie, you've got bigger fish to fry.

She'd lost her part-time job. She'd have to find something, and soon. Sierra would have her hands full with five classes—provided she'd signed up for them yesterday as Annie had told her to do.

Dylan buttoned his white shirt and ran his hands through his freshly washed hair. Annie was coming. Luke had gone for a haircut and supper at the Tin Roof, so it would just be the two of them tonight.

His heart gave a couple hard thumps, and he told himself it was on Braveheart's behalf. He was just excited for his buddy's progress.

Despite their success, being with her had become awkward, and tonight was bound to be worse because everything had changed. His first clue was when Annie had sat with Shay at church instead of Oakley. Then he'd heard from Brenda Peterson that Oakley had proposed and Annie had turned him down. She was apparently free as a wild mustang.

That only made her a bigger threat to his sanity. But even after that kiss—especially after that kiss—he wasn't signing away his heart. He'd decided that long before he'd ever met Annie.

Besides, she wasn't interested in taking things to the next level anyway. Didn't she want to pretend the kiss had never even happened?

That should make things nice and simple. But if that were the case, why had he donned his favorite shirt, taken the extra time to shave for the second time that day?

He heard a car coming down the drive and looked out the window to see Annie's old truck approaching, raising a cloud of dust behind it. Despite his previous warnings, anticipation filled his chest.

She was exiting the truck as he ambled down the porch steps. "Afternoon, Annie."

"Ready to get started?"

"Always." He flashed his best smile and got no response. But he was used to that with Annie.

"We're going to teach him to find water," Annie said. "So can you make sure the waterer is filled?"

"Sure thing."

He pulled the hose over to the metal tub in the pasture, remembering the last time he'd held the hose. His lips lifted in a bittersweet smile as he recalled chasing Annie around the truck, recalled the water dripping off her nose, recalled the way her eyes had gone from laughing to wanting in the space of a few heart-beats. His heart twisted.

He dropped the nozzle and found Annie in the barn, talking to Braveheart as she attached the lead to the bridle.

She handed him the lead. "Let's take him out to the turnout point."

Dylan followed her directions, wondering what was wrong. Annie was all business, but wasn't that typical since the kiss? And judging by his dangerous thoughts moments ago, maybe that was for the best.

They reached the turnout point.

"Always stop here. It lets him know where Point A is. Point B will be the waterer. Go ahead and lead him toward it."

"Walk," he said.

Annie continued talking quietly. "You'll need to do this a few times a day. Be consistent, and he'll be finding water on his own in a couple of months. Then you can leave him in the pasture even when it's hot."

Dylan stopped when they reached the waterer.

Annie leaned down and tapped the metal tub a few times, then swished the water with her hand.

Braveheart's ears turned, and he nickered.

"He doesn't have to drink but be sure you tap the sides and swish the water each time."

They led him back to the turnout point.

"Let's try it again."

After working with Braveheart awhile, they led him back to his stall and removed his bridle. Dylan could tell Annie had something on her mind, but it wasn't his business. Maybe she was upset about her breakup with Oakley. Or maybe Sierra was giving her fits again.

He hung the lead and pulled his hat lower as they left the barn. The sun had dropped behind the mountains, taking the hottest part of the day with it. The air smelled of sweet hay and grass.

"I'll get some coffee on and meet you on the porch," he said.

"Wait, Dylan."

He faced Annie. She looked at her boots, then lifted her chin and tossed her hair over her shoulder.

"I won't be needing your help with the column anymore."

There was pride in her posture, but something else in her eyes. He wondered if the tension between them had become too much. Something tugged in his gut.

"Why's that?" He'd managed a casual tone, though sudden thoughts of no more time with Annie left his throat dry and made his lungs feel hot and heavy.

She gave a brittle laugh and a little shrug. "I kinda got fired."

Anger brewed fast as a summer storm. "What?"

"Seems my answers weren't what the readers were looking for. The complaints haven't stopped."

"That doesn't mean she has to fire you. She should give you more time."

The corner of Annie's lip tucked in. "I think it's best for everyone if I move out of the love advice business. Anyway, it'll be fine. I'll find another job."

His anger drained away, replaced by something else. This was all his fault. She'd used his answers, after all. Gone against her own instincts most of the time.

He tugged his hat lower, all the better to hide. He'd let her believe he was Mr. Love. He should've told her the truth instead of letting his foolish pride have its way. She'd helped him with his blind horse, and in return, he'd gotten her fired.

"This is my fault."

Her brows twitched. "No, Dylan. It's not."

"It is too, Annie. You don't understand." He walked toward her truck, ducking his head. He felt like a real jerk. Some expert.

When he turned, she was there behind him.

Annie tilted her head, studying his face. "What do you mean?"

He sucked in a deep breath and let it out on a sigh. "Thing is, Annie . . . I'm not the expert you think I am. I'm about the last person who should've been helping you."

"Please. You've probably been in love at least a dozen times."

He ducked his head, looking like a child sitting in the principal's office. She had to know what was behind that look. She raised her brows, waiting.

"I'm more a footloose-and-fancy-free guy, in case you haven't noticed."

"You *have* been in love before."

He rubbed the back of his neck. "Just once. Didn't go well."

She crossed her arms. This was getting more interesting by the moment. "Do tell."

He leaned on her truck and hitched his boot on the runner, and she wondered if he was going to shut down.

But after a moment he began talking. "Her name was Merilee. Met her down in Texas."

Annie was mesmerized as he told her how he'd fallen for a college student. About their long dates and how things had gotten out of hand physically. His cheeks colored at the confession.

She was surprised he was so forthcoming, but sometimes Dylan's mouth ran away from him. And she was too intrigued to stop him.

"So after graduation, she went back to her hometown for a couple months. I decided while she was gone that I wanted to marry her. I missed her, knew I wanted to spend the rest of my life with her. So I sold my horse and bought her a ring."

Cowboys didn't sell their horses for their girls, at least not the ones she'd known. At least John hadn't done anything so sacrificial. She would've felt even more awful.

Dylan cleared his throat, pulling her eyes to his. Those brown eyes of his drew her right in.

"What happened?" A light breeze blew her hair off her shoulders. The daylight waned, and the light near his barn flickered on.

She was afraid for a minute that he'd stop the story right there, and she was desperate to know the rest.

He tugged on the brim of his hat and continued. "When Merilee got back, I took her out for a nice evening. Something seemed off, but I thought it was just all the time apart. I popped the question over by the river, a spot we liked to frequent."

"She said no?" Annie wondered if he'd looked as vulnerable that night as he did right now. Or if hope had shone in his eyes at the thought of a bright future, the way John's had.

"She said she was pregnant."

Annie tried to keep the surprise from her face. He'd fathered a child? Just like his brother? Did Dylan have a kid out there somewhere who didn't know his dad too?

"It wasn't mine." The pain was evident in his eyes, even all these years later.

"Oh." Despite herself, she hurt for him. Wanted to reach out and hug him.

"Her old boyfriend. Apparently they reconnected when she went back home and . . ." He shrugged.

Something tugged in her stomach at the betrayal he must've felt. "That's awful."

She could hardly imagine Dylan so deeply in love, so vulnerable to a woman. To be full of hope, then have it dashed so cruelly. What kind of girl would do such a thing to a man she professed to love?

"After I recovered, I told her I'd marry her anyway, raise the baby as my own. But she married the baby's father instead."

She winced. It was the opposite of what his brother had done to Sierra. She wondered if Merilee had soured Dylan on love. Maybe that was why he flitted from woman to woman like a bee over a flower garden. Maybe he'd decided love was more trouble than it was worth.

He gave a wry grin. "Shoulda told you up front I wasn't the best person to help with a lovelorn column. The one time I managed to find that something special, well . . . it didn't turn out so well."

Annie smiled. "You still had more experience than me."

Their eyes locked, and she felt the smile slide from her face. Her heart kicked up into her throat. His eyes still bore the traces of vulnerability but now held something else she couldn't define.

"I heard about Oakley."

She'd wondered when he was going to bring that up. "Figured as much."

"Sorry it didn't work out." He sounded sincere, and one look into his eyes was one look too many.

Annie dug for her keys, her face growing warm. "I should probably be leaving."

"I could still start that coffee . . ."

The fact that she was tempted told her all she needed to know. She turned toward her truck. "I should get back."

He followed her to the driver's side. "I'm sorry again, about the column."

She waved him off, ready to be gone, away from his confusing presence. "It's fine."

"What about Braveheart? I'll pay you whatever you want if you'll keep working with him."

"No, no. I'll see the job through. Shouldn't take much longer; he's doing really well." She climbed into the driver's seat and he shut the door behind her.

"I'll fix your sister's car then, for free. In return for your help."

"It might be expensive."

Dylan shrugged. "I have a friend who owns an auto shop in Bozeman. He gives me a good deal on parts."

It would have to wait until Luke was far away from Moose Creek. "Well, all right then. Deal."

After a final wave she pulled out. In her rearview mirror Dylan grew farther and farther away until he disappeared into the darkness.

Annie's fingers ached from squeezing the steering wheel and she loosened them. What was wrong with her? Why'd he work her up in knots this way? Why'd she continually find herself drawn to him? To his strength and his vulnerability? Why'd she long to comfort him for a pain he'd suffered years ago?

He might be a cowboy, but it was clearer than ever that he was a wounded cowboy. Maybe he was a better man than she'd given him credit for.

Not that it mattered. All that mattered now was hiding Ryder and Sierra from Dylan's brother.

Dear Poleaxed,

    As you're learning, sometimes things are not as they seem.
Not even close.

29

Annie woke but kept her eyes closed, hoping to fall back to sleep. She had a full schedule tomorrow, and it started at the crack of dawn. It couldn't be much past midnight.

Despite her need for sleep, her mind drifted over the conversation she'd had with Sierra that evening. Annie had expected her to be upset about the lost opportunity at the newspaper, not to mention the lost income. But no.

"I never wanted to work for that paper anyway," Sierra had said. "You'd know that if you'd ever stopped to ask—which you didn't."

Sometimes Sierra made her want to pull out her hair. Did the girl not see Annie was trying to help her? Didn't she know Annie only wanted the best for her? It was as if she were still a rebellious teenager, not a twenty-year-old young woman and a mother to boot. But she tried to cut her sister some slack. She was under a lot of stress right now with Luke still in town.

Annie heard a noise and lifted her head from the pillow.

Voices. Sierra must be on the phone. She looked at the clock. It was past midnight. Pretty late for a phone call, but then, Sierra didn't have to be up early.

Footsteps sounded. Was someone here with her, or was Sierra just up and about? Annie hoped she hadn't brought a man over. She knew that being in hiding had been hard for Sierra, but still.

She turned down the covers and sat up in bed. Ryder didn't need to wake up and find some man in the house.

She heard Sierra's voice again and realized it was coming from the porch. Annie sat still, listening. A moment later she heard the low rumble of a male voice.

What was going on? Sierra had been watching TV with Ryder when Annie had turned in. She suddenly remembered the phone calls Sierra had avoided. Was her sister in some kind of trouble?

Annie swung her legs over the bed, tugging her nightgown into place, then grabbed her cell phone from the nightstand. The hardwood floor was cold against her bare feet, and the bits of grit sticking to them reminded her she needed to sweep.

The living room lights were out, and she peeked through the sheers, but the porch was dark too. Should she interrupt? She remembered Sierra's complaints about her interference and stilled, the phone clutched to her chest.

Instead she leaned closer, listening. Maybe she could hear what was going on first. But at the first sign of threat, she was calling the sheriff. She looked around the darkened room for a weapon and grabbed the heavy clay paperweight Ryder had made for her.

"You should leave," Sierra was saying. Her shadow moved to the door.

"Wait. Please." He reached for Sierra. His form seemed tall and solid on the darkened porch. "I just want to talk."

"You've said enough."

"I love you, Sierra. That's never changed."

The doorknob clicked and the door opened.

Annie eased back against the wall.

"Go home, Luke, and don't come back," Sierra whispered, then closed the door.

Luke was here? What did he want with Sierra now, after all this time?

"Luke's here?" Annie whispered harshly.

Sierra jumped at the sound of Annie's voice.

"Why didn't you tell me he'd seen you?" Annie whispered.

Sierra's mouth worked wordlessly.

Annie pushed off the wall, tossing her phone on the sofa. She kept the paperweight, had visions of smashing it over Luke's head, Dylan's brother or no. Ryder had been without a father because that—that *cowboy* wouldn't man up. Even now he only seemed to care about Sierra.

Annie reached for the door. "Well, now that he found the guts to face you, I have a few things to say to him."

"No, Annie!" Sierra blocked her way.

"Move it, Sierra! He left you and Ryder high and dry, and I'm going to give him a piece of my mind."

Annie grabbed for the doorknob. Sierra pressed against it, but Annie was stronger.

"Please, you can't!"

"Oh yes, I can!"

She wrestled the knob from Sierra.

Her sister grabbed her arm. "He doesn't know! He doesn't know about Ryder."

At the terror in Sierra's voice, Annie stilled. The words sank in, making her knees go weak. "What?"

The only sound in the room was their heavy breathing, the ticking of the grandfather clock. Then the sound of an engine start-ing. A moment later it faded into silence.

"I—I never told him."

Annie lowered her hand, staring at her sister's dark form. "Yes, you did. You called him." She'd been right there in the room almost five years ago, had forced Sierra to make the call. "He said he'd be in touch, and then he changed his number. You couldn't find him . . ."

But Annie was beginning to see that all that wasn't true.

Sierra had gone as stagnant as Whippoorwill Pond on a still August day.

Annie backed away, the truth sinking in. When her legs hit the sofa, she sank onto it. All this time? All the financial struggles? And he didn't even know? Ryder didn't know his dad because Sierra hadn't bothered to tell him?

"Why? Why in heaven's name didn't you tell him?" She struggled to keep her voice down. Struggled to keep the anger and disappoint-ment from letting loose the scream that rose in her throat.

"You wouldn't understand."

"Try me!" Annie knotted her hands in her lap. "Is he trouble? Is he abusive or cruel? Are you afraid of him?"

"No!"

"Is he married?"

"Of course not!"

"Then there's no excuse for this, Sierra! You don't have a man's baby and not tell him!"

Sierra crossed her arms and sniffled.

Annie drew a deep breath, then three more. She had to calm down or they'd wake Ryder.

"We've done all right, haven't we?" A tear sparkled on Sierra's lower lashes. "I know it's been hard, and you've gone to a lot of trouble for me, but we've managed okay."

"The man has a child he doesn't know about. Cowboy or not, he deserves to know."

"I know that, okay?" she said on a choked sob. "I know. I just couldn't tell him. I couldn't, Annie!"

Annie sucked in a breath and blew it out slowly, then flipped on the dim reading light. They needed to talk this out. Calmly. She drew air into her lungs one more time. Two.

"Come on. Come sit. Talk to me."

Sierra dropped into the recliner across from her. The sound of her weeping caught at Annie.

Sierra had refused to talk about the relationship when she'd turned up pregnant. Annie hadn't forced it once they'd lost contact with the father. And then Grandpa died, and they were reeling over that loss. Annie'd had her plate full just trying to settle his estate and keep their heads above water.

"I can't believe he found me," Sierra said, whimpering.

Annie frowned. "Found you?"

"I—I didn't give him my real number when we parted that summer."

"Why not?"

Sierra shrugged.

"I don't understand." Did she feel ambivalent toward Luke the way Annie had felt toward John? "You didn't care for him? Didn't want to see him again?" But that made no sense. Sierra had been despondent when she'd returned from the trip. Annie had suspected she was lovesick even before she'd known about the pregnancy.

"I loved him. Don't you see?"

"No, I don't. It doesn't make sense."

"I didn't want to be in love! Not with him or anyone else. It never would've worked out. It never does."

"Of course it does."

"Look at Mom. Good grief, Annie, love only made her miserable. Why would I want any part of that?"

It was so similar to what she'd thought earlier about Dylan. How he'd been hurt by Merilee and was afraid to love again. How had she missed in her own sister what had been so obvious in Dylan?

"I didn't mean to fall in love with Luke. It was just a fun little summer fling, and then next thing I knew, I was in too deep, and I couldn't make the feelings go away. It was all my fault."

Annie softened at her sister's sorrow. "Not *all* your fault, honey."

"I pushed him too far. When the mission trip was over, I decided that was going to be it. A clean cut. Better I break it off than have him hit the trail later. I gave him a fake address and phone number so he couldn't find me."

She wiped her face. "And then I found out I was pregnant. What was I supposed to do?"

"Oh, Sierra." She'd been so young, only sixteen. "I wish you'd told me."

Sierra looked across the space, her face looking older than its twenty years. "You can't fix everything, Annie."

Annie leaned forward, planted her elbows on her bare knees. Maybe not. But she could help Sierra figure out where to go from here. She remembered Luke's words on the porch. He'd said he loved Sierra. Annie didn't know how that was possible after almost five years, but then, what did she know about love? According to her "Dear Annie" readers, not much.

"Has he been looking for you all this time?"

Sierra shrugged. "He didn't at first. He said he felt guilty and figured I did too. But then he started looking for me and couldn't find me. When he came here, he stumbled across your column, saw your byline, and remembered I had a sister named Annie. He asked Dylan about us."

Dylan? It would only be a matter of time before he put two and two together. "Dylan knows about you and Luke?"

Sierra shook her head. "He didn't say anything to Dylan. He only found out you had a sister named Sierra, and then he knew how to find me."

Annie thought the guy must either be crazy in love or just plain crazy to keep looking. Either way he had to be told about Ryder. He might even want a part in Ryder's life.

"You have to tell him."

Sierra's head snapped up. "No. I don't have to tell him. You stay out of this, Annie."

How could Sierra be so stubborn? So wrong? "He deserves to know. Ryder's his *child*. What if someone tried to keep Ryder from you?"

"This is none of your business. Stay out of it for once, Annie." Her voice was cold and hard. She nailed Annie with a look. "I mean it."

"What if he tells Dylan, have you thought of that? It won't take Dylan long to remember you have a son just about the right age to be Luke's."

"He won't tell Dylan. I made Luke promise not to tell him about us."

Annie rolled her eyes. "A promise. I'm sure he'd never go back on his word."

"That's for me to worry about, Annie."

"I *would* be worried if I were you."

"I'm not telling Luke. So you can get off the throttle. My son is a happy, well-adjusted little boy. He's doing just fine without a father. Luke would leave, just like Daddy did, and where would that leave Ryder?"

"Sierra . . ."

"Think about it, Annie. Isn't it better to never have had a father than to be abandoned by the one who was supposed to love you?"

Annie hated to admit it, but Sierra had a point. Didn't she know as well as anyone what that felt like? They both did. It left a child feeling worthless. She didn't want that for Ryder.

"What if it didn't turn out that way?" Annie said. "What if Luke wanted to be a dad? What if he stuck around and made Ryder's life better?"

"He won't. I know him, and you don't." Sierra popped up from the recliner, leaving it rocking frantically in the dark, quiet room. "This is not your secret to tell, so you just stay out of it, Annie. I can handle my own life."

Annie watched Sierra stalk down the darkened hallway, heard her shut the door quietly behind her, and wondered how their lives had gotten so out of control.

Dear Scared in Saco,

Whoever said we have nothing to fear but fear itself has never been in love.

30

The jukebox cranked out a new tune as Dylan sank into a seat between his brother and Wade. He'd had to persuade Luke to come. The kid seemed down in the dumps lately, though he refused to say why. Maybe it was a girl from back home. Maybe he was homesick.

Beside him, Wade was watching Abigail perform a line dance with Shay to the snappy tune they'd selected. Shay looked like she'd rather be riding atop a saddle of burrs than learning a line dance.

"Where're the kiddos?" Dylan asked. Maybe he'd ask Maddy to dance, get his mind off his troubles.

"Miss Lucy's got 'em."

So much for that.

Luke picked at a thread on his cuff, looking like he'd rather be cleaning out a barn full of moldy stalls.

"Why don't you find a dancing partner?" Dylan said to Luke, scoping out the room. He nodded toward the wall. "That one's got her eye on you."

Luke looked, then shrugged. "I was thinking about heading back, actually. Could you get a ride if I take your truck?"

"Sure, I'll run him home," Wade said.

"Great."

Dylan fished for his keys, frowning. Luke hadn't even given the pretty blonde a second glance. "You sure?"

"Think I'll take a ride on one of your horses, if you don't mind. There's a little daylight left."

"Help yourself."

He watched Luke skirt the tables and leave the restaurant, then his eyes darted toward the far wall where Annie usually sat. The tables were filled, but Annie was nowhere to be found. Now that she and Oakley had split up, he didn't expect he'd see her around here much. Wouldn't see her much at all now that she'd lost her column. It was only a matter of time before she finished with Braveheart, and then he'd only see her at church. He told himself he was glad. He'd let his feelings get out of hand.

"So," Wade said. "You're dateless tonight, huh?"

Dylan shrugged, looking around. "Plenty of fillies to while away the night with."

Wade's lips twitched, but Dylan wasn't in the mood to guess why. He took a swig of his drink instead.

"And yet, here you sit."

Dylan opened the snack menu and pretended to check it over. He didn't want to talk about women. Especially one particular woman. A woman who was more present, though she wasn't here, than any woman in the room.

"Guess you heard about Annie and John Oakley," Wade said.

"Yup."

He couldn't forget the way their eyes had locked the night before. It had taken everything in him not to pull her into his arms and make her remember the passion between them. If he couldn't forget it, why should he let her?

"Something going on there?"

"Nope."

Wade smirked. "Really."

Dylan clenched his jaw. Fact was, he was coming to the conclusion that he'd already let things get too far with Annie. His heart ached when he thought of her. He was starting to wonder if he was in love with her.

The thought darted straight toward his heart and pierced it dead center. Bull's-eye. There was no wondering about it. He had fallen in love with her. Somehow. Somewhere along the way. He hadn't meant for it to happen, sure hadn't wanted it.

"Nothing to say?"

He had to forget about Annie. But saying it and doing it were two different things, and he couldn't seem to get any fire behind the idea.

"Moving on to greener pastures," Dylan said.

Too bad no one else could hold a candle to Annie.

"You know," Wade said. "Gonna say something here."

Dylan scowled. "You have to?"

"I'm remembering a night in my barn a couple years ago when you had a few words for me."

"That was different. You and Abigail were meant to be. Just had your foolish pride standing in the way."

"I've seen the way you look at her, the way she looks at you."

The thought made his limbs go weak.

"She's free from Oakley. There's nothing standing in your way now. Nothing but your fear."

Dylan ground his teeth together. He'd already relived the whole Merilee episode with Annie, really didn't want to go there with Wade too. His friend knew better than anyone what she'd put him through.

"She's not Merilee, buddy. Sometimes you just have to cowboy up and take a chance, that's all."

"Are we done now?"

Abigail approached and pulled Wade from his seat. "Come on, handsome."

Wade took her hand and gave Dylan a pointed look over his shoulder. *All this could be yours, too, if you just laid down that fear of yours*, his eyes seemed to say.

Yeah, buddy, I get it.

Dear Anxious,

You can't control your boyfriend or anyone else. Except your-
self, if you're lucky.

31

*T*he next week Annie stood in the middle of the pasture working
with Braveheart on the long line. A single line had caused the
horse to turn inside, following her voice rather than circling. So
she'd put another line around his body, keeping it high, above his
hocks, to keep him in square. It had taken awhile for him to adapt to
the extra line, but he was coming along.

"That's it, buddy, you're doing great."

She wished things were going as well with Sierra. She'd been
torn about keeping Ryder from Luke. She'd even considered an
ultimatum: either Sierra told Luke the truth or she would. But
Annie could never follow through on that threat.

Besides, maybe her sister was right. Ryder *was* doing fine, and what if Luke only hurt him? Still, she couldn't escape the fact that it just felt wrong.

Fortunately, between work and trying to find another part-time job, Annie had been home to do little other than sleep. And mercifully, Luke hadn't been around when she'd come to work with Braveheart.

"How's it going?" Dylan asked, climbing the fence. He waited to approach until she directed Braveheart to stop. The nape of Dylan's hair was damp, his sleeves rolled up on his arms.

"I was wondering where you were." She'd been hoping he wouldn't show up. Being with him only made her feel guilty.

"Miss me?"

"Hmmph." She wasn't willing to admit, even to herself, that he might be right. "He's doing better than last week, don't you think?"

"Sure is." His eyes twinkled, and she told herself it was because he was pleased with Braveheart.

He talked to the horse and patted his neck, but when he looked at her, she read the admiration on his face.

"You added a second lunge line. Very clever."

The compliment warmed her more than it should. "It keeps him in line."

He winked. "And aren't you good at that."

She notched her chin up, ignoring the flutter in her stomach. "Someone has to do it."

He grinned.

Maybe spilling his heart about Merilee had shifted something in him. He was right back to the old Dylan. Maybe he felt safer behind his Casanova façade, and frankly, it was easier for her too. So long as he kept his distance.

Her phone vibrated in her pocket, and Annie checked the screen. It was Sierra's school. She frowned.

"Go ahead. I've got Braveheart."

"Thanks." She answered the phone.

"Miss Wilkerson? This is Elaine Conroy from the registrar's office at MSU. How are you today?"

"I'm fine, thanks."

"I've been trying to reach Sierra Wilkerson to let her know tomorrow is the last day for registration. You're listed as a contact, so I was wondering if you might pass that along?"

"She hasn't registered?"

"No, ma'am. I see she's only got five classes left. Is she planning to attend this fall?"

"Yes, she is."

"Well, she'll want to come to the registrar's office tomorrow. Online registration is closed and classes start on Monday. As it is, she may have difficulty scheduling her remaining classes."

"I'll let her know. Thanks so much for calling."

Annie pocketed her phone. What in the world? Annie had been reminding her for weeks, but with the distraction of Luke's arrival, she hadn't double-checked. Sierra must've forgotten.

"Everything okay?"

Annie sighed. "Sierra. I don't know what I'm going to do with that girl." She had half a mind to call her now. But she needed to handle this face-to-face, and she needed some time to cool her heels.

"Anything I can do?"

"Not unless you want to nag a twenty-year-old into registering for classes."

He gave that crooked grin and his dimples appeared. "Not my specialty."

Annie couldn't think about Braveheart anymore. She needed to get home and deal with Sierra. "Would you mind if we wrap it up?"

"Sure." He took Braveheart's lines and led him back to the barn.

"What a week. What a month," Annie said as she unclipped the lunge lines from the bridle and handed them to Dylan. "I just need to get her through one more semester, and she'll be on her way."

"You sure take on a lot."

"She's my sister. Besides, I promised my grandfather."

She'd never told anyone, not even Shay, about the deathbed promise. She wondered why she'd told Dylan. Maybe it was the connection between their grandfathers. Maybe it was because he'd opened up about his heartbreak.

"Promised him what?"

Annie patted Braveheart, then followed Dylan to the tack room. "Sierra's always been a little too much like our mother. Grandpa was worried about her, especially after she turned up pregnant. When he got sick, I promised him I wouldn't let anything happen to her. That I'd help her get on her own two feet and see her settled."

He hung the lines on the hook. "That's a lot to take on. You were young."

"Not really. I was twenty."

"Same as Sierra now."

The realization took her back. But it was hardly the same. Annie had been independent and responsible at twenty. She'd already started her business and owned a home.

"She'll figure it out."

"I hope so."

"She gonna bring her car over soon? I feel guilty taking your time and giving you nothing in return."

Annie barely stopped the flinch. Sierra didn't need to be anywhere near here, not until Luke left.

"It's still making noises?"

"Yeah. She'll bring it by before college starts. Otherwise it's going to break down halfway between Bozeman and here, and then she'll be up a creek."

He walked her to her truck. He'd only been with her ten minutes and she'd been dumping on him the whole time. He wasn't Miss Lucy, for heaven's sake.

She turned at the driver's door, contrite. "Sorry."

He cocked a smile. "For what?"

"Dumping on you."

"I dumped on you last time."

Their eyes locked. His brown eyes grew serious. They were the color of cocoa in the evening light, deep and warm. His hand lifted, reached toward her. Then he dropped it, stuffing it into his pocket instead.

She wondered what he'd had in mind before he thought better of it. She wondered if it was the fear in his heart that held him back. She supposed it didn't matter now.

Besides, she had her hands way too full with Sierra to worry about what Dylan might be thinking. She broke eye contact and slipped into the truck.

When Annie got home, however, Sierra wasn't there. Annie started supper and went to work on the growing pile of laundry. The clothes were in the dryer, and the chicken was in the oven by the time Sierra strolled in with Ryder.

"Aunt Annie!" Ryder hugged her around the legs, his cowboy hat lurching back. She'd hardly had any time with the boy the past couple of weeks.

"Hey, Bed Head. I've missed you."

"I spent the day with Miss Lucy! Wanna play Chutes and Ladders?"

"Sure, after supper. Why don't you go outside and swing for a while. I need to talk to your mama, okay?" She wondered where Sierra had been if Miss Lucy had been babysitting.

Ryder had run off by the time Sierra entered the kitchen, her defined brows popping up. "What'd I do now?"

"Where've you been?"

"Relax, I just went to Bridgett's house. No chance of seeing Luke there, and I'm dying of boredom here." She crossed her arms.

This wasn't how Annie wanted to broach the conversation about school, with Sierra already on the defense.

She turned down the rice and faced her sister. "I was hoping to talk about school. The registrar's office called today."

Sierra lifted her chin. "And?"

"They said you need to register tomorrow—it's the last day. Classes start Monday." She locked her lips into a calm smile, determined not to let this spill into another pointless speech.

"I know that, Annie."

"Do you know that you won't graduate in December if any of those classes are full?"

"I believe you've made me aware of that. Several times."

Annie frowned at her. "Then what's the holdup? You're only a few months from your degree; why are you risking everything? Soon you'll be able to get a job doing just what you want. Have you even checked with Martha about babysitting?"

Sierra leaned against the door frame and gave a wry laugh.

"What does that mean?"

She waited, but Sierra only pressed her lips together.

"So you'll register for your classes tomorrow, and hopefully they'll all be open. It'll get you out of the house too. Doesn't a trip to Bozeman sound nice? I suppose I could call Martha for you."

When the buzzer sounded, Annie turned off the stovetop. The chicken still had a few more minutes, so she reset the timer.

"I'm not registering for classes, Annie."

She turned. Sierra had her elfin chin up, that stubborn look on her face. "You have to. Tomorrow's the last day."

Sierra straightened. "I'm quitting school."

Annie's stomach dropped to her toes. "What? Don't be ridiculous! You have one semester left."

"I don't want to be a journalist anymore."

"You don't want to— That's crazy, Sierra. You've been in school for three and a half years! It's taken most of what Grandpa left us to get you through—"

Sierra whirled around. "I knew you'd bring that up!"

Annie followed her into the living room. "You're being unreasonable."

"I'm trying to tell you what I want. I want to be a photographer."

Annie rolled her eyes. "A photographer!"

"Remember that guy I was seeing—that friend of Dylan's from the rodeo? Well, he's interning as a photographer in Texas, and he taught me a lot while he was here. That's what we were doing, why we were out all night. He showed me how to take night pictures and—"

"See?" She pointed at Annie's face. "That's why I didn't tell you. But it doesn't matter what you think, Annie. I'm an adult, and I can make my own decisions, and I'm not going back to school!"

"You have a child to support, are you forgetting about that? We don't have the money for another four-year program or even a two-year program."

"I have other options, if you'd just listen. I have a friend who's a photographer. He has a studio and everything, and he's willing to let me intern. He thinks I've got talent."

"You are one semester away—"

"From a degree I don't want!"

"Well, it would've been nice if you'd have figured that out thirty thousand dollars ago!"

Sierra growled, turning down the hall.

Annie followed, stopping at Sierra's bedroom door. "It's just one semester. Can't you just suck it up so you'll have a degree to fall back on if this photography thing doesn't work?"

"You're already expecting me to fail. Well, I won't. I have a plan, Annie. Believe it or not, I'm capable of making a plan and carrying it out."

Like her plan for a journalism degree? Not to mention all the jobs she'd been fired from. Annie clamped her mouth shut.

"You think I'm a failure."

"No, I don't."

"Aren't I a good mom? Haven't I done a good job with Ryder?"

"You're a great mom. But you need a way to make a living. A degree would give you that. Just sign up for the classes, Sierra, and get your degree! Later you can—"

"You're not my mom, Annie! I'm so tired of you trying to control me. I feel trapped, and I'm sick of it!"

"Well, you *should* feel grateful."

"Stop telling me how to feel!" Sierra's face bloomed with color. She whipped out her suitcase and jerked a drawer open. "I have to get out of here. I need to be alone." She shut the door in Annie's face.

"You can't risk being seen in town."

"Again—none of your business!"

Annie returned to the kitchen, her legs shaking. She turned off the buzzer that she hadn't noticed until now and removed the chicken. The smell of oregano and thyme turned her stomach.

Mechanically, she checked on Ryder, who was on his tire swing, then cut open the hot bag of rice and dumped it into a bowl. She set the table. For three? For one? Where was Sierra planning to go? Probably back to Bridgett's house. Maybe Annie could talk some sense into her before she left.

She set the table for three and was putting the food out when Sierra entered with her suitcase and Ryder's Batman bag. Without a word she carried the bags out the back door and knelt down to talk to Ryder at the swing. A moment later he climbed down and followed Sierra around the side of the house.

Not even a good-bye? She obviously wasn't planning to return before tomorrow. When would she convince Sierra to register? She had to try one more time or at least confirm Sierra would be home tomorrow.

Annie was walking out of the house as Sierra tried to start her car, but it wasn't turning over.

Thank You, Jesus. A reprieve. She drew a breath and let it out, but her sister and Ryder continued to sit there. Well, let her stew. Maybe she'd calm down and be able to discuss this rationally. Annie was glad her own keys were safely tucked in her pocket. Sierra was too angry to ask for them.

Annie went back inside. She wasn't hungry anymore. She covered the chicken and rice and placed it in the warm oven, then headed for the shower. She'd feel better after the day's dirt and grime were gone.

After the shower she dressed in a pair of shorts and a T-shirt.

The house was still quiet, and a peek out the window revealed Sierra and Ryder on the porch steps. She heard his low chatter and Sierra's monosyllabic responses.

Maybe they were all ready for supper now. Her own stomach had settled. She was removing the food from the oven when she heard the rumble of a vehicle in the drive. It suddenly occurred to her that Sierra wasn't just cooling off, but waiting for Bridgett.

Annie set down the food and darted for the front door. Ryder was climbing into a blue truck, Sierra on his heels. She didn't recognize the truck or the man in the driver's seat.

Annie scrambled across the porch. "Wait, Sierra!"

Her sister climbed in.

"Wait. Let's talk about this." Annie's heart pounded as her bare feet took the steps.

"I'll call you later."

"Do you even know this guy?" she called.

The door slammed, and the truck swung around, offering her a full view of Sierra's stubborn face. "Give me some credit, Annie," she said through the window.

And then the truck was rumbling down the drive. A man she didn't know, taking her sister and nephew who knew where. Annie put her hands on her heated cheeks.

Oh, God, keep them safe. What can I do now? What should I do?

But there was nothing to do. The truck was already turning onto the main road, headed toward town, of all places. She couldn't call the sheriff. Sierra was an adult, and she'd left willingly.

Annie staggered up the porch steps and back into the house.

Dear Uncertain,

I don't know that love is something you can define with words, but when you find it, you'll know.

32

*A*nnie paced the house, not settling anywhere, like an antsy horse. Where had she gone wrong with Sierra? She'd known the girl had gotten off course, not attending church regularly, getting fired from jobs.

But this.

Quitting school when she was so close, completely changing her career path, wasting all that money. What was she thinking? And now she'd run off with some man Annie had never seen, taking her four-year-old child with her.

Lord, help her. Help me. I don't know what to do with her. Haven't I tried to keep her in line, tried to help her toward a successful future? And all for her to throw it away?

It was as if Sierra were twelve instead of twenty. But there was more at stake than pierced ears or a bad grade on an English test.

She tried Sierra's phone, but it rang through to voice mail. She took a deep breath.

"Sierra, call me. Please. We need to talk." She closed the phone and went back to pacing. She wasn't sure how much time had passed when she heard a car door slam.

Sierra! Thank God. She'd come back.

Annie ran to the front door and flung it open. But it wasn't her sister jogging up the porch steps. It was Dylan. Her hopes shrank even as her heart fluttered beneath her ribs. She sank against the door frame as the adrenaline rush faded.

"Thought I might take a look at Sierra's car yet tonight and see if—" Dylan pulled his hat. "What's wrong?"

"Sierra . . . She just . . . Some cowboy took her and Ryder, and I don't know where they went or who they're with. And she's quitting college."

Dylan settled his hands on her shoulders. "Easy now, you're shaking."

Annie turned back into the house and Dylan followed, shutting the door.

Between the Luke debacle and the news Sierra had just spilled, she felt like their lives had spun out of control.

She palmed her cheeks and found them wet. "How did things become such a mess? I feel like someone lit a stick of dynamite under our lives."

Dylan pulled her to the couch. "Come on, honey. Sit down, tell me what happened."

Annie followed his lead, glad to let someone else take control for a change.

"First of all," he said, "are they in danger? Do we need to call the sheriff?"

Annie shook her head. "I don't know. She tried to leave and her car wouldn't start. They were on the porch, she was mad at me, and I thought she was just blowing off steam, but then some truck showed up and took off with them."

"Tell me exactly what happened. Did she get in willingly?"

Annie nodded. "I called for her to come back and asked if she even knew who that was, and she said to give her some credit." Annie sniffled. "Then they were gone."

"Okay, so she must've called the guy to come for her, right?"

Annie nodded.

"She must know him fairly well then. She's a good mom. She wouldn't put Ryder in jeopardy."

"Not intentionally. But what if she doesn't know him as well as she thinks?" Annie didn't even want to think about what could happen. "If he were a local, I'd have recognized him. What if he's just some drifter she doesn't really know?"

"What did he look like?"

Annie shrugged. "I couldn't see him through the windows. He wore a cowboy hat, maybe average sized?"

"That's half the men in Park County. What about the truck?"

"It was a blue Dodge. Old, maybe an early '90s model."

"Doesn't sound familiar."

More tears leaked from her eyes. Dylan put his arm around her. "Come on, Annie, that doesn't mean anything. Sierra's the friendly sort, she knows a lot of people. It might be someone from college."

That was true. She didn't know many of Sierra's college friends, since MSU was in Bozeman.

"How long ago did they leave?"

"Twenty minutes? Half an hour?"

"Maybe he took her to a friend's house."

"Bridgett!" Annie retrieved her phone and dialed. Bridgett answered in two rings. "Hey, Bridge, this is Annie. Is Sierra there?"

"Hi, Annie. No, not here . . ."

"Have you heard from her in the last half hour?"

"What's going on?"

Annie filled her in. Bridgett didn't know anyone with a truck of that description. Annie asked her to call if she heard from Sierra and closed the phone.

"No luck." She clasped her trembling hands in her lap. What if that man did something to Sierra or Ryder?

Oh, God, I'll never forgive myself. Why did I have to be so pushy? Please protect them and bring them home safely. Why had she let things escalate? She knew better.

Dylan turned her face toward his. He dashed away fresh tears with his thumbs. "Hey, now . . . they'll be fine. Sierra's a grown woman, and she called for the ride. I'm sure it's a college friend or something."

"But she was so mad . . ." Would Sierra do something foolish in her anger? She could be so impulsive.

"Want to talk about it?"

Annie filled him in on their argument. "She said I wasn't her mom and she was sick of me trying to control her. I just want what's best for her. Why can't she see that?" Fresh tears surfaced and Annie covered her face.

"Aw, come here." He drew her into his arms.

She turned her face into his chest and clutched his shirt. It felt so good to have his strong arms around her. To lean on someone else. Not just someone else. Dylan. She felt his fingers in her hair, and that felt good too.

"You have been a mom to her," he whispered. "She was only sixteen when your grandpa died, and she was pregnant. She needed you."

"I've done my best." She sniffled. "I really have. I love her so much. Where did I go wrong?"

"You've done great."

"But now I've lost her."

"No, you haven't. She's just older, wants her independence. Maybe it's time to let go a bit, let her make her own decisions. Every good parent has to let go at some point."

His gentle tone made the unwanted words go down easier. "I failed my grandpa."

"No, honey. You helped your sister get on her feet. Helped her raise her son. You've gone above and beyond. You can only do so much. At some point you have to let her spread her wings and fly."

"But she flew straight into a stranger's truck."

She heard his low chuckle rumble through his chest. "You have to trust her, sugar. I'm sure it's hard, but put her in God's hands. He can handle her. My mom told me that when I left home, her prayer life increased exponentially."

It wasn't what she wanted to hear, but she couldn't deny that Sierra was a legal adult. Somehow her sister had grown up right under her nose, and Annie had failed to notice.

Have I been holding on too tight, God? Is it time to turn her over to You?

One thing was sure. Her way wasn't working. She'd pushed and prodded, and all she'd done was get Sierra's back up. Sierra was the same age Annie had been when she'd taken Sierra into her home.

Hadn't Annie been capable of making her own decisions? So her sister was a little flighty, a little too much like their mother. That didn't take away her right to be her own person, to make her own choices. Even if they weren't always the wisest ones.

Annie drew in a breath, taking in the scent of musk and leather that was all Dylan. She became aware of his hand on her shoulder, caressing. Aware of the steady beat of his heart under her ear. It was rhythmic, hypnotizing.

She should pull away. Thank him for talking her off the ledge. But she couldn't deny the urge to stay put.

Just a few more seconds wouldn't hurt. She was only accepting his comfort, and it felt so good to be in his arms, to feel safe, protected, cared for. She closed her eyes and drew in another breath of him. His shirt felt soft against her cheek. It was damp with her tears, but he didn't seem bothered that she'd sniveled all over him.

She loosened her hold on his shirt and smoothed it down. Against her ear his heart thumped faster at her touch.

"Annie . . ." Her name rumbled through his chest and sent a shiver down her spine. He tightened his arms around her, settled them back against the sofa, dropped a kiss on top of her head.

Chills raced down her arms at his touch and she burrowed in tighter. Sweet heaven. She wanted to sink into his embrace and forget about the rest of the world awhile. He felt so good. So strong and solid.

He put his hand against her cheek. His palm was rough and cool against her heated face. His thumb moved lazily.

Then he pulled back.

Not yet. Just a little longer.

But instead of setting her away, he framed her face. His eyes caught and held hers. Brown, like melted chocolate, and as somber as she'd ever seen them. Something else was in there too, something deep and unfathomable, something mesmerizing.

He pulled her close and his lips closed over hers. They moved slowly, softly.

She melted into his arms, touched his face, felt the scrape of his jaw against her palm. Images flashed to her mind. Their last kiss, their playful interlude with the hose. The sight of him with baby Cody in his arms. The vulnerability on his face as he spoke of his lost love.

The images converged with the feelings his kiss provoked, building inside her. When he deepened the kiss, she hung on tight and went right with him, down under the surface.

"Annie . . . ," he murmured between kisses.

The feel of her name on his lips was intoxicating.

"Annie . . ."

When he pulled away, it was only to kiss her closed eyes, her nose. Her heart pounded like a hundred mustangs running wild across her chest, and when she opened her eyes, she wanted to drown in those puppy dog eyes of his.

"Annie . . . I love you."

The words pulled her toward the surface. Toward reality. It was all coming back now, trickling in . . .

Sierra and Ryder.

Luke.

And the secret she kept from Dylan.

What was she doing?

"I've been afraid," he said. "Afraid to feel like this again. I've fought it hard, but I just can't anymore. I finally found a woman worth risking my heart for, and she's you, Annie." His thumbs moved over her cheeks. "You do things to me no woman has ever done—"

"No, Dylan, don't—"

He shook his head, and a lock of hair fell over his forehead. "I'm not just talking about chemistry. You stole my heart." He smiled in that charming way of his, his eyes gleaming. "And I don't want it back, Annie. You hear me? I don't want it back."

Her heart twisted. She shook her head, pulled away. "We can't."

He reached out, fingered a lock of her hair. "You care for me too, don't deny it."

The words might've struck her as cocky once upon a time. Now they just pricked her heart with their truth. She couldn't, *wouldn't*, lie to him. She was stuck. He'd held out his heart to her, and now she had to stomp all over it. Just like Merilee had done.

And the real zinger was . . . she loved him too. If she didn't know it before this moment, she knew it now. She'd rather face a pit of rattlesnakes than break his heart.

"Annie?"

She looked away, unable to bear the confusion in his eyes. Down at her trembling fingers. "I can't, Dylan. I'm so sorry . . ."

His hand closed over hers. "Is it . . . Are you afraid I can't commit? Because I can, Annie. I know you haven't seen that side of me, but I'm a loyal man."

She shook her head. Even if he weren't Ryder's uncle, he would always be a cowboy. How many strikes could one man have against him? "It's just . . . impossible between us."

His hand moved over hers enticingly. Making her lose her train of thought, drawing her eyes back to his. He'd pull her right back in if she didn't move and fast.

Annie stood and crossed the room.

"What do you mean, impossible?"

She opened her mouth, but the explanation died in her throat. She couldn't tell him about Luke and Sierra, about Ryder. That wasn't her secret to tell. Sierra might be an adult, but she was still her sister, and Annie wouldn't betray her.

He stood. "Impossible how?"

She took another step back, needing space. "I just . . . It won't work, Dylan. I can't really explain it, and I'm sorry for that, but you just have to—" The lump in her throat choked off anything else she might've said.

"We can take it slow."

She shook her head.

"I'm in no hurry, Annie. As slow as you like, and we'll see what—"

"No, Dylan."

His brows pulled low, his eyes turned fervent as he approached.

She backed up, but he followed her step for step. Her back hit the wall. Dylan continued until he was a breath away. His eyes held hers prisoner, locking onto hers tighter than shackles.

He palmed the wall over her head. "Say it then. Tell me you don't care. That there's nothing between us. Say it, Annie."

Her lungs froze, the air inside them seeping out through her parted lips. Those words wouldn't come out. They were a lie.

She wanted to say the other words, the ones he wanted to hear. She longed to see his frown turn to dimples when she confessed her love for him. But she thought of Sierra, and the words crumbled in her throat.

She dropped her gaze. "What you want is impossible," she whispered. "I'm sorry."

She felt his warm breath fan her face. She would not look up. She would not reach out and touch his face one last time. She clenched her fists at her sides.

"I need to be alone now." The words scraped across her throat.

Please, God, let him leave. Before I do something to betray my sister. Before I mess things up more than I already have.

He hadn't moved. She couldn't breathe with him so close. Couldn't think. "Please, Dylan. Just go." Her eyes burned at the words.

A heartbeat later he lowered his arm, straightened. His sigh was loud in the quietness of the house. "All right, Annie. If that's the way you want it."

He paused a beat as if waiting for her to change her mind.

She bit her lip before she could cry out that no, that's not the way she wanted it at all. She wanted him to wrap her up in his arms and never let go.

But then he stepped back, moved away. He opened the door and walked through it. She didn't breathe again, didn't let the tears go until she heard the quiet click of the door closing behind him.

Dear A Mess in Missoula,

    *Change is never easy, but the hardest kind of transformation
is the kind that happens on the inside.*

33

Annie took another spin through town, this time checking the café parking lot and the side streets to the east. There was no sign of Sierra. She had to face it. Her sister wasn't in Moose Creek.

She turned into a parking slot in front of the Mocha Moose. After last night's sleep, or lack thereof, she was in desperate need of caffeine.

She was leaving the shop with her cup of java when she ran smack into Miss Lucy on the sidewalk. She steadied the cup, preventing a spill.

"Sorry!" they said simultaneously.

"Oh, honey," Miss Lucy said after they'd steadied each other. "I heard about Sierra. Have you heard from her?"

Seeing the compassion in Miss Lucy's eyes, Annie's eyes stung, threatening to spill over right there on Main Street. She shook her head.

"Come with me." Miss Lucy led her to the Doll House and ushered her into the shop. The scent of new fabric and glue permeated the store, and the blast of air-conditioning made her shiver.

"Sit down now. Tell me what happened."

Annie sat and her nervous energy spilled out in the form of words. She didn't stop with the story of Sierra's leaving. It flowed right into Dylan's proclamation of love, and that led right into Sierra's secret. Annie spilled it all, trusting Miss Lucy implicitly, her thoughts gushing out like water from a broken jar.

"Oh my," Miss Lucy said when she'd finally run out of words. "What a mess."

Hearing it all spoken at once only helped Annie see it afresh, and Miss Lucy was right. "Why is this happening? My sister is missing, and my life is falling apart at the seams."

"I know it feels that way. But have faith. It'll all work out as God intends."

"I'm so worried about Sierra and Ryder. I'll never forgive myself if something happens to them."

Miss Lucy took her hand. "I've been praying for her since I heard. I'm sure she's fine. She can be a little hasty, but she's got a good head on her shoulders. She wouldn't endanger her boy."

Annie hoped she was right. As impulsive as Sierra could be, she'd never been reckless with Ryder.

"About that other thing . . ."

"Other thing?"

"Your young man."

Dylan. Annie slanted a grin at Miss Lucy. "He's hardly that. I just told you about Luke and Ryder. Have you ever seen such a dead-end relationship as mine and Dylan's?"

"Luke's on his way back to Texas even as we speak. I ran into Dylan this morning. He's the one who asked me to pray for Sierra— and for you."

That knowledge warmed her through. "But he and Luke are brothers. We couldn't hide the truth forever. And even if it wasn't for that, you know how I feel about cowboys."

Miss Lucy's lips pursed, accentuating the lines fanning outward. "Yes, I do."

The weight of the last twenty-four hours pressed down on Annie, crushing her. Her shoulders slumped with the burden. "Despite all my efforts to guide Sierra, I failed. Despite my determination not to fall for a cowboy, I fell. I did the one thing I never wanted to do and *didn't* do the one thing I promised to do. All my efforts to keep Sierra from becoming like our mother, and look at me . . . *I'm* the one who's become her."

"Oh, honey, you couldn't be further from the truth."

"I'm head over heels for a cowboy, just like her."

"Maybe so, but that's not uncommon. Let's face it, you can't throw a rock around here without hitting one."

"Are we destined to make our parents' mistakes? I knew the truth, I guarded myself against it, and it still happened."

"What truth do you mean?"

"You know, Miss Lucy. Cowboys. They're unfaithful. They leave. Sure, they can be charming and hardworking and otherwise fine, upstanding citizens, but put them in a thousand-square-foot house with a wife and two kids and see how fast they beat a path for the door."

"Oh, honey."

"It's *true*."

Miss Lucy shook her head. Her eyes looked large and sad behind her Coke-bottle glasses. "It's not true. And when you talk like that, it hurts my feelings. My dear Murray was a cowboy, and he was the most faithful man that ever walked God's green earth."

Annie felt a stab of guilt. She wouldn't argue with Miss Lucy, but that was one man. So Miss Lucy had found the anomaly. That didn't mean anything.

"You witnessed a string of deadbeats parading through your life when you were young, and yes, they were cowboys. I understand how it might make an impression. But it's a false impression."

Annie locked the denial behind tight lips. She respected Miss Lucy, but the woman was wrong. Some stereotypes were stereo-types for a reason.

"It's not a matter of cowboys, dear. Your mother, God rest her soul, had awful poor judgment in men. If there was a loser in a fifty-mile radius, she'd have him wrapped around her little finger in five seconds flat."

"You can't tell me most cowboys are faithful. Every last one of those men betrayed my mom."

Miss Lucy tilted her head, her face gentling. "Like you did John? Oh, I know it was only a kiss, honey, but it was a small betrayal nonetheless."

The woman's words were like a kick in the solar plexus. Annie took a sip of her coffee, trying to soothe the sting. It didn't work.

"I hope you'll forgive me. I didn't mention it to make you feel bad, dear. I only want you to see that everybody makes mistakes. But each person has the right to stand on his own merits, not be herded into some category. You wouldn't want someone to judge you by that one mistake, much less judge a whole segment of the population."

Maybe so, but as she'd said . . . it had only been a kiss. And Annie had realized what she'd done, had felt remorse. That wasn't the same thing. Even her own father had never looked back.

"I see the reluctance on your face. But, Annie, God loves everyone, even cowboys. And He works in their lives just like He works in yours and mine. Who are we to judge?"

No one could accuse Miss Lucy of beating around the bush.

Is that what I've been doing, Lord? Judging people? It was a nasty thought, one she wanted to shrug off as quickly as possible.

The bell rang over the door, and a family entered, their little girl running to the display window and pointing at a prairie doll in a ruffled yellow calico.

Annie stood, trying to shake off the feelings Miss Lucy had dredged up. She tried for a smile, uncertain whether she was grateful for the talk or not.

"I'll let you get to your customer."

"Wait here. It won't take long."

"That's okay, I have some work to do." Inside and out, it would seem.

Annie left the store in a daze. She felt like she'd just had her bell rung, and maybe she had. The rebuke, no matter how gently delivered, had stung.

She got in her car and turned the key. She thought of Dylan and the way she'd perceived him before she'd known him. Yes, her impression of him had changed along the way. She didn't think her feelings could've grown into love otherwise. She'd come to see him as a man who helped his friends. A man who listened, really listened when you talked. Sure, he liked to have fun. Sure, he was a cowboy. But he was unlike any cowboy she'd ever met.

Her eyes fell on the worn copy of *Pride and Prejudice* poking from her purse. Was she like Elizabeth Bennet, judging Dylan the way Elizabeth had judged Mr. Darcy—presuming him to be haughty before she even knew him?

Yes, she was. She was no better than Elizabeth Bennet. One would think she'd read the novel enough times to recognize when prejudice reared its ugly head. Apparently not. She'd judged not only Dylan, but every man in cowboy boots all her life, and had never once considered she might be wrong.

How's that for ironic, Lord? I've been both prideful and prejudiced. No wonder the novel struck a chord with her. How could Dylan even stand her, much less love her?

Annie tore her eyes from the faded cover. *I've been wholly unlovely, God. Forgive me. Help me to see people as they really are and not as I've believed them to be. Help me to see myself for who I really am, not for what I believed myself to be.*

Dear Hesitant in Helena,

Secrets have a way of coming out into the open. Almost always,
they're better told than discovered.

34

D ylan pulled out of his driveway and turned toward Bozeman where Luke would board a plane to Texas. He'd miss his little brother. Luke had been a big help around the ranch. The kid could hold his own in the saddle.

Luke stretched out in the passenger seat. "You've been quiet today."

His brother was one to talk. "A lot on my mind." Dylan couldn't think of anything except Annie lately. All day, moving cattle, all he thought about was Annie. Annie's smile, Annie's touch, Annie's kiss. Annie, Annie, Annie.

And their supposedly impossible relationship.

She just didn't love him, that's what it was. If she felt the way he did, she wouldn't let anything stand between them. And that was the thought that had put a hole in his gut all day.

"Anything you want to talk about?"

"You been watching too many Lifetime movies."

Luke shrugged. "Sometimes it helps."

Dylan knew Sierra hadn't returned. He'd managed to draw that tidbit out of Abigail, who'd heard it from Shay. Annie was probably biting her nails to the quick and wearing holes in her knees. He whispered another prayer for her, for Sierra and the whole mess of their relationship.

As they approached town, he kept his eyes peeled for an old blue Dodge. It was late on Friday, and with the glut of tourists, he couldn't scan fast enough.

"Keep your eyes open for a blue Dodge pickup, would you?"

Luke looked out his window. "What for?"

"Friend of mine, her sister's missing. She took off with some guy."

"What friend?"

He slowed as he went through town. The bank parking lot was empty. Not even John Oakley was working. No blue trucks down Church Street.

"Annie—the woman who helps me with Braveheart." Maybe he should call around. Someone might know something.

"Annie Wilkerson? You mean Sierra's missing?"

"You met her?"

Luke's brows knotted. "She's—What happened? Tell me now."

Dylan frowned at Luke's urgency. "What's going on?"

"Just tell me what happened! Stop the truck."

Dylan gave Luke another look, then pulled into the parallel slot in front of the Mocha Moose.

"Annie and her sister got into it last night, and Sierra took off with some guy in a blue truck."

"A boyfriend?"

Dylan shook his head, eyeing Luke. Something was going on here. "Don't really know. Annie tried calling her sister; no answer though. You know something, Luke? If you have information—"

"No, but we have to find her! Did Annie call the sheriff?"

"Sierra's an adult, and she left of her own free will."

Luke looked out the window. "With a stranger!"

"A stranger to Annie. What's this all about, Luke? I thought I asked you to stay away from Sierra." Last thing he needed was to give Annie another reason to be cross with him.

Luke pressed his lips together. "I don't want to get into it right now. We just need to find her!"

"All right, all right, settle down."

"An old blue truck? You know about everyone in town, don't you?"

"Annie thinks it might be someone from MSU."

"That's in Bozeman, right? We should look there."

"Luke, we don't have time for this. You have a flight in two hours."

"I don't care about my flight. I'm not leaving until we find Sierra."

Dylan looked at his brother's set jaw. His brother who, by all appearances, seemed smitten with the girl. But how was that possible? He'd been in town less than a month. They'd been apart much of the time. He supposed it was possible he'd been seeing Sierra.

"What are you waiting for?"

Dylan put the truck in reverse and pulled onto Main Street. "It'll be a needle in a haystack. Bozeman isn't exactly Moose Creek."

They could drive around the campus, around the housing area.

Most of the students in residence were surely on campus by now. How else could he find that truck?

A service station. His old buddy, the one he got parts from, ran one near the campus. Maybe the guy got it serviced there or filled up there regularly. If he went to MSU, it was likely.

He pulled out his phone.

"Who you calling?"

Dylan held up a finger. "Is Matt in?" he asked when someone answered.

"One minute."

"Calling a buddy of mine over there."

"Hello?"

"Hey, Matt, Dylan Taylor here."

"Dylan, good to hear from you. What's up? Finally ran into a mechanical problem you couldn't fix yourself?"

"No, I need your help with something else. Friend of mine might be in trouble. She took off with a guy in an old blue Dodge, probably early '90s. You work on anything like that? We think the owner is an MSU student."

"Let me check with my mechanics. Hold on a sec."

Dylan pulled onto I-90, heading toward Bozeman. "He's checking."

Luke squirmed in his seat.

The campus community wasn't that big. If he was on campus, maybe they could check on Sierra and get Luke to the airport before his plane left.

Several long minutes later, Matt came back on the line. "You might be in luck. Eddie remembers a truck like that. Guy comes in regular for oil changes. Can't be sure it's him though."

"Can I get an address?"

"Only for you, buddy. You didn't get it here though."

"You have my word."

It took awhile for Matt to look up the address. Once he found it, he rambled it off, along with directions. Luke took it down on the back of an old receipt.

"Thanks, man. Owe you one."

He glanced at the clock. They weren't far from Bozeman now.

"Can't you go faster?"

"I'm already topping the speed limit. Relax. I'm sure she's fine. You wanna tell me what's going on between you two?"

Luke looked out the window where the August brown buttes rolled by. "Not really."

"Suit yourself. But I'm getting you to your flight on time. I know you don't have the money to waste."

The rest of the ride was tense and quiet. When he reached the campus exit, he took the ramp and followed Luke's directions to a neighborhood not far from MSU. He pulled down the street, looking for the right address. The streetlights hadn't come on yet, making the numbers difficult to read in the twilight.

"There's the truck!" Luke said, leaning forward.

It was parked in front of a brown two-story. Dylan pulled up behind it. The house squatted on a corner lot close to the street. A few trees shaded the withered grass, and a set of crumbling porch steps led to the front door.

Luke's seat belt was already off, his door open.

Dylan grabbed his arm. "Let me handle this."

Dylan proceeded up the short walk and onto the porch with Luke following. The front door was open, the sound of a TV commercial leaking out. A window air conditioner hummed from an upstairs window.

A small sign beside the door read *Claybourne Portrait Studio. Use side door.*

Dylan knocked on the screen door. He looked at Luke, whose feet danced beneath him. He was asking for trouble. "Settle down and step aside." He wasn't sure what had gotten into his easygoing brother.

A young man appeared on the other side of the screen. He had a slim build, wore a T-shirt and jeans. His short hair was artfully tousled. "Yeah?"

"Hey," Dylan said. "We're friends of Sierra's. Need to talk to her, if you don't mind."

The guy eyed them. "She know you're coming?"

It was the right place. Dylan smiled, did his best to look harmless, especially with Luke strung tight as a wire beside him. "No, but she won't mind."

Without looking away, the man called over his shoulder. "Sierra . . . some friends here to see you."

A moment later Sierra came into view. She looked perfectly healthy, her auburn hair swept into a ponytail.

She tilted her head, no doubt confused, when she spotted Dylan. She smiled anyway, opening the door. "Hey, Dylan, come on in."

Dylan moved into the living room.

When Sierra saw Luke, she stopped short. Her eyes widened, her jaw went slack. "Luke." She looked between them. "What are you doing here?"

"Who's this guy?" Luke nodded his head toward the guy as he stepped through the door. "Did he hurt you?"

"What do *you* think, dude?" the man said.

Luke was on him before Dylan could move, had him pinned to the wall in one second flat. "You better not have laid a hand on her, that's what I think."

"Stop it, Luke," Sierra said.

Dylan reached for his brother.

Ryder flew into the room. "Look, Mommy!" he said, waving a paper.

Luke's eyes swung toward the boy, the guy's shirt still in his fists.

Sierra's eyes went wide as silver dollars. She looked at Luke, frozen in place. For reasons Dylan didn't understand, the air thickened with tension.

"You have a kid?" Luke said. He loosened his hold on the punk. He moved back, his shoulders drooping.

Sierra's mouth opened. Closed.

Ryder clung to her leg, holding up a drawing. "Look, Mommy."

But she didn't look. Couldn't seem to look at anyone but Luke.

"You have a kid with *him*?" Luke nodded toward the other man, his pain-filled eyes fastened on Sierra's.

The guy pushed Luke away belatedly and straightened his shirt. "He's not mine, dude . . . he's yours."

Dear Muddled,

The messes we make with our lives are like knots of yarn. With enough time, enough patience, most of them can be untangled.

35

Dylan looked between his brother and Sierra as the guy's words registered. It made no sense. How could Luke be Ryder's father?

But Luke had gone still as an August afternoon, and Sierra wasn't denying the crazy words.

"What's going on?" Dylan asked.

"Sierra?" Luke said. His Adam's apple bobbed.

Sierra's mouth worked. Her arm found Ryder and wrapped protectively around his shoulder.

The boy seemed to realize something more important than his picture was going on. He lowered the paper, looking at them.

"Ryder . . . ?" Sierra's voice quavered. "Can you go draw Mommy another picture?"

Dylan looked at the boy closely. Looked at the dark curls at his nape. His wide-set green eyes.

"Come on, buddy," the other man said. "Let's go color. I'll let you have the markers this time."

"Yippee!" Ryder followed him into the next room.

Sierra watched him go. A beat of silence stretched into a long pause. Her face had gone as white as the wall behind her.

"I—I guess we need to talk," Sierra said.

"What's going on, Sierra?" Luke asked.

Dylan stepped toward the door. "I'll just wait in the truck."

He left the house in a daze. Was it possible? He didn't see how. Luke hadn't visited him since he'd moved to Moose Creek, except the one time, and it *had* been several years ago. But he'd only been at his place a few days before leaving for the summer mission trip up in Missoula . . .

He got in the truck and propped his elbow on the windowsill. Was it possible he'd met Sierra there? That they'd fallen in love that summer? But why hadn't she told Luke about the pregnancy? And if Luke cared as much as he seemed to, why hadn't he married her?

The screen door creaked as Luke and Sierra left the house. Sierra folded onto a chair, but Luke remained standing.

Dylan slouched in the seat, trying to make himself inconspicuous. He couldn't help overhearing bits of their conversation.

"Is it true?"

A long pause ensued, and Dylan thought he'd missed the answer.

"Yes," she said finally, her voice wobbling on the word.

Unbelievable. Luke had a son. Dylan was an uncle. He let that thought sink in, wash over him. He felt so much. Affection at the thought of Ryder. A sudden affinity with the little guy he'd taught to rope. No wonder it had come so naturally. It was in the kid's blood.

But he was also angry and frustrated. How could Sierra have kept this from Luke?

Dylan glanced at the clock. The airline ticket was going to go unused. No way would Luke leave now, and Dylan couldn't blame him.

When he glanced toward the porch a few minutes later, Sierra's arms were wrapped around her waist.

She swiped away tears. "I don't blame you for hating me," she was saying. "I'd hate me too."

Luke rubbed the back of his neck. "I don't hate you, Sierra, not even close. I'm just frustrated. I have a son, and I lost the first four years of his life."

"I know. I'm so sorry."

Luke paced to the other side of the porch, tension in the straight line of his back, in the set of his jaw. He returned to her seconds later. "What now? I want to know Ryder. I want to be his father."

"You're leaving . . ."

He shook his head. "Not now. No way am I leaving him." He reached for her. "Or you. I want you back, Sierra. You know it's true. I never felt about any woman the way I feel about you. I'd marry you tomorrow, God as my witness."

Tears poured down her face. She held herself rigid. "I can't, Luke."

"Why not? Don't you remember how it was with us? I haven't forgotten. Those memories keep me awake at night. Tell me I'm not the only one."

"I'm just—I'm so afraid. You make me—" She covered her mouth with her fingers.

"What, Sierra?"

"You make me feel too much."

At her words Dylan's frustration began to drain. Fear was something he understood. Hadn't his own fear consumed him? It had been a high wall around his heart, keeping out any hope of love.

Until Annie.

Luke was brushing Sierra's tears away. "Have faith, sweetheart. We'll take it slow. I won't rush you."

Sierra gave a wry laugh. "I'm not fit to be your wife, Luke."

Dylan couldn't hear his response. He looked out the front windshield. He was sure his brother was reminding her of his own unworthiness and God's unmerited grace.

Funny how Luke's words about taking it slow echoed his own words to Annie the night before. He hoped Luke had better luck convincing Sierra of their future than Dylan had had with her sister.

Annie's words came back to him now, the ones that had haunted him all day. *"It's impossible between us."*

Impossible.

He'd turned those words every which way all day, but they hadn't made sense. Now, though, something clicked into place.

Impossible . . .

Of course. She'd known about Ryder. She'd been keeping Sierra's secret. Protecting her sister . . . it was what Annie did. His heart rate kicked up a notch. Could he be right? Was Sierra's secret the only thing standing between him and Annie?

His breath caught in his lungs. *Please, God. Let it be true.*

Dylan glanced at the porch as Luke opened his arms. Sierra went into his embrace.

God had somehow brought the two of them—the three of them—back together. Couldn't He break down any remaining walls around Annie? Dylan was suddenly eager to leave. Eager to tell her he knew. That it was all going to work out somehow.

Luke lowered his head for a kiss, and Dylan looked away. He wondered what would happen next. When they'd tell Ryder, and whether their relationship could survive the rocky start. One thing was sure, his brother seemed determined. And when Luke was determined, there was little he couldn't accomplish.

They went back in the house and returned several minutes later with Ryder and two small suitcases.

Ryder hopped in the truck as Luke stored their bags in the back.

"Scooch all the way over," Sierra said, climbing in next, then buckling Ryder.

"Hey, buddy," Dylan said.

Luke got in behind Sierra, a determined look on his face.

"Where to?" Dylan asked.

"Home, please." Sierra sounded like she had the world's worst cold. Her eyes were bloodshot, her face pale, but there was a brave smile playing on her lips that reminded him of Annie.

Annie. She was worried sick.

He frowned at Sierra. "Call your sister."

She gave a wobbly smile as she retrieved her phone and dialed.

Dylan started the truck and pulled onto the street.

"Hey, Annie . . . No, I'm fine . . . I know, I'm sorry."

Dylan relaxed just knowing Annie's mind was put to rest. He couldn't wait to get there. Couldn't wait to get this straightened out. If he was right.

Please, God. I love her so much.

Sierra took Ryder's hand. "Well . . . I'll explain later . . . Okay."

Dylan held out his hand for the phone.

"Hang on a sec," Sierra said, then handed over the phone. "She's at your place, with Braveheart," she told Dylan.

Dylan took the phone. "Stay put, Annie. I'm coming home."

Dear Troubled,

Love is often fraught with obstacles. The question is, which ones are worth moving?

 **36**

$\mathcal{A}$nnie had been so relieved to hear Sierra's voice. To know they were okay. She'd sounded a little odd, but at least they were coming home.

What she didn't understand was why Dylan was with them. Miss Lucy had said he was taking Luke to the airport, which was why Annie had gone to his place on a Friday night.

Annie halted Braveheart and praised him for a job well done. She patted the horse, her mind still on the phone call.

Had Dylan run into Sierra after dropping Luke at the airport and convinced her to come home? Why had he told Annie to stay put? There'd been something in his voice, something she couldn't get a handle on. It was almost like they had something to settle. But last night they'd said everything, hadn't they?

The memory of his kiss had haunted her into the early morning hours. The look on his face when she'd hurt him. Today her work hadn't had her full attention. Instead, regret and longing filled her to overflowing.

She'd had an ongoing conversation with God. Why was it, just when she'd found the love she'd been seeking all her life, he turned out to be the one man she couldn't have?

Annie scratched the horse's withers, his favorite spot. *How am I going to face him week after week, God? How am I going to run into him at the market, at the Chuckwagon, at church, feeling what I do and knowing I can't have him? Why did You give me these feelings, Lord?*

Her eyes burned with the tears she hadn't let herself shed. She blinked hard. She would not cry. He was on his way even now. He'd found Sierra somehow and was bringing her home. Annie would keep a safe distance, thank him politely, and leave.

Then she would focus on changing her ways with Sierra. By letting her sister set her own course, staying out of her business. She would encourage, she would be supportive, but she would lock her lips unless Sierra asked for her opinion. And she would pray—yes, there'd be lots of that.

Her love compelled her to do more, but she'd learn to let go. With God's help, she would turn the reins over. How else would her baby sister learn to ride solo?

Annie took Braveheart for another circle, praising him when he followed her guidance. Her goal had been to saddle up Braveheart and see how he responded. When she'd put the bareback saddle on him, he'd mouthed for the bit. The horse wanted to ride again. Dylan would be overjoyed. But for now, she'd been reining him from the ground.

As nicely as the horse was responding, she was certain he'd let

Dylan ride soon. Pleased with his progress, she led him back to the barn, removed his tack, and put him in his stall.

She heard the truck coming down the drive before she saw it. Annie's heart thumped like hooves over dry ground. She could handle this. At least Sierra and Ryder would be there to serve as buffers. The waning daylight would hopefully hide any traces of her earlier emotional struggle.

She left the barn as Dylan cut the engine. The door opened. Dylan stepped out, his eyes trained on her.

Annie's gaze cut to the other side of the cab, but it was empty. "Where are they?"

He closed the door, walked around the truck. "Took 'em home."

She swallowed hard. "Oh."

Dylan approached with that easy stride of his. Annie wrapped her arms around herself.

"Luke was with them."

Annie's mouth went slack. Luke? What was going on? "What do you mean? I thought he was on his way home."

Dylan stopped a few feet away. "Think he found himself a new home."

Dylan knew. She could see it in his eyes. The secret was out. Panic settled in. Everything inside quivered like the aftershocks of a great quake.

"I think that boy's in love with your sister."

Annie hoped it was true. But what if, after the shock wore off, after the novelty of being a father wore off, Luke left them both high and dry? What if he hurt Ryder the way their dad had hurt them?

This was happening too fast. And Ryder was with them now. What did the child know? Surely they wouldn't tell him tonight.

They had to give him time to get to know Luke before springing the news on him. Surely they wouldn't . . .

She had to get over there, now. "I have to go."

Annie retrieved her keys, heading toward her truck.

"No, Annie . . ."

Slow down, Sierra, she'd say. *Think it through. You have to handle this carefully.*

She reached for the truck door, her mind spinning.

Stop, beloved. The whisper came quietly into her heart.

She stopped cold. Her fist tightened on the keys.

They need me, God. I have to help her, make sure she handles this right. It's too important to mess up. How else will she have the wisdom to take things slow? She's like a whirlwind, God, fast and impulsive. She'll jump right in now that Luke knows, and not even consider the consequences. I know her, Lord. Who else knows her like me?

I do.

The words hit their mark. The air rushed from her lungs. Guilt pricked her heart. Of course God knew Sierra. Hadn't He formed her?

Had Annie really thought she knew Sierra better than God? Believed she could handle her sister better than the One who'd designed the universe, who'd set the stars in the sky?

She let loose of the door handle. She was only kidding herself. She'd never been in control of Sierra, not really. Hadn't the girl always done as she pleased?

But God had made Sierra. Surely He could direct her. Annie had decided as much the night before, but here she was, trying to take the reins again. She closed her eyes, disappointed in herself. Clearly this was a one-day-at-a-time kind of thing.

Okay, God, she's Yours. For real this time. Please guide her. Help me to step back and get out of Your way.

Annie turned, leaned on the truck door, and heaved a deep sigh. It was all in God's hands. He would work it out.

"Well done, big sister," Dylan said.

She hadn't heard him approach. Hadn't realized he'd been aware of her struggle. She didn't like how he seemed to read her mind, or how close he'd come to stand, barely an arm's length away.

"It's not easy," she said.

His eyes locked onto hers. "It never is."

She had a feeling they weren't talking about Sierra anymore.

"Guess I have a new nephew to spoil," he said.

He had a right to be angry with her and Sierra. But if he was, she couldn't see it in his eyes. They roamed over her face like the gentlest caress. They pulled at her, threatened to draw her in.

It sank in then, what it all meant. They were aunt and uncle to the same child.

"They'll be all right," he said. "Luke will be there for Ryder."

"You don't know that."

"Well, I know this." He stepped forward until they were toe-to-toe. His eyes were like a beacon of light. "I love his aunt."

Annie's heart twisted at the welcome words. Even so, fear trickled in despite her decision to lay down her prejudice.

"Dylan . . ."

"What is it, Annie? What's holding you back?"

She took a deep breath. "I'm afraid."

Dylan put his hands on the truck beside her, leaned in.

"I know about fear, Annie. So does your sister. Even Braveheart . . . you helped him find his way when he was terrified to take a step. He learned to trust you. You can learn to trust me too; I'm a loyal man. It takes a leap of faith to work past fear. I'm asking you to make that leap."

Her heart beat up into her throat. His musky scent filled her lungs, intoxicated her. Made her remember other times. His integrity at the cabin. On the porch, a baby in his arms. On the phone, helping a lovesick teenaged girl. He was a better man than she'd ever given him credit for.

His thumb stroked her cheek, lit a fire of need inside her. The way he made her feel, this cowboy. The way he held her, safe and secure in his arms. She closed her eyes against the feeling, against the sight of him.

As darkness closed in, she thought of Braveheart. Unsighted, dependent upon others for his every need. If it had been this hard for the horse to trust, she was amazed by his courage. Amazed by Dylan's courage too, for taking a risk on her.

"Open your eyes," he whispered. "Tell me you love me."

She did as he said and fell into his gaze. Even as the fear swelled inside, she said the words. "I do. So much."

His eyes lit. A tiny smile formed as he threaded his fingers into her hair. "That's all I need to know."

His lips fell onto hers, moving tenderly, sweeping away all her fears. She melted into his arms. His hands were magic, his body strong and solid. She wound her arms around his waist and hung on tight, feeling braver as joy flooded her soul. The scariest thing about a leap of faith was the first step.

He broke the kiss, pulled her into his chest, and lifted her off her feet. "Ah, Annie. You make me a happy man."

She could hear the rush of his heart, a rhythmic beat she found comforting. So much had happened in the past twenty-four hours. So many obstacles overcome. Obstacles she'd believed were insurmountable.

"I never would've believed," she said. "I thought it was impossible."

"I have a Friend in high places," he whispered into her hair. "Impossibilities are His specialty."

"I noticed," she said as her feet hit the ground again.

He was looking at her in that way she loved. That way that made her feel she was the only woman in the world.

She thought of Sierra and Luke and Ryder. She hadn't even thanked Dylan for bringing her sister home.

Dylan pulled her closer.

"Wait. You haven't told me what happened. How you found Sierra, and how you found out about her and Luke and—"

He put his fingers over her lips. "Later, woman," he said, then covered her lips with his own.

Epilogue

The March wind tugged at Annie's hair. The afternoon sun flooding from a clear blue sky was a welcome sight after the long, cold winter.

She crossed her arms against the chill and called into the house. "You about ready, Ryder?"

"We're finishing up his bag," Dylan said.

They would be here any minute. Annie drew in a deep breath and let it out. Three days ago Sierra and Luke had become husband and wife after a seven-month courtship. Luke had worked on Dylan's ranch through the winter, and Sierra had spent the fall and winter in a paid internship at her friend's studio. She was ready to strike out on her own with a portfolio full of beautiful portraits.

As for Annie and Dylan, they'd settled into the kind of relationship she'd once only dreamed of.

The screen door squeaked, then a few seconds later Dylan's arms came around her. He pulled her into his chest and kissed her temple.

"Stop worrying," he said. "They're gonna be fine."

She relaxed into his embrace, sighing. "So far away."

"Only an hour."

Still, she was used to her sister being right down the hall. Used to Ryder's big hugs every night when she came home.

Annie's eyes burned at the thought. "That's forever away."

His arms tightened.

Ever since Luke had scored a job as manager at a ranch in Cody, Wyoming, Sierra had been eager to start her own business in a town big enough to support it. Never mind that she was leaving her big sister behind.

In the distance Luke's truck pulled into the drive and Annie straightened. Time to do this. She'd try to keep her tears at bay—no sense ruining Sierra's grand adventure.

Moments later Sierra popped from the truck and trotted toward the house. Fresh from a short honeymoon up at Big Sky, her face glowed and her eyes sparkled.

Annie and Dylan came off the porch and greeted them.

"Missed you, sis," Sierra said as she hugged Annie.

Ryder barged through the screen door. "Mommy! Daddy!" He flew down the steps, dropping his overstuffed bag in the grass, and threw his arms around both of them. A moment later Luke scooped him up, and Ryder wound his arms around his dad's neck.

As Annie had hoped, they'd waited several weeks before telling Ryder who Luke was. By then they'd already formed a close friendship. Annie had to admit Luke was good for her nephew. She'd never seen him as happy as when his daddy tussled with him on the floor or saddled up behind him.

Ryder gave his parents an exuberant synopsis of their last three days. Annie smiled, watching them together. Luke had swept into her sister's life and loved the fear away, much as Dylan had done for her.

Amazing. *Impossibilities really are Your specialty, aren't they, God?*

Awhile later, after they'd caught up and loaded the rest of their belongings, Luke pulled out his keys. "We'd better hit the road, darlin'."

They all exchanged hugs, Annie saving Sierra for last.

"We'll be back in two weeks," Sierra reminded her.

"I know."

"We'll be fine."

"I know that too." *Please, God. Go with them. Keep them safe.*

Sierra squeezed tight. "Thanks for everything, Annie. You're the best sister anyone could ask for."

The words threatened her determination to hold it together. Annie blinked against the sting in her eyes. "Right back atcha, sis."

If her eyes were a tiny bit glassy when they drew apart, it was only because she was so happy for them.

Moments later they waved from the truck as it rolled down the lane. Dylan took Annie's hand as they walked toward the house, up the porch steps.

At the top Annie turned into his arms, not wanting to face the quiet house, the empty rooms. "I don't want to go in yet."

Dylan pulled her against his chest. "Proud of you. I know that wasn't easy."

No more toys scattered on the floor. No more cereal bowls in the sink. She couldn't even stand the thought of supper alone every night. The tears Annie had held at bay spilled over.

"It won't be the same anymore."

He tightened his arms. "Life is full of changes—some of them very good."

She sniffled and thumped her fist on his chest. "Your brother just had to come steal her away."

He chuckled, dropping a kiss on her head. "She looked pretty happy about it."

He had her there. "Yeah. She did."

Luke balanced out Sierra in many ways. Sierra brought fun and spontaneity into his life, and he brought stability into hers.

"They're a good match," she said.

"Kinda like us."

She smiled against his chest. "Kinda like." They'd been officially dating for seven months, and she was surer of that than ever.

Dylan thumbed her tears away, then kissed her, his lips lingering on hers for a few moments before growing more persistent.

Ah, the man knew how to distract her. Annie gave herself fully to the kiss, and he responded in kind. When he drew away, it was only so he could look deeply into her eyes. Those brown eyes were serious now, shining with love and ardor.

"You know I love you," he said.

"I love you too." So much. She couldn't believe how much things had changed in a year. How much *she'd* changed.

"I've been thinking lately . . ."

"Uh-oh."

His eyes took on a twinkle. "I have this question . . . for Dear Annie, you know. Only trouble is, they canceled her column."

Annie smiled. "You could always ask her in person."

His brows lifted, and he nodded approvingly. "That's an excellent idea. Okay, here goes. See, there's this woman—I've fallen in love with her. She's beautiful inside and out, and she loves me too. But lately I'm thinking . . ." He frowned, shook his head, and heaved a great sigh. "It's just not enough."

She wasn't fooled by his woebegone expression. "Not enough, huh?"

"Not nearly enough. Not enough time. Not enough kisses. Not enough . . . Annie. See my problem?"

Annie's lips twitched. "I think I do."

"So I was wondering if I should, you know . . ." He paused, a vulnerable look sneaking into his eyes. "Ask her to marry me."

Joy flooded through her, lifting her lips.

"I mean," he continued, a flush filling his cheeks, "I know she's the one for me, and I think she feels the same way, but sometimes a guy can feel vulnerable about putting himself out there. Plus her sister just left town, so she's kind of distracted and a little blue. It's a big commitment—one I'm not the least afraid to make, but I'm not sure how she might—"

"Hush."

His brows lifted. "Beg pardon?"

Annie looked deeply into his eyes. "Dear Annie thinks you should ask her—with all due haste."

"All due haste?"

Annie nodded slowly, not even fighting the smile.

Without breaking eye contact Dylan dropped to his knee, pulling off his hat in the same motion.

The look in his eyes made her breath catch. Her heart flopped over in her chest. She covered it with her hand.

"Annie Wilkerson," he said softly, "I love you more than I can say, and nothing would make me happier than a lifetime filled with you. Your smile, your hugs, your laughter . . . Will you marry me?"

Annie's eyes filled again. Happy tears. She nodded. "I will."

He stood slowly, pulling her into his arms where she felt safe and loved. "I do love you, sweet Annie," he whispered before kissing her again.

She gave herself over to the kiss as happiness bloomed inside her. When he pulled her closer, that familiar spark ignited in her midsection and spread through her veins, making her limbs go weak.

Sometimes a girl needed a little spark in her life. And Annie knew that, even after a lifetime together, no matter how many kisses they exchanged or how much laughter they shared, she would never get enough of him—that was the trouble with cowboys.

Dear friend,

$\mathcal{I}$ knew from the moment Dylan galloped onto the page in *A Cowboy's Touch* that he had a story to tell. I only had to find the right woman for him. Then Annie appeared on the page, and I knew Dylan had met his match.

Annie's struggle to let go of Sierra was very real to me. As I was writing the story, I was getting ready to let my first chick out of the nest. Working through this issue with Annie helped me to leave our oldest son in God's hands as he went off to college. I hope walking with Annie on her spiritual journey helped you along on yours too.

I can hardly believe the Big Sky series is over; it went so fast! I hope your visit to Moose Creek was as enjoyable as mine. Thank you for coming along and for making the ride worthwhile. I value each of you so much!

In His grace,
Denise

Reading Group Guide

1. Which character did you most relate to and why?
2. Annie and Sierra shared the same childhood experiences, yet they viewed love differently. Why do you think that is? Have you experienced anything similar with your siblings?
3. How did Dylan's past experience with love affect his ability to love again?
4. Sometimes Annie tried to manipulate Sierra into attending church. Why do you think such tactics are usually ineffective, despite the best of intentions?
5. If you've read *Pride and Prejudice*, how is Annie similar to Elizabeth Bennet? How is she different?
6. In what ways was Braveheart symbolic in the story?
7. Annie's childhood caused her to develop a prejudice toward cowboys. Have you ever clung to a false belief? How did you discover it was false, and what did you do to overcome it?
8. Miss Lucy confronted Annie about her prejudice toward cowboys. What does the Bible say about confronting each other? Do you think Miss Lucy handled it well? Should she have confronted Annie sooner?
9. Sierra accused Annie of judging her early in the story. Where is the line between judging and confronting in love?

10. Annie struggled to let go of Sierra and let her sister lead her own life. What do you need to let go of? What are some steps you can take to leave it in God's hands?

*Hear "Smitten," the song Annie
and Dylan danced to, at
www.SmittenVermont.com*

If your book club of 15 or more would like to read this book, Denise would be happy to schedule a call-in to answer any questions your group may have. Contact her at denise@denisehunterbooks.com.

Acknowledgments

*W*riting a book is a team effort, and I'm so grateful for the entire team at Thomas Nelson Fiction, led by Publisher Allen Arnold: Katie Bond, Amanda Bostic, Ruthie Dean, Natalie Hanemann, Jodi Hughes, Ami McConnell, Becky Monds, Eric Mullet, Ashley Schneider, and Kristen Vasgaard.

Thanks especially to my editor, Natalie Hanemann, who helped shape this story, notified me of gaping holes, and otherwise helped me fashion this into a more enjoyable read. I'm forever grateful to the talented LB Norton, whose eye for detail has saved me from countless mistakes!

Author Colleen Coble is my first reader. Thank you, friend! She, along with friends and authors Diann Hunt and Kristin Billerbeck, is a great help at the brainstorming stage of every story. Love you, girls!

I'm grateful to my agent, Karen Solem, who handles all the left-brained matters so I can focus on the right-brained stuff.

To Billy and Marci Whitehurst, who opened their Montana home and ranch for a city girl and her husband. Thanks for taking the time to show me the cowboy way of life.

A research trip to Montana would've been impossible without my sister-in-law Gina Sinclair, brother-in-law Mark Sinclair, and niece Mindy Sinclair. Thanks so much for coming to take over our daily lives for a few days so Kevin and I could gallivant all over Big Sky Country. We're so grateful to call you family.

Thanks to my Facebook friends at Denise Hunter Readers Circle who helped me title this book, name the town of Moose Creek, and name the series itself. Thanks for all your input!

To my family, Kevin, Justin, Chad, and Trevor. I love each one of you so much! Thanks for putting up with me!

Lastly, thank you, friend, for letting me share this story with you. I wouldn't be doing this without you! I've enjoyed connecting with readers like you through my Facebook group. Visit my website at www.DeniseHunterBooks.com or just drop me a note at Denise@DeniseHunterBooks.com. I'd love to hear from you!

The Big Sky Romance Series

Available in print and e-book

An excerpt from *The Convenient Groom*

he red light on Kate Lawrence's cell phone blinked a staccato warning. But before she could retrieve the message, her maid of honor, Anna Doherty, waved her pale arms from the beach, stealing her attention.

Anna's smooth voice sounded in her headset. "Kate, can you come here? We've got a few glitches."

"Be right there." Kate tucked her clipboard in the crook of her elbow, took the steps down Jetty Pavilion's porch, and crossed the heel-sinking sand of the Nantucket shoreline. In six hours, thirty-four guests would be seated there in the rows of white chairs, watching Kate pledge her life to Bryan Montgomery under a beautiful hand-carved gazebo.

Where was the gazebo anyway? She checked her watch, then glanced toward the Pavilion, where workers scurried in white uniforms. No sign of Lucas.

She approached Anna, who wore worry lines as naturally as she wore her Anne Klein pantsuit. Anna was the best receptionist Kate could ask for. Her capable presence reassured the troubled couples she ushered through Kate's office.

Right now, Anna's long brown hair whipped across her face like a flag gone awry, and she batted it from her eyes with her freckled hand. "Soiree's just called. Their delivery truck is in for service, and the flowers will be a little late. Half an hour at the most."

Kate jotted the note on her schedule. "That's okay." She'd factored in cushion time.

"Murray's called, and the tuxes haven't been picked up except for your dad's."

Bryan and his best man had been due at Murray's at nine thirty. An hour ago. "I'll check on that. What else?"

Anna's frown lines deepened, and her eyes blinked against the wind. "The carriage driver is sick, but they're trying to find a replacement. The Weatherbys called and asked if they could attend last minute—they were supposed to go out of town, but their plans changed."

Kate nodded. "Fine, fine. Call and tell her they're welcome. I'll notify the caterer."

"Your publicist—Pam?—has been trying to reach you. Did you check your cell? She said she got voice mail. Anyway, your book copies did arrive this morning. She dropped this off." Anna pulled a hardback book from under her clipboard. "Ta-da!"

"My book!" Kate stared at the cover, where the title, *Finding Mr. Right-for-You*, floated above a cartoon couple. The man was on his knee, proposing. Below them, a colorful box housed the bold letters of Kate's name. She ran her fingers over the glossy book jacket, feeling the raised bumps of the letters, savoring the moment.

"Pam wants a quick photo shoot before the guests arrive. You holding the book, that kind of thing. You should probably call her."

Kate jotted the note. While it was on her mind, she reached down and turned on her cell.

"Ready for more great news?" Anna asked. Her blue eyes glittered like diamonds. The news had to be good.

"What?"

"The *New York Times* is sending a reporter and a photographer. They want to do a feature story on your wedding and your book."

Fresh air caught and held in Kate's lungs. Rosewood Press was probably turning cartwheels. "That's fabulous. They'll want an interview." She scanned her schedule, looking for an open slot. After the reception? She hated to do it, but Bryan would understand. The *New York Times*. It would give Kate's initial sales the boost they needed. Maybe enough to make the bestseller list.

"Here's the number." Anna handed her a yellow Post-It. "That tabloid guy has been hanging around all morning, trying to figure out who the groom is. I told him he'd find out in six hours like everyone else. The rest of the media is scheduled to arrive an hour before the wedding, and Pam's having an area set up over there for them." Anna gestured behind the rows of chairs to a square blocked off with white ribbon.

"Good. I want them to be as inconspicuous as possible. This is my wedding, and a girl only gets married once, after all."

"One would hope," Anna said. "Is there anything else I can do?"

Kate gave her a sideways hug, as close to an embrace as she'd ever given her assistant, her fingers pressing into Anna's fleshy shoulder. "You're a godsend. I don't know what I'd do without you."

"Oh! I know what I forgot to tell you. The gazebo. It should have been here by now. I tried to call Lucas, but I got the machine, and I don't have his cell number."

"His shop's closed today, and he doesn't have a cell." The man didn't wear a watch, much less carry a phone. She should've known better than to put something this crucial in his hands. Kate checked her watch. "I'll run over and check on it."

ॐ   ॐ   ॐ

The drive to town was quick and effortless, but Kate's mind swam with a hundred details. She jotted reminders on her clipboard when she stopped for pedestrians, occasionally admiring the cover of her book.

She couldn't believe what a wonderful day it was. She had a book coming out, she was about to walk down the aisle, and the weather couldn't be more perfect. *Thank You, God, for the beautiful day, for the man I'm about to marry, for the book deal.* Eveything was in perfect order.

She called Pam for a quick recap about the *New York Times* reporter, and by the time she hung up, she was pulling into a parallel slot on Main Street, in front of Lucas's storefront.

The sign above the picture window read "Cottage House Furniture." On the second floor of the Shaker building, the wooden shingle for her own business dangled from a metal pole: "Kate Lawrence, Marriage Counseling Services." She needed to remind Lucas to remove it; otherwise he'd leave it hanging for another year or until someone else rented the space.

Kate exited her car and slid her key into the rusty lock of the shop's door. Once inside, she passed the stairs leading to her office and walked through the darkened maze of furniture to the back, where she hoped to find Lucas. She bumped an end table with her shin. *Ow!* That would leave a mark.

The high-pitched buzz of a power tool pierced the darkness, a good sign. "Lucas?" She rapped loudly on the metal door with her knuckles. The noise stopped.

"Come in."

She opened the door. Lucas Wright looked up from his spot on the cement floor at the base of the gazebo, his too-long hair hanging over one eye. He looked her over, then turned back to the spindle and ran his thick hand over it as if testing the curves.

"Aren't you supposed to be at the beach?" he asked.

Kate crossed her arms. "I could ask you the same thing."

He stood, agile for his size, and backed away from the gazebo. Sawdust from the floor clung to his faded jeans and black T-shirt. "I was just finishing."

"You were supposed to be there an hour ago. The gazebo needs to be put in place before the sound system, and the florist has to decorate it, and there are people waiting to do their jobs."

He faced her, looking into her in that way of his that made her feel like he could see clean through her. "Today's the big day, huh?" Putting his tool on his workhorse, he dusted off his hands, moving in slow motion as though he'd decided tonight wouldn't arrive until next week.

Kate checked her watch. "Do you think you can get this down to the beach sometime today?"

Walking around the piece, he studied it, hands on his hips, head cocked. "You like it?"

For the first time since the week before, Kate looked at the gazebo—the white lattice top, the hand-carved spindles, the gentle arch of the entry. At the top of the arch, a piece of wood curved gracefully, etched with clusters of daisies. The gazebo's simple lines were characteristic of Lucas's work, but she'd never known him to use such exquisite detail. The piece had an elegance that surpassed her expectations. He did beautiful work; she'd give him that.

"I do. I love the etching." She sighed. Just when he irritated the snot out of her, he did something like this, caught her off guard.

She always felt like she was tripping down the stairs when she was with him.

Focus! "It needs to find its way to the beach. Pronto."

"Yes, ma'am." His salute was unhurried.

Before she could offer a retort, her cell phone pealed and buzzed simultaneously, and she pulled it from her capri pocket.

"Hello?"

"Kate?"

"Bryan." Turning away from Lucas and toward the door, she eyed a crude desk with a metal folding chair that bore countless rusty scratches. "Good morning." A smile crept into her voice. It was their wedding day. The day they'd planned for nearly two years. "Did you sleep well?" She hadn't. She'd rumpled the sheets until nearly two o'clock, but that was to be expected.

The silence on the other end, however, was not. "Bryan?" Had she lost the signal?

"Um, Kate, did you get my message?"

There'd been a blinking red light this morning. She'd assumed it was Pam's voice mail and hadn't checked. Suddenly, she wished she had.

"No. What's wrong?"

"Are you sitting down?"

"No, I'm not sitting down. Just tell me." An ugly dread snaked down her spine and settled there, coiled and waiting.

"I'm on my way back to Boston," he said. "I left a message this morning. You must've had your phone off."

Kate's stomach stirred. She stared at the wall in front of her—a pegboard with a zillion holes, metal prongs poking from it, tools and cords everywhere. "What happened?" Some emergency, maybe?

What emergency could trump our wedding?

"I can't marry you, Kate."

The words dropped, each one crumbling under its own weight. The stirring in her stomach intensified. "That's not funny, Bryan." It was a terrible joke. He'd never been good with jokes. His punch lines left you leaning forward, waiting for the rest.

"I'm in love with someone else."

Pain. A huge wooden spoon, tossing the contents of her stomach. Her legs wobbled, trembling on the wedge heels of her sandals, and she clutched the cold metal of the folding chair. "What?" Was that her voice, weak and thready? Someone had vacuumed all the moisture from her mouth, sucked the air from her lungs.

"I'm so sorry," Bryan was saying. "I know this is awful. You don't deserve this, but I can't marry you. It happened slowly, and I didn't realize what was going on until recently. I tried to put it out of my mind, but I just can't. And I can't marry you knowing how I feel. I'm so sorry, Kate."

"What?" It was the only word her mind could form at the moment.

"I know there's no excuse. I should have told you before now, but I thought it would go away. I thought I was just having cold feet or something, but it's more than that."

"We've been together for two years, Bryan."

It was a stupid thing to say, but it was all she could think of. Memories played across the screen of her mind in fast-forward. The day they'd met in line at Starbucks in downtown Boston when Kate had gone there for a conference. Their first date at the Colonial Theatre. The long-distance courting and weekend visits. The e-mails, the phone calls, the engagement, the book. It all whizzed by, coming to a screeching halt here, at this moment. Here, in Lucas's dusty workshop. Here, in front of the special gazebo they were to be married in.

"I've already called my family and told them. I know there's a lot to do, and I'll help any way you want me to. And then there's your book . . . I'm so sorry."

Sorry. You're sorry? She pictured the precise rows of white chairs, the tent being erected as they spoke, the celebrity preacher, the photographers.

The *New York Times.*

She closed her burning eyes. Everything would have to be canceled.

At that thought, humiliation arrived on the scene, sinking in past the pain of betrayal. The weight of it pushed at her shoulders, and she grabbed the hair at her nape. *Think, Kate! This is no time to lose it.*

"Stop, Bryan. Just stop and think about what you're doing. Maybe you're letting your issues with your parents' divorce affect your decisions. This kind of fear is perfectly natural before a wedding, and maybe—"

"No, it's not that—"

"How do you know?" She forced reason into her tone. Used her soothing voice—the one she used when things got heated between one of her couples. "We love each other. We're perfect for each other. You've said it a hundred times."

"There's something missing, Kate."

She wobbled again and steadied herself with a hand on the chair. "Something missing"? What was that supposed to mean?

As her mind grappled with that seemingly unanswerable question, she felt a hand at her back, leading her into the chair.

She was sitting, her head as fuzzy as a cotton-candy machine, her emerald-cut engagement ring blurring before her eyes.

"What do you mean there's something missing? The only thing missing is the groom. For our wedding that starts in five hours. Five hours, Bryan." Now she felt the hysteria building and took a full breath, nearly choking on the way the oxygen stretched her lungs.

"I'll help in any way I can."

"You can help by showing up for our wedding!"

Her mind ran through the list of people she'd have to call. Her dad, the guests, her publisher. She thought of the money Rosewood Press had spent on this elaborate beach wedding. They'd flown in friends and family from all over the country, paid for the photographer, flowers, caterer, the wedding attire. Kate had only wanted a simple wedding, but with the release of the book, the marketing department had other ideas. "An elegant wedding and a surprise groom just as the book releases. We can ask Reverend James McFadden to perform the ceremony! Think of the publicity, Kate!"

A knot started in her throat and burned its way to her heart.

"I'll always care about you," Bryan said.

The words fell, as empty as a discarded soda bottle on a deserted beach.

Enough.

The adrenaline coursing through her veins drained suddenly, leaving her once again weak and shaky. She couldn't talk to him anymore. She wasn't going to break down on the phone, wasn't going to beg him to come back. It wouldn't accomplish a thing anyway. She'd heard this tone of Bryan's voice before. He was a man who knew what he wanted. And what he didn't want.

And he didn't want Kate. She suddenly knew that fact as surely as she knew tomorrow would be more impossible to face than today.

She cleared her throat. "I have to go."

"Kate, tell me what I can do. My family will pitch in too. I want to help fix things."

She wanted to tell him there was no fixing this. There was no fixing her heart or the impending collision of her life and her career. Instead, numb, she closed the phone, staring straight ahead at the holes on the pegboard until they blended together in a blurry haze.

He was leaving her. The man she loved was walking away. This wasn't supposed to be happening. Not to her. She'd been so careful, and for what? A hollow spot opened up in her stomach, wide and gaping.

Instead of the headlines reading "Marriage Expert Finds Her Mr. Right," they would read "Marriage Expert Jilted at the Altar."

Kate had never considered herself prideful, but the thought of facing the next twenty-four hours made cyanide seem reasonable. *How can this be happening, God? To me, of all people?* She'd written a book on the subject of finding the right mate and had managed to find the wrong one instead. By tomorrow the whole world would know.

The story continues in *The Convenient Groom* by Denise Hunter.

NANTUCKET LOVE STORIES

Four Women. *Four Love Stories.*

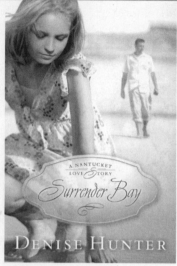

One Island. *Escape to Nantucket.*

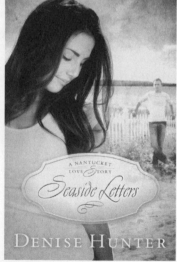

She wished she could go back and change things . . . but life doesn't give do-overs. Could anything but good-byes be waiting on the other side of *Sweetwater Gap*?

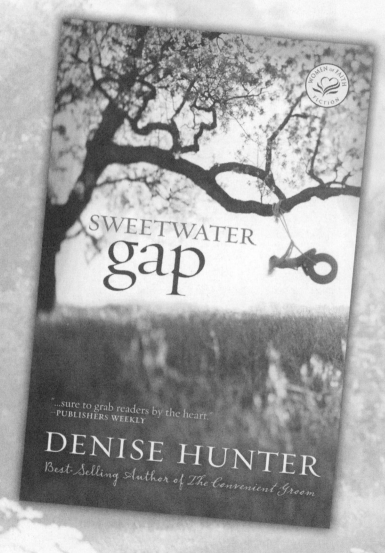

Available in print and e-book

Don't miss the first installment in
Denise Hunter's new series:

The Chapel Springs Romance series

Barefoot Summer

Available July 2013

9781595548030-D

*F*our friends devise a plan to turn Smitten, Vermont, into the country's premier romantic getaway—while each searches for her own true love along the way.

THOMAS NELSON
Since 1798

There's a mystery brewing in Smitten, Vermont—
the little town with a big heart.

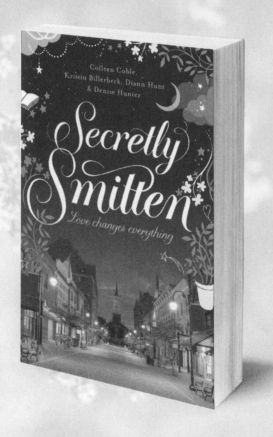

Available July 2013

About the Author

Author photo by Amber Zimmerman

*D*enise Hunter is the best-selling author of many novels, including *Surrender Bay* and *The Accidental Bride*. She lives in Indiana with her husband, Kevin, and their three sons. In 1996 Denise began her first book, a Christian romance novel, writing while her children napped. Two years later it was published, and she's been writing ever since. Her books contain a strong romantic element, and her husband, Kevin, says he provides all her romantic material, but Denise insists a good imagination helps too! Visit her website at www.DeniseHunterBooks.com.